The Author

STEPHEN LEACOCK was born in Swanmore, Hampshire, England, in 1869. His family emigrated to Canada in 1876 and settled on a farm north of Toronto. Educated at Upper Canada College and the University of Toronto, Leacock pursued graduate studies in economics at the University of Chicago, where he studied under Thorstein Veblen.

Even before he completed his doctorate, Leacock accepted a position as sessional lecturer in political science and economics at McGill University. When he received his Ph.D. in 1903, he was appointed to the full position of lecturer. From 1908 until his retirement in 1936, he chaired the Department of Political Science and Economics.

Leacock's most profitable book was his textbook, *Elements of Political Science*, which was translated into seventeen languages. The author of nineteen books and countless articles on economics, history, and political science, Leacock turned to the writing of humour as his beloved avocation. His first collection of comic stories, *Literary Lapses*, appeared in 1910, and from that time until his death he published a volume of humour almost every year.

Leacock also wrote popular biographies of his two favourite writers, Mark Twain and Charles Dickens. At the time of his death, he left four completed chapters of what was to have been his autobiography. These were published posthumously under the title *The Boy I Left Behind Me*.

Stephen Leacock died in Toronto, Ontario, in 1944.

THE NEW CANADIAN LIBRARY

General Editor: David Staines

STEPHEN LEACOCK

Arcadian Adventures
with the Idle Rich

With an Afterword by Gerald Lynch

M&S

Canadian Cataloguing in Publication Data

Leacock, Stephen, 1869-1944
Arcadian adventures with the idle rich

(New Canadian Library)
Bibliography: p.
ISBN 0-7710-9966-5

I. Title.   II. Series.

PS8523.E15A9 1989   C813'.52   C88-094968-6
PR9199.2.L42A9 1989

Typesetting by Pickwick
Printed and bound in Canada

McClelland & Stewart Inc.
The Canadian Publishers
481 University Avenue
Toronto, Ontario
M5G 2E9

Contents

Contents

ONE

A Little Dinner with Mr. Lucullus Fyshe

THE MAUSOLEUM Club stands on the quietest corner of the best residential street in the City. It is a Grecian building of white stone. About it are great elm trees with birds – the most expensive kind of birds – singing in the branches.

The street in the softer hours of the morning has an almost reverential quiet. Great motors move drowsily along it, with solitary chauffeurs returning at 10.30 after conveying the earlier of the millionaires to their down-town offices. The sunlight flickers through the elm trees, illuminating expensive nursemaids wheeling valuable children in little perambulators. Some of the children are worth millions and millions. In Europe, no doubt, you may see in the Unter den Linden avenue or the Champs Elysées a little prince or princess go past with a clattering military guard to do honour. But that is nothing. It is not half so impressive, in the real sense, as what you may observe every morning on Plutoria Avenue beside the Mausoleum Club in the quietest part of the city. Here you may see a little toddling princess in a rabbit suit who owns fifty distilleries in her own right. There, in a lacquered perambulator, sails past a little hooded head that controls from its cradle an entire New Jersey corporation. The United States attorney-general is suing her as she sits, in a vain attempt to make her dissolve herself into constituent companies. Near by is a child of four, in a khaki suit, who represents the merger of two trunk line railways. You may meet in the flickered sunlight any number of little princes and princesses far more real than the poor survivals of Europe. Incalculable infants wave their fifty-dollar ivory rattles in an inarticulate greeting to one another. A million dollars of preferred stock laughs merrily in recognition of a majority control going past in a go-cart drawn by an imported nurse. And through it all the sunlight falls through the elm-trees, and the birds sing and the motors hum, so that the whole world as seen from the boulevard of Plutoria Avenue is the very pleasantest place imaginable.

Just below Plutoria Avenue, and parallel with it, the trees die out and the brick and stone of the City begins in earnest. Even from the Avenue you see the tops of the sky-scraping buildings in the big commercial streets, and can hear or almost hear the roar of the elevated railway, earning dividends. And beyond that again the City sinks lower, and is choked and crowded with the tangled streets and little houses of the slums.

In fact, if you were to mount to the roof of the Mausoleum Club itself on Plutoria Avenue you could almost see the slums from there. But why should you? And on the other hand, if you never went up on the roof, but only dined inside among the palm-trees, you would never know that the slums existed – which is much better.

There are broad steps leading up to the club, so broad and so agreeably covered with matting that the physical exertion of lifting oneself from one's motor to the door of the club is reduced to the smallest compass. The richer members are not ashamed to take the steps one at a time, first one foot and then the other; and at tight money periods, when there is a black cloud hanging over the Stock Exchange, you may see each and every one of the members of the Mausoleum Club dragging himself up the steps after this fashion, his restless eyes filled with the dumb pathos of a man wondering where he can put his hand on half a million dollars.

But at gayer times, when there are gala receptions at the

club, its steps are all buried under expensive carpet, soft as moss and covered over with a long pavilion of red and white awning to catch the snowflakes; and beautiful ladies are poured into the club by the motorful. Then indeed it is turned into a veritable Arcadia; and for a beautiful pastoral scene, such as would have gladdened the heart of a poet who understood the cost of things, commend me to the Mausoleum Club on just such an evening. Its broad corridors and deep recesses are filled with shepherdesses such as you never saw, dressed in beautiful shimmering gowns, and wearing feathers in their hair that droop off sideways at every angle known to trigonometry. And there are shepherds too with broad white waistcoats and little patent leather shoes and heavy faces and congested cheeks. And there is dancing and conversation among the shepherds and shepherdesses, with such brilliant flashes of wit and repartee about the rise in Wabash and the fall in Cement that the soul of Louis Quatorze would leap to hear it. And later there is supper at little tables, when the shepherds and shepherdesses consume preferred stocks and gold-interest bonds in the shape of chilled champagne and iced asparagus, and great platefuls of dividends and special quarterly bonuses are carried to and fro in silver dishes by Chinese philosophers dressed up to look like waiters.

But on ordinary days there are no ladies in the club, but only the shepherds. You may see them sitting about in little groups of two and three under the palm-trees drinking whiskey and soda; though of course the more temperate among them drink nothing but whiskey and Lithia water, and those who have important business to do in the afternoon limit themselves to whiskey and Radnor, or whiskey and Magi water. There are as many kinds of bubbling, gurgling, mineral waters in the caverns of the Mausoleum Club as ever sparkled from the rocks of Homeric Greece. And when you have once grown used to them, it is as impossible to go back to plain water as it is to live again in the forgotten house in a side street that you inhabited long before you became a member.

Thus the members sit and talk in undertones that float to the ear through the haze of Havana smoke. You may hear the older men explaining that the country is going to absolute ruin, and the younger ones explaining that the country is forging ahead as it never did before; but chiefly they love to talk of great national questions, such as the protective tariff and the need of raising it, the sad decline of the morality of the working man, the spread of syndicalism and the lack of Christianity in the labour class, and the awful growth of selfishness among the mass of the people.

So they talk, except for two or three that drop off to directors' meetings, till the afternoon fades and darkens into evening, and the noiseless Chinese philosophers turn on soft lights here and there among the palm-trees. Presently they dine at white tables glittering with cut glass and green and yellow Rhine wines; and after dinner they sit again among the palm-trees, half hidden in the blue smoke, still talking of the tariff and the labour class and trying to wash away the memory and the sadness of it in floods of mineral waters. So the evening passes into night, and one by one the great motors come throbbing to the door, and the Mausoleum Club empties and darkens till the last member is borne away and the Arcadian day ends in well-earned repose.

"I want you to give me your opinion very, very frankly," said Mr. Lucullus Fyshe on one side of the luncheon table to the Rev. Fareforth Furlong on the other.

"By all means," said Mr. Furlong.

Mr. Fyshe poured out a wineglassful of soda and handed it to the rector to drink.

"Now tell me very truthfully," he said, "is there too much carbon in it?"

"By no means," said Mr. Furlong.

"And – quite frankly – not too much hydrogen?"

"Oh, decidedly not."

"And you would not say that the percentage of sodium bicarbonate was too great for the ordinary taste?"

"I certainly should not," said Mr. Furlong, and in this he spoke the truth.

"Very good then," said Mr. Fyshe, "I shall use it for the Duke of Dulham this afternoon."

He uttered the name of the Duke with that quiet, democratic carelessness which meant that he didn't care whether half a dozen other members lunching at the club could hear or not. After all, what was a duke to a man who was president of the People's Traction and Suburban Co. and the Republican Soda and Siphon Co-operative, and chief director of the People's District Loan and Savings? If a man with a broad basis of popular support like that was proposing to entertain a duke, surely there could be no doubt about his motives? None at all.

Naturally, too, if a man manufactures soda himself, he gets a little over-sensitive about the possibility of his guests noticing the existence of too much carbon in it.

In fact, ever so many of the members of the Mausoleum Club manufacture things, or cause them to be manufactured, or – what is the same thing – merge them when they are manufactured. This gives them their peculiar chemical attitude towards their food. One often sees a member suddenly call the head waiter at breakfast to tell him that there is too much ammonia in the bacon; and another one protest at the amount of glucose in the olive oil; and another that there is too high a percentage of nitrogen in the anchovy. A man of distorted imagination might think this tasting of chemicals in the food a sort of nemesis of fate upon the members. But that would be very foolish, for in every case the head waiter, who is the chief of the Chinese philosophers mentioned above, says that he'll see to it immediately and have the percentage removed. And as for the members themselves, they are about as much ashamed of manufacturing and merging things as the Marquis of Salisbury is ashamed of the founders of the Cecil family.

What more natural therefore than that Mr Lucullus Fyshe, before serving the soda to the Duke, should try it on somebody else? And what better person could be found for this than Mr. Furlong, the saintly young rector of St. Asaph's, who had enjoyed the kind of expensive college education calculated to develop all the faculties. Moreover, a rector of the Anglican Church who has been in the foreign mission field is the kind of person from whom one can find out, more or less incidentally, how one should address and converse with a duke, and whether you call him, "Your Grace," or "His Grace," or just "Grace," or "Duke," or what. All of which things would seem to a director of the People's Bank and the president of the Republican Soda Co. so trivial in importance that he would scorn to ask about them.

So that was why Mr. Fyshe had asked Mr. Furlong to lunch with him, and to dine with him later on in the same day at the Mausoleum Club to meet the Duke of Dulham. And Mr. Furlong, realising that a clergyman must be all things to all men and not avoid a man merely because he is a duke had accepted the invitation to lunch, and had promised to come to dinner, even though it meant postponing the Willing Workers' Tango Class of St. Asaph's until the following Friday.

Thus it had come about that Mr. Fyshe was seated at lunch, consuming a cutlet and a pint of Moselle in the plain, downright fashion of a man so democratic that he is practically a revolutionary socialist, and doesn't mind saying so; and the young rector of St. Asaph's was sitting opposite to him in a religious ecstasy over a *salmi* of duck.

"The Duke arrived this morning, did he not?" said Mr. Furlong.

"From New York," said Mr. Fyshe; "he is staying at the Grand Palaver. I sent a telegram through one of our New York directors of the Traction, and his Grace has very kindly promised to come over here to dine."

"Is he here for pleasure?" asked the rector.

"I understand he is –" Mr. Fyshe was going to say

"about to invest a large part of his fortune in American securities," but he thought better of it. Even with the clergy it is well to be careful. So he substituted "is very much interested in studying American conditions."

"Does he stay long?" asked Mr. Furlong.

Had Mr. Lucullus Fyshe replied quite truthfully, he would have said, "Not if I can get his money out of him quickly," but he merely answered, "That I don't know."

"He will find much to interest him," went on the rector in a musing tone. "The position of the Anglican Church in America should afford him an object of much consideration. I understand," he added, feeling his way, "that his Grace is a man of deep piety."

"Very deep," said Mr. Fyshe.

"And of great philanthropy?"

"Very great."

"And I presume," said the rector, taking a devout sip of the unfinished soda, "that he is a man of immense wealth?"

"I suppose so," answered Mr. Fyshe quite carelessly; "all these fellows are." – Mr. Fyshe generally referred to the British aristocracy as "these fellows" – "Land, you know, feudal estates; sheer robbery, I call it. How the working class, the proletariat, stand for such tyranny is more than I can see. Mark my words, Furlong, some day they'll rise and the whole thing will come to a sudden end."

Mr. Fyshe was here launched upon his favourite topic; but he interrupted himself, just for a moment, to speak to the waiter.

"What the devil do you mean," he said, "by serving asparagus half cold?"

"Very sorry, sir," said the waiter, "shall I take it out?"

"Take it out? Of course take it out, and see that you don't serve me stuff of that sort again, or I'll report you."

"Very sorry, sir," said the waiter.

Mr. Fyshe looked at the vanishing waiter with contempt upon his features. "These pampered fellows are getting unbearable," he said. "By Gad, if I had my way I'd fire the whole lot of them: lock 'em out, put 'em on the street. That would teach 'em. Yes, Furlong, you'll live to see it that the whole working class will one day rise against the tyranny of the upper classes, and society will be overwhelmed."

But if Mr. Fyshe had realised that at that moment, in the kitchen of the Mausoleum Club, in those sacred precincts themselves, there was a walking delegate of the Waiters' International Union leaning against a sideboard, with his bowler hat over one corner of his eye, and talking to a little group of the Chinese philosophers, he would have known that perhaps the social catastrophe was a little nearer than even he suspected.

"Are you inviting any one else to-night?" asked Mr. Furlong.

"I should have liked to ask your father," said Mr. Fyshe, "but unfortunately he is out of town."

What Mr. Fyshe really meant was, "I am extremely glad not to have to ask your father, whom I would not introduce to the Duke on any account."

Indeed, Mr. Furlong, senior, the father of the rector of St. Asaph's, who was President of the New Amalgamated Hymnal Corporation, and Director of the Hosanna Pipe and Steam Organ, Limited, was entirely the wrong man for Mr. Fyshe's present purpose. In fact, he was reputed to be as smart a man as ever sold a Bible. At this moment he was out of town, busied in New York with the preparation of the plates of his new Hindu Testament (copyright); but had he learned that a duke with several millions to invest was about to visit the city, he would not have left it for the whole of Hindustan.

"I suppose you are asking Mr. Boulder," said the rector.

"No," answered Mr. Fyshe very decidedly, dismissing the name absolutely.

Indeed, there was even better reason not to introduce Mr. Boulder to the Duke. Mr. Fyshe had made that sort of mistake once, and never intended to make it again. It was only a year ago, on the occasion of the visit of young

Viscount FitzThistle to the Mausoleum Club, that Mr. Fyshe had introduced Mr. Boulder to the Viscount and had suffered grievously thereby. For Mr. Boulder had no sooner met the Viscount than he invited him up to his hunting-lodge in Wisconsin, and that was the last thing known of the investment of the FitzThistle fortune.

This Mr. Boulder of whom Mr. Fyshe spoke might indeed have been seen at that moment at a further table of the lunch room eating a solitary meal, an oldish man with a great frame suggesting broken strength, with a white beard and with falling under-eyelids that made him look as if he were just about to cry. His eyes were blue and far away, and his still, mournful face and his great bent shoulders seemed to suggest all the power and mystery of high finance.

Gloom indeed hung over him. For, when one heard him talk of listed stocks and cumulative dividends, there was as deep a tone in his quiet voice as if he spoke of eternal punishment and the wages of sin.

Under his great hands a chattering viscount, or a sturdy duke, or a popinjay Italian marquis was as nothing.

Mr. Boulder's methods with titled visitors investing money in America were deep. He never spoke to them of money, not a word. He merely talked of the great American forest – he had been born sixty-five years back, in a lumber state – and, when he spoke of primeval trees and the howl of the wolf at night among the pines, there was the stamp of reality about it that held the visitor spellbound; and when he fell to talking of his hunting-lodge far away in the Wisconsin timber, duke, earl, or baron that had ever handled a double-barrelled express rifle listened and was lost.

"I have a little place," Mr. Boulder would say in his deep tones that seemed almost like a sob, "a sort of shooting box, I think you'd call it, up in Wisconsin; just a plain place" – he would add, almost crying – "made of logs."

"Oh, really," the visitor would interject, "made of logs. By Jove, how interesting!"

All titled people are fascinated at once with logs, and Mr. Boulder knew it – at least subconsciously.

"Yes, logs," he would continue, still in deep sorrow; "just the plain cedar, not squared, you know, the old original timber; I had them cut right out of the forest."

By this time the visitor's excitement was obvious. "And is there game there?" he would ask.

"We have the timber wolf," said Mr. Boulder, his voice half choking at the sadness of the thing, "and of course the jack wolf and the lynx."

"And are they ferocious?"

"Oh, extremely so – quite uncontrollable."

On which the titled visitor was all excitement to start for Wisconsin at once, even before Mr. Boulder's invitation was put in words.

And when he returned a week later, all tanned and wearing bush-whackers' boots, and covered with wolf bites, his whole available fortune was so completely invested in Mr. Boulder's securities that you couldn't have shaken twenty-five cents out of him upside down.

Yet the whole thing had been done merely incidentally – round a big fire under the Wisconsin timber, with a dead wolf or two lying in the snow.

So no wonder that Mr. Fyshe did not propose to invite Mr. Boulder to his little dinner. No, indeed. In fact, his one aim was to keep Mr. Boulder and his log house hidden from the Duke.

And equally no wonder that as soon as Mr. Boulder read of the Duke's arrival in New York, and saw by the *Commercial Echo and Financial Undertone* that he might come to the City looking for investments, he telephoned at once to his little place in Wisconsin – which had, of course, a primeval telephone wire running to it – and told his steward to have the place well aired and good fires lighted; and he especially enjoined him to see if any of the shanty men thereabouts could catch a wolf or two, as he might need them.

"Is no one else coming then?" asked the rector.

"Oh yes. President Boomer of the University. We shall

be a party of four. I thought the Duke might be interested in meeting Boomer. He may care to hear something of the archaeological remains of the continent."

If the Duke did so care, he certainly had a splendid chance in meeting the gigantic Dr. Boomer, the president of Plutoria University.

If he wanted to know anything of the exact distinction between the Mexican Pueblo and the Navajo tribal house, he had his opportunity right now. If he was eager to hear a short talk – say half an hour – on the relative antiquity of the Neanderthal skull and the gravel deposits of the Missouri, his chance had come. He could learn as much about the stone age and the bronze age, in America, from President Boomer, as he could about the gold age and the age of paper securities from Mr. Fyshe and Mr. Boulder.

So what better man to meet a duke than an archaeological president?

And if the Duke should feel inclined, as a result of his American visit (for Dr. Boomer, who knew everything, understood what the Duke had come for) inclined, let us say, to endow a chair in Primitive Anthropology, or do any useful little thing of the sort, that was only fair business all round; or if he even was willing to give a moderate sum towards the general fund of Plutoria University – enough, let us say, to enable the president to dismiss an old professor and hire a new one – that surely was reasonable enough.

The president, therefore, had said yes to Mr. Fyshe's invitation with alacrity, and had taken a look through the list of his more incompetent professors to refresh his memory.

The Duke of Dulham had landed in New York five days before and had looked round eagerly for a field of turnips, but hadn't seen any. He had been driven up Fifth Avenue and had kept his eyes open for potatoes, but there were none. Nor had he seen any shorthorns in Central Park, nor any Southdowns on Broadway. For the Duke, of course, like all dukes, was agricultural from his Norfolk jacket to his hobnailed boots.

At his restaurant he had cut a potato in two and sent half of it to the head waiter to know if it was Bermudian. It had all the look of an early Bermudian, but the Duke feared from the shading of it that it might be only a late Trinidad. And the head waiter sent it to the chef, mistaking it for a complaint, and the chef sent it back to the Duke with a message that it was not a Bermudian but a Prince Edward Island. And the Duke sent his compliments to the chef, and the chef sent his compliments to the Duke. And the Duke was so pleased at learning this that he had a similar potato wrapped up for him to take away, and tipped the head waiter twenty-five cents, feeling that in an extravagant country the only thing to do is to go the people one better. So the Duke carried the potato round for five days in New York and showed it to everybody. But beyond this he got no sign of agriculture out of the place at all. No one who entertained him seemed to know what the beef that they gave him had been fed on; no one, even in what seemed the best society, could talk rationally about preparing a hog for the breakfast table. People seemed to eat cauliflower without distinguishing the Denmark variety from the Oldenburg, and few, if any, knew Silesian bacon even when they tasted it. And when they took the Duke out twenty-five miles into what was called the country, there were still no turnips, but only real estate, and railway embankments, and advertising signs; so that altogether the obvious and visible decline of American agriculture in what should have been its leading centre saddened the Duke's heart. Thus the Duke passed four gloomy days. Agriculture vexed him, and still more, of course, the money concerns which had brought him to America.

Money is a troublesome thing. But it has got to be thought about even by those who were not brought up to it. If, on account of money matters, one has been driven to come over to America in the hope of borrowing money, the awkwardness of how to go about it naturally makes one gloomy and preoccupied. Had there been broad fields of turnips to walk in and Holstein cattle to punch in the ribs, one might have managed to borrow it in the course of gentlemanly intercourse, as from one cattle-man to another. But in New York, amid piles of masonry and roaring street-traffic and glittering lunches and palatial residences, one simply couldn't do it.

Herein lay the truth about the Duke of Dulham's visit and the error of Mr. Lucullus Fyshe. Mr. Fyshe was thinking that the Duke had come to *lend* money. In reality he had come to *borrow* it. In fact, the Duke was reckoning that by putting a second mortgage on Dulham Towers for twenty thousand sterling, and by selling his Scotch shooting and leasing his Irish grazing and sub-letting his Welsh coal rent he could raise altogether a hundred thousand pounds. This, for a duke, is an enormous sum. If he once had it he would be able to pay off the first mortgage on Dulham Towers, buy in the rights of the present tenant of the Scotch shooting and the claim of the present mortgagee of the Irish grazing, and in fact be just where he started. This is ducal finance, which moves always in a circle.

In other words the Duke was really a poor man – not poor in the American sense, where poverty comes as a sudden blighting stringency, taking the form of an inability to get hold of a quarter of a million dollars, no matter how badly one needs it, and where it passes like a storm-cloud and is gone, but poor in that permanent and distressing sense known only to the British aristocracy. The Duke's case, of course, was notorious, and Mr. Fyshe ought to have known of it. The Duke was so poor that the Duchess was compelled to spend three or four months every year at a fashionable hotel on the Riviera simply to save money, and his eldest son, the young Marquis of Beldoodle, had to put in most of his time shooting big game in Uganda, with only twenty or twenty-five beaters, and with so few carriers and couriers and such a dearth of elephant men and hyena boys that the thing was a perfect scandal. The Duke indeed was so poor that a younger son, simply to add his efforts to those of the rest, was compelled to pass his days in mountain climbing in the Himalayas, and the Duke's daughter was obliged to pay long visits to minor German princesses, putting up with all sorts of hardship. And while the ducal family wandered about in this way – climbing mountains, and shooting hyenas, and saving money, the Duke's place or seat, Dulham Towers, was practically shut up, with no one in it but servants and housekeepers and gamekeepers and tourists; and the picture galleries, except for artists and visitors and villagers, were closed; and the town house, except for the presence of servants and tradesmen and secretaries, was absolutely shut. But the Duke knew that rigid parsimony of this sort, if kept up for a generation or two, will work wonders, and this sustained him; and the Duchess knew it, and it sustained her; in fact, all the ducal family, knowing that it was only a matter of a generation or two, took their misfortune very cheerfully.

The only thing that bothered the Duke was borrowing money. This was necessary from time to time when loans or mortgages fell in, but he hated it. It was beneath him. His ancestors had often taken money, but had never borrowed it, and the Duke chafed under the necessity. There was something about the process that went against the grain. To sit down in pleasant converse with a man, perhaps almost a gentleman, and then lead up to the subject and take his money from him, seemed to the Duke's mind essentially low. He could have understood knocking a man over the head with a fire shovel and taking his money, but not borrowing it.

So the Duke had come to America, where borrowing is notoriously easy. Any member of the Mausoleum Club, for instance, would borrow fifty cents to buy a cigar, or fifty thousand dollars to buy a house, or five millions to buy a railroad with complete indifference, and pay it back, too, if he could, and think nothing of it. In fact, ever so many of the Duke's friends were known to have borrowed money in America with magical ease, pledging for it their seats or their pictures, or one of their daughters – anything.

So the Duke knew it must be easy. And yet, incredible as it may seem, he had spent four days in New York, entertained everywhere, and made much of, and hadn't borrowed a cent. He had been asked to lunch in a Riverside palace, and, fool that he was, had come away without so much as a dollar to show for it. He had been asked to a country house on the Hudson, and, like an idiot – he admitted it himself – hadn't asked his host for as much as his train fare. He had been driven twice round Central Park in a motor and had been taken tamely back to his hotel not a dollar the richer. The thing was childish, and he knew it. But to save his life the Duke didn't know how to begin. None of the things that he was able to talk about seemed to have the remotest connection with the subject of money. The Duke was able to converse reasonably well over such topics as the approaching downfall of England (they had talked of it at Dulham Towers for sixty years), or over the duty of England towards China, or the duty of England to Persia, or its duty to aid the Young Turk Movement, and its duty to check the Old Servia agitation. The Duke became so interested in these topics and in explaining that while he had never been a Little Englander he had always been a Big Turk, and that he stood for a Small Bulgaria and a Restricted Austria, that he got further and further away from the topic of money, which was what he really wanted to come to; and the Duke rose from his conversations with a look of such obvious distress on his face that everybody realised that his anxiety about England was killing him.

And then suddenly light had come. It was on his fourth day in New York that he unexpectedly ran into the Viscount Belstairs (they had been together as young men in Nigeria, and as middle-aged men in St. Petersburg), and Belstairs, who was in abundant spirits and who was returning to England on the *Gloritania* at noon the next day, explained to the Duke that he had just borrowed fifty thousand pounds, on security that wouldn't be worth a halfpenny in England.

And the Duke said with a sigh, "How the deuce do you do it, Belstairs?"

"Do what?"

"Borrow it," said the Duke. "How do you manage to get people to talk about it? Here I am wanting to borrow a hundred thousand, and I'm hanged if I can even find an opening."

At which the Viscount had said, "Pooh, pooh! you don't need any opening. Just borrow it straight out – ask for it across a dinner table, just as you'd ask for a match; they think nothing of it here."

"Across the dinner table?" repeated the Duke, who was a literal man.

"Certainly," said the Viscount. "Not too soon, you know – say after a second glass of wine. I assure you it's absolutely nothing."

And it was just at that moment that a telegram was handed to the Duke from Mr. Lucullus Fyshe, praying him, as he was reported to be visiting the next day the City where the Mausoleum Club stands, to make acquaintance with him by dining at that institution.

And the Duke, being as I say a literal man, decided that just as soon as Mr. Fyshe should give him a second glass of wine, that second glass should cost Mr. Fyshe a hundred thousand pounds sterling.

And oddly enough, at about the same moment, Mr. Fyshe was calculating that provided he could make the Duke drink a second glass of the Mausoleum champagne, that glass would cost the Duke about five million dollars.

So the very morning after that the Duke had arrived on the New York express in the City; and being an ordinary, democratic, commercial sort of place, absorbed in its own affairs, it made no fuss over him whatever. The morning edition of the *Plutopian Citizen* simply said, "We understand that the Duke of Dulham arrives at the Grand Palaver this morning," after which it traced the Duke's pedigree back to Jock of Ealing in the twelfth century and let the matter go at that; and the noon edition of the *People's Advocate* merely wrote, "We learn that Duke Dulham is in town. He is a relation of Jack Ealing." But the *Commercial Echo and Financial Undertone*, appearing at four o'clock, printed in its stock market columns the announcement: "We understand that the Duke of Dulham, who arrives in town to-day, is proposing to invest a large sum of money in American Industrials."

And of course that announcement reached every member of the Mausoleum Club within twenty minutes.

The Duke of Dulham entered the Mausoleum Club that evening at exactly seven of the clock. He was a short, thick man with a shaven face, red as a brick, and grizzled hair, and from the look of him he could have got a job at sight in any lumber camp in Wisconsin. He wore a dinner jacket, just like an ordinary person, but even without his Norfolk coat and his hobnailed boots there was something in the way in which he walked up the long main hall of the Mausoleum Club that every imported waiter in the place recognised in an instant.

The Duke cast his eye about the club and approved of it. It seemed to him a modest, quiet place, very different from the staring ostentation that one sees too often in a German hof or an Italian palazzo. He liked it.

Mr. Fyshe and Mr. Furlong were standing in a deep alcove or bay where there was a fire and india-rubber trees and pictures with shaded lights and a whiskey-and-soda table. There the Duke joined them. Mr. Fyshe he had met already that afternoon at the Palaver, and he called him "Fyshe" as if he had known him forever; and indeed, after a few minutes he called the rector of St. Asaph's simply "Furlong," for he had been familiar with the Anglican clergy in so many parts of the world that he knew that to attribute any peculiar godliness to them, socially, was the worst possible taste.

"By Jove," said the Duke, turning to tap the leaf of a rubber-tree with his finger, "that fellow's a Nigerian, isn't he?"

"I hardly know," said Mr. Fyshe, "I imagine so"; and he added, "You've been in Nigeria, Duke?"

"Oh, some years ago," said the Duke, "after big game, you know – fine place for it."

"Did you get any?" asked Mr. Fyshe.

"Not much," said the Duke; "a hippo or two."

"Ah," said Mr. Fyshe.

"And, of course, now and then a giro," the Duke went on, and added, "My sister was luckier, though; she potted a rhino one day, straight out of a doolie; I call that rather good."

Mr. Fyshe called it that too.

"Ah, now here's a good thing," the Duke went on, looking at a picture. He carried in his waist-coat pocket an eye-glass that he used for pictures and for Tamworth hogs, and he put it to his eye with one hand, keeping the other in the left pocket of his jacket; "and this – this is a very good thing."

"I believe so," said Mr. Fyshe.

"You really have some awfully good things here," continued the Duke. He had seen far too many pictures in too many places ever to speak of "values" or "compositions" or anything of that sort. The Duke merely looked at a picture and said, "Now here's a good thing," or "Ah! here now is a very good thing," or "I say, here's a really good thing."

No one could get past this sort of criticism. The Duke had long since found it bullet-proof.

"They showed me some rather good things in New York," he went on, "but really the things you have here seem to be awfully good things."

Indeed, the Duke was truly pleased with the pictures, for something in their composition, or else in the soft, expensive light that shone on them, enabled him to see in the distant background of each a hundred thousand sterling. And that is a very beautiful picture indeed.

"When you come to our side of the water, Fyshe," said the Duke, "I must show you my Botticelli."

Had Mr. Fyshe, who knew nothing of art, expressed his real thought, he would have said, "Show me your which?" But he only answered, "I shall be delighted to see it."

In any case there was no time to say more, for at this moment the portly figure and the great face of Dr. Boomer, president of Plutoria University, loomed upon them. And with him came a great burst of conversation that blew all previous topics into fragments. He was introduced to the Duke, and shook hands with Mr. Furlong, and talked to both of them, and named the kind of cocktail that he wanted, all in one breath, and in the very next he was asking the Duke about the Babylonian hieroglyphic bricks that his grandfather, the thirteenth Duke, had brought home from the Euphrates, and which every archaeologist knew were preserved in the Duke's library at Dulham Towers. And though the Duke hadn't known about the bricks himself, he assured Dr. Boomer that his grandfather had collected some really good things, quite remarkable.

And the Duke, having met a man who knew about his grandfather, felt in his own element. In fact, he was so delighted with Dr. Boomer and the Nigerian rubber-tree and the shaded pictures and the charm of the whole place and the certainty that half a million dollars was easily findable in it, that he put his eye-glass back in his pocket and said,

"A charming club you have here, really most charming."

"Yes," said Mr. Fyshe, in a casual tone, "a comfortable place, we like to think."

But if he could have seen what was happening below in the kitchens of the Mausoleum Club, Mr. Fyshe would have realised that just then it was turning into a most uncomfortable place.

For the walking delegate with his hat on sideways, who

had haunted it all day, was busy now among the assembled Chinese philosophers, writing down names and distributing strikers' cards of the International Union and assuring them that the "boys" of the Grand Palaver had all walked out at seven, and that all the "boys" of the Commercial and the Union and of every restaurant in town were out an hour ago.

And the philosophers were taking their cards and hanging up their waiters' coats and putting on shabby jackets and bowler hats, worn sideways, and changing themselves by a wonderful transformation from respectable Chinese to slouching loafers of the lowest type.

But Mr. Fyshe, being in an alcove and not in the kitchens, saw nothing of these things. Not even when the head waiter, shaking with apprehension, appeared with cocktails made by himself, in glasses that he himself had had to wipe, did Mr. Fyshe, absorbed in the easy urbanity of the Duke, notice that anything was amiss.

Neither did his guests. For Dr. Boomer, having discovered that the Duke had visited Nigeria, was asking him his opinion of the famous Bimbaweh remains of the lower Niger. The Duke confessed that he really hadn't noticed them, and the Doctor assured him that Strabo had indubitably mentioned them (he would show the Duke the very passage), and that they apparently lay, if his memory served him, about half-way between Oohat and Ohat; whether above Oohat and below Ohat or above Ohat and below Oohat he would not care to say for a certainty; for that the Duke must wait till the president had time to consult his library.

And the Duke was fascinated forthwith with the president's knowledge of Nigerian geography, and explained that he had once actually descended from below Timbuctoo to Oohat in a doolie manned only by four swats.

So presently, having drunk the cocktails, the party moved solemnly in a body from the alcove towards the private dining-room upstairs, still busily talking of the Bimbaweh remains, and the swats, and whether the doolie was, or was not, the original goatskin boat of the book of Genesis.

And when they entered the private dining-room with its snow-white table and cut glass and flowers (as arranged by a retreating philosopher now heading towards the Gaiety Theatre with his hat over his eyes), the Duke again exclaimed,

"Really, you have a most comfortable club – delightful."

So they sat down to dinner, over which Mr. Furlong offered up a grace as short as any that are known even to the Anglican clergy. And the head waiter, now in deep distress – for he had been sending out telephone messages in vain to the Grand Palaver and the Continental, like the captain of a sinking ship – served oysters that he had opened himself and poured Rhine wine with a trembling hand. For he knew that unless by magic a new chef and a waiter or two could be got from the Palaver, all hope was lost.

But the guests still knew nothing of his fears. Dr. Boomer was eating his oysters as a Nigerian hippo might eat up the crew of a doolie, in great mouthfuls, and commenting as he did so upon the luxuriousness of modern life.

And in the pause that followed the oysters he illustrated for the Duke with two pieces of bread the essential difference in structure between the Mexican *pueblo* and the tribal house of the Navajos, and lest the Duke should confound either or both of them with the adobe hut of the Bimbaweh tribes he showed the difference at once with a couple of olives.

By this time, of course, the delay in the service was getting noticeable. Mr. Fyshe was directing angry glances towards the door, looking for the reappearance of the waiter, and growling an apology to his guests. But the president waved the apology aside.

"In my college days," he said, "I should have considered a plate of oysters an ample meal. I should have asked for nothing more. We eat," he said, "too much."

This, of course, started Mr. Fyshe on his favourite topic.

"Luxury!" he exclaimed, "I should think so! It is the curse of the age. The appalling growth of luxury, the piling up of money, the ease with which huge fortunes are made" (Good! thought the Duke, here we are coming to it), "these are the things that are going to ruin us. Mark my words, the whole thing is bound to end in a tremendous crash. I don't mind telling you, Duke – my friends here, I am sure, know it already – that I am more or less a revolutionary socialist. I am absolutely convinced, sir, that our modern civilisation will end in a great social catastrophe. Mark what I say" – and here Mr. Fyshe became exceedingly impressive – "a great social catastrophe. Some of us may not live to see it, perhaps; but you, for instance, Furlong, are a younger man; you certainly will."

But here Mr. Fyshe was understating the case. They were all going to live to see it, right on the spot.

For it was just at this moment, when Mr. Fyshe was talking of the social catastrophe and explaining with flashing eyes that it was bound to come, that it came; and when it came it lit, of all places in the world, right there in the private dining-room of the Mausoleum Club.

For the gloomy head waiter re-entered and leaned over the back of Mr. Fyshe's chair and whispered to him.

"Eh? what?" said Mr. Fyshe.

The head waiter, his features stricken with inward agony, whispered again.

"The infernal, damn scoundrels!" said Mr. Fyshe, starting back in his chair. "On strike: in this club! It's an outrage!"

"I'm very sorry, sir. I didn't like to tell you, sir. I'd hoped I might have got help from the outside, but it seems, sir, the hotels are all the same way."

"Do you mean to say," said Mr. Fyshe, speaking very slowly, "that there is no dinner?"

"I'm sorry, sir," moaned the waiter. "It appears the chef hadn't even cooked it. Beyond what's on the table, sir, there's nothing."

The social catastrophe had come.

Mr. Fyshe sat silent with his fist clenched. Dr. Boomer, with his great face transfixed, stared at the empty oyster-shells, thinking perhaps of his college days. The Duke, with his hundred thousand dashed from his lips in the second cup of champagne that was never served, thought of his politeness first and murmured something about taking them to his hotel.

But there is no need to follow the unhappy details of the unended dinner. Mr. Fyshe's one idea was to be gone: he was too true an artist to think that finance could be carried on over the table-cloth of a second-rate restaurant, or on an empty stomach in a deserted club. The thing must be done over again; he must wait his time and begin anew.

And so it came about that the little dinner-party of Mr. Lucullus Fyshe dissolved itself into its constituent elements, like broken pieces of society in the great cataclysm portrayed by Mr. Fyshe himself.

The Duke was bowled home in a snorting motor to the brilliant rotunda of the Grand Palaver, itself waiterless and supperless.

The rector of St. Asaph's wandered off home to his rectory, musing upon the contents of its pantry.

And Mr. Fyshe and the gigantic Doctor walked side by side homewards along Plutoria Avenue, beneath the elm trees.

Nor had they gone any great distance before Dr. Boomer fell to talking of the Duke.

"A charming man," he said, "delightful. I feel extremely sorry for him."

"No worse off, I presume, than any of the rest of us," growled Mr. Fyshe, who was feeling in the sourest of democratic moods; "a man doesn't need to be a duke to have a stomach."

"Oh, pooh, pooh!" said the president, waving the topic aside with his hand in the air; "I don't refer to that. Oh, not at all. I was thinking of his financial position – an ancient family like the Dulhams; it seems too bad altogether."

For, of course, to an archaeologist like Dr. Boomer an intimate acquaintance with the pedigree and fortunes of the greater ducal families from Jock of Ealing downwards was nothing. It went without saying. As beside the Neanderthal skull and the Bimbaweh ruins it didn't count.

Mr. Fyshe stopped absolutely still in his tracks. "His financial position?" he questioned, quick as a lynx.

"Certainly," said Dr. Boomer; "I had taken it for granted that you knew. The Dulham family are practically ruined. The Duke, I imagine, is under the necessity of mortgaging his estates; indeed, I should suppose he is here in America to raise money."

Mr. Fyshe was a man of lightning action. Any man accustomed to the Stock Exchange learns to think quickly.

"One moment!" he cried; "I see we are right at your door. May I just run in and use your telephone? I want to call up Boulder for a moment."

Two minutes later Mr. Fyshe was saying into the telephone, "Oh, is that you, Boulder? I was looking for you in vain to-day – wanted you to meet the Duke of Dulham, who came in quite unexpectedly from New York; felt sure you'd like to meet him. Wanted you at the club for dinner, and now it turns out that the club's all upset – waiters' strike or some such rascality – and the Palaver, so I hear, is in the same fix. Could you possibly –"

Here Mr. Fyshe paused, listening a moment and then went on, "Yes, yes; an excellent idea – most kind of you. Pray do send your motor to the hotel and give the Duke a bite of dinner. No, I won't join you, thanks. Most kind. Good-night –"

And within a few minutes more the motor of Mr. Boulder was rolling down from Plutoria Avenue to the Grand Palaver Hotel.

What passed between Mr. Boulder and the Duke that evening is not known. That they must have proved congenial company to one another there is no doubt. In fact, it would seem that, dissimilar as they were in many ways, they found a common bond of interest in sport. And it is quite likely that Mr. Boulder may have mentioned that he had a hunting-lodge – what the Duke would call a shooting-box – in Wisconsin woods, and that it was made of logs, rough cedar logs not squared, and that the timber wolves and others which surrounded it were of a ferocity without parallel.

Those who know the Duke best could measure the effect of that upon his temperament.

At any rate, it is certain that Mr. Lucullus Fyshe at his breakfast-table next morning chuckled with suppressed joy to read in the *Plutopian Citizen* the item:

"We learn that the Duke of Dulham, who has been paying a brief visit to the City, leaves this morning with Mr. Asmodeus Boulder for the Wisconsin woods. We understand that Mr. Boulder intends to show his guest, who is an ardent sportsman, something of the American wolf."

And so the Duke went whirling westwards and northwards with Mr. Boulder in the drawing-room end of a Pullman car, that was all littered up with double-barrelled express rifles and leather game bags, and lynx catchers and wolf traps and Heaven knows what. And the Duke had on his very roughest sporting suit, made, apparently, of alligator hide; and as he sat there with a rifle across his knees, while the train swept onward through open fields and broken woods, the real country at last, towards the Wisconsin forest, there was such a light of genial happiness in his face that had not been seen there since he had been marooned in the mud jungles of Upper Burmah.

And opposite, Mr. Boulder looked at him with fixed, silent eyes, and murmured from time to time some renewed information of the ferocity of the timber wolf.

But of wolves other than the timber wolf, and fiercer still,

into whose hands the Duke might fall in America, he spoke
never a word.

Nor is it known in the record what happened in Wisconsin, and to the Mausoleum Club the Duke and his visit
remained only as a passing and a pleasant memory.

TWO

The Wizard of Finance

Down in the City itself, just below the residential street where the Mausoleum Club is situated, there stands overlooking Central Square the Grand Palaver Hotel. It is, in truth, at no great distance from the club, not half a minute in one's motor. In fact, one could almost walk it.

But in Central Square the quiet of Plutoria Avenue is exchanged for another atmosphere. There are fountains that splash unendingly and mingle their music with the sound of the motorhorns and the clatter of the cabs. There are real trees and little green benches, with people reading yesterday's newspaper, and grass cut into plots among the asphalt. There is at one end a statue of the first governor of the state, life-size, cut in stone; and at the other a statue of the last, ever so much larger than life, cast in bronze. And all the people who pass by pause and look at this statue and point at it with walking sticks, because it is of extraordinary interest; in fact, it is an example of the new electro-chemical process of casting by which you can cast a state governor any size you like, no matter what you start from. Those who know about such things explain what an interesting contrast the two statues are; for in the case of the governor of a hundred years ago one had to start from plain, rough material and work patiently for years to get the effect, whereas now the material doesn't matter at all, and with any sort of scrap, treated in the gas furnace under tremendous pressure, one may make a figure of colossal size like the one in Central Square.

So naturally, Central Square with its trees and its fountains and its statues is one of the places of chief interest in the City. But especially because there stands along one side of it the vast pile of the Grand Palaver Hotel. It rises fifteen stories high and fills all one side of the square. It has, overlooking the trees in the square, twelve hundred rooms with three thousand windows, and it would have held all George Washington's army. Even people in other cities who have never seen it know it well from its advertising; "the most homelike hotel in America," so it is labelled in all the magazines, the expensive ones, on the continent. In fact, the aim of the company that owns the Grand Palaver – and they do not attempt to conceal it – is to make the place as much a home as possible. Therein lies its charm. It is a home. You realise that when you look up at the Grand Palaver from the square at night when the twelve hundred guests have turned on the lights of the three thousand windows. You realise it at theatre time when the great strings of motors come sweeping to the doors of the Palaver, to carry the twelve hundred guests to twelve hundred seats in the theatres at four dollars a seat. But most of all do you appreciate the character of the Grand Palaver when you step into its rotunda. Aladdin's enchanted palace was nothing to it. It has a vast ceiling with a hundred glittering lights, and within it night and day is a surging crowd that is never still and a babel of voices that is never hushed, and over all there hangs an enchanted cloud of thin blue tobacco smoke such as might enshroud the conjured vision of a magician of Bagdad or Damascus.

In and through the rotunda there are palm-trees to rest the eye and rubber-trees in boxes to soothe the mind, and there are great leather lounges and deep arm-chairs, and here and there huge brass ash-bowls as big as Etruscan tear-jugs. Along one side is a counter with grated wickets like a bank, and behind it are five clerks with flattened hair and tall collars, dressed in long black frock-coats all day like members of a legislature. They have great books in front of them in which they study unceasingly, and at their lightest thought they strike a bell with the open palm of their hand, and at the sound of it a page boy in a monkey suit, with G.P. stamped all over him in brass, bounds to the desk and off again, shouting a call into the unheeding crowd vociferously. The sound of it fills for a moment the great space of the rotunda; it echoes down the corridors to the side; it floats, softly melodious, through the palm-trees of the ladies' palm room; it is heard, fainter and fainter, in the distant grill, and in the depths of the barber shop below the level of the street the barber arrests a moment the drowsy hum of his shampoo brushes to catch the sound – as might a miner in the sunken galleries of a coastal mine cease in his toil a moment to hear the distant murmur of the sea.

And the clerks call for the pages, the pages call for the guests, and the guests call for the porters, the bells clang, the elevators rattle, till home itself was never half so home-like.

"A call for Mr. Tomlinson! A call for Mr. Tomlinson!"

So went the sound, echoing through the rotunda.

And as the page boy found him and handed him on a salver a telegram to read, the eyes of the crowd about him turned for a moment to look upon the figure of Tomlinson, the Wizard of Finance.

There he stood in his wide-awake hat and his long black coat, his shoulders slightly bent with his fifty-eight years. Anyone who had known him in the olden days on his bush farm beside Tomlinson's Creek in the country of the Great Lakes would have recognised him in a moment. There was still on his face that strange, puzzled look that it habitually wore, only now, of course, the financial papers were calling it "unfathomable." There was a certain way in which his eye roved to and fro inquiringly that might have looked like perplexity, were it not that the *Financial Undertone* had recognised it as the "searching look of a captain of industry." One might have thought that for all the goodness in it there was something simple in his face, were it not that the *Commercial and Pictorial Review* had called the face "inscrutable," and had proved it so with an illustration that left no doubt of the matter. Indeed, the face of Tomlinson of Tomlinson's Creek, now Tomlinson the Wizard of Finance, was not commonly spoken of as a *face* by the paragraphers of the Saturday magazine sections, but was more usually referred to as a mask; and it would appear that Napoleon the First had had one also. The Saturday editors were never tired of describing the strange, impressive personality of Tomlinson, the great dominating character of the newest and highest finance. From the moment when the interim prospectus of the Erie Auriferous Consolidated had broken like a tidal wave over Stock Exchange circles, the picture of Tomlinson, the sleeping shareholder of uncomputed millions, had filled the imagination of every dreamer in a nation of poets.

They all described him. And when each had finished he began again.

"The face," so wrote the editor of the "Our Own Men" section of *Ourselves Monthly*, "is that of a typical American captain of finance, hard, yet with a certain softness, broad but with a certain length, ductile but not without its own firmness."

"The mouth," so wrote the editor of the "Success" column of *Brains*, "is strong but pliable, the jaw firm and yet movable, while there is something in the set of the ear that suggests the swift, eager mind of the born leader of men."

So from state to state ran the portrait of Tomlinson of Tomlinson's Creek, drawn by people who had never seen him; so did it reach out and cross the ocean, till the French journals inserted a picture which they used for such occasions, and called it *Monsieur Tomlinson, nouveau capitaine de la haute finance en Amérique*; and the German weeklies, inserting also a suitable picture from their stock, marked it

Herr Tomlinson, Amerikanischer Industrie-und Finanz-capitän. Thus did Tomlinson float from Tomlinson's Creek beside Lake Erie to the very banks of the Danube and the Drave.

Some writers grew lyric about him. What visions, they asked, could one but read them, must lie behind the quiet, dreaming eyes of that inscrutable face?

They might have read them easily enough, had they but had the key. Anyone who looked upon Tomlinson as he stood there in the roar and clatter of the great rotunda of the Grand Palaver with the telegram in his hand, fumbling at the wrong end to open it, might have read the visions of the master-mind had he but known their nature. They were simple enough. For the visions in the mind of Tomlinson, Wizard of Finance, were for the most part those of a wind-swept hillside farm beside Lake Erie, where Tomlinson's Creek runs down to the low edge of the lake, and where the off-shore wind ripples the rushes of the shallow water: that, and the vision of a frame house, and the snake fences of the fourth concession road where it falls to the lakeside. And if the eyes of the man are dreamy and abstracted, it is because there lies over the vision of this vanished farm an infinite regret, greater in its compass than all the shares the Erie Auriferous Consolidated has ever thrown upon the market.

When Tomlinson had opened the telegram he stood with it for a moment in his hand, looking the boy full in the face. His look had in it that peculiar far-away quality that the newspapers were calling "Napoleonic abstraction." In reality he was wondering whether to give the boy twenty-five cents or fifty.

The message that he had just read was worded, "Morning quotations show preferred A.G. falling rapidly recommend instant sale no confidence send instructions."

The Wizard of Finance took from his pocket a pencil (it was a carpenter's pencil) and wrote across the face of the message,

"Buy me quite a bit more of the same yours truly."

This he gave to the boy. "Take it over to him," he said, pointing to the telegraph corner of the rotunda. Then after another pause he mumbled, "Here, sonny," and gave the boy a dollar.

With that he turned to walk towards the elevator, and all the people about him who had watched the signing of the message knew that some big financial deal was going through – a *coup*, in fact, they called it.

The elevator took the Wizard to the second floor. As he went up he felt in his pocket and gripped a quarter, then changed his mind and felt for a fifty-cent piece, and finally gave them both to the elevator boy, after which he walked along the corridor till he reached the corner suite of rooms, a palace in itself, for which he was paying a thousand dollars a month ever since the Erie Auriferous Consolidated Company had begun tearing up the bed of Tomlinson's Creek in Cahoga County with its hydraulic dredges.

"Well, mother," he said as he entered.

There was a woman seated near the window, a woman with a plain, homely face such as they wear in the farm kitchens of Cahoga County, and a set of fashionable clothes upon her such as they sell to the ladies of Plutoria Avenue.

This was 'mother,' the wife of the Wizard of Finance and eight years younger than himself. And she too was in the papers and the public eye; and whatsoever the shops had fresh from Paris, at fabulous prices, that they sold to mother. They had put a Balkan hat upon her with an upright feather, and they had hung gold chains on her, and everything that was most expensive they had hung and tied on mother. You might see her emerging any morning from the Grand Palaver in her beetle-back jacket and her Balkan hat, a figure of infinite pathos. And whatever she wore, the lady editors of *Spring Notes* and *Causerie du Boudoir* wrote it out in French, and one paper had called her a *belle châtelaine*, and another had spoken of her as a *grande dame*, which the Tomlinsons thought must be a misprint.

But in any case, for Tomlinson the Wizard of Finance it was a great relief to have as his wife a woman like mother, because he knew that she had taught school in Cahoga County and could hold her own in the city with any of them.

So mother spent her time sitting in her beetle jacket in the thousand-dollar suite, reading new novels in brilliant paper covers. And the Wizard on his trips up and down to the rotunda brought her the very best, the ones that cost a dollar fifty, because he knew that out home she had only been able to read books like Nathaniel Hawthorne and Walter Scott, that were only worth ten cents.

"How's Fred?" said the Wizard, laying aside his hat, and looking towards the closed door of an inner room. "Is he better?"

"Some," said mother. "He's dressed, but he's lying down."

Fred was the son of the Wizard and mother. In the inner room he lay on a sofa, a great hulking boy of seventeen in a flowered dressing-gown, fancying himself ill. There was a packet of cigarettes and a box of chocolates on a chair beside him, and he had the blind drawn and his eyes half-closed to impress himself.

Yet this was the same boy that less than a year ago on Tomlinson's Creek had worn a rough store suit and set his sturdy shoulders to the buck-saw. At present Fortune was busy taking from him the golden gifts which the fairies of Cahoga County, Lake Erie, had laid in his cradle seventeen years ago.

The Wizard tip-toed into the inner room, and from the open door his listening wife could hear the voice of the boy saying, in a tone as of one distraught with suffering:

"Is there any more of that jelly?"

"Could he have any, do you suppose?" asked Tomlinson coming back.

"It's all right," said mother, "if it will sit on his stomach."

For this, in the dietetics of Cahoga County, is the sole
test. All those things can be eaten which will sit on the
stomach. Anything that won't sit there is not eatable.

"Do you suppose I could get them to get any?" questioned Tomlinson. "Would it be all right to telephone down
to the office, or do you think it would be better to ring?"

"Perhaps," said his wife, "it would be better to look out
into the hall and see if there isn't someone round that would
tell them."

This was the kind of problem with which Tomlinson and
his wife, in their thousand-dollar suite in the Grand Palaver, grappled all day. And when presently a tall waiter in
dress-clothes appeared, and said, "Jelly? Yes, sir, immediately, sir; would you like, sir, Maraschino, sir, or Porto-
vino, sir?" Tomlinson gazed at him gloomily, wondering if
he would take five dollars.

"What does the doctor say is wrong with Fred?" asked
Tomlinson, when the waiter had gone.

"He don't just say," said mother; "he said he must keep
very quiet. He looked in this morning for a minute or two,
and he said he'd look in later in the day again. But he said to
keep Fred very quiet."

Exactly! In other words Fred had pretty much the same
complaint as the rest of Dr. Slyder's patients on Plutoria
Avenue, and was to be treated in the same way. Dr. Slyder,
who was the most fashionable practitioner in the City,
spent his entire time moving to and fro in an almost noiseless motor earnestly advising people to keep quiet. "You
must keep very quiet for a little while," he would say with a
sigh, as he sat beside a sick-bed. As he drew on his gloves in
the hall below he would shake his head very impressively
and say, "You must keep him very quiet," and so pass out,
quite soundlessly. By this means Dr. Slyder often succeeded in keeping people quiet for weeks. It was all the
medicine that he knew. But it was enough. And as his
patients always got well – there being nothing wrong with
them – his reputation was immense.

Very naturally the Wizard and his wife were impressed

with him. They had never seen such therapeutics in Cahoga County, where the practice of medicine is carried on with forceps, pumps, squirts, splints, and other instruments of violence.

The waiter had hardly gone when a boy appeared at the door. This time he presented to Tomlinson not one telegram but a little bundle of them.

The Wizard read them with a lengthening face. The first ran something like this, "Congratulate you on your daring market turned instantly"; and the next, "Your opinion justified market rose have sold at 20 points profit"; and a third, "Your forecast entirely correct C.P. rose at once send further instructions."

These and similar messages were from brokers' offices, and all of them were in the same tone; one told him that C.P. was up, and another T.G.P. had passed 129, and another that T.C.R.R. had risen ten – all of which things were imputed to the wonderful sagacity of Tomlinson. Whereas if they had told him that X.Y.Z. had risen to the moon he would have been just as wise as to what it meant.

"Well," said the wife of the Wizard as her husband finished looking through the reports, "how are things this morning? Are they any better?"

"No," said Tomlinson, and he sighed as he said it; "this is the worst day yet. It's just been a shower of telegrams, and mostly all the same. I can't do the figuring of it like you can, but I reckon I must have made another hundred thousand dollars since yesterday."

"You don't say so!" said mother, and they looked at one another gloomily.

"And half a million last week, wasn't it?" said Tomlinson as he sank into a chair. "I'm afraid, mother," he continued, "it's no good. We don't know how. We weren't brought up to it."

All of which meant that if the editor of the *Monetary Afternoon* or *Financial Sunday* had been able to know what was happening with the two wizards, he could have written up a news story calculated to electrify all America.

For the truth was that Tomlinson, the Wizard of Finance, was attempting to carry out a *coup* greater than any as yet attributed to him by the Press. He was trying to lose his money. That, in the sickness of his soul, crushed by the Grand Palaver, overwhelmed with the burden of high finance, had become his aim, to be done with it, to get rid of his whole fortune.

But if you own a fortune that is computed anywhere from fifty millions up, with no limit at the top, if you own one-half of all the preferred stock of an Erie Auriferous Consolidated that is digging gold in hydraulic bucketfuls from a quarter of a mile of river bed, the task of losing it is no easy matter.

There are men, no doubt, versed in finance, who might succeed in doing it. But they have a training that Tomlinson lacked. Invest it as he would in the worst securities that offered, the most rickety of stock, the most fraudulent bonds, back it came to him. When he threw a handful away, back came two in its place. And at every new *coup* the crowd applauded the incomparable daring, the unparalleled prescience of the Wizard.

Like the touch of Midas, his hand turned everything to gold.

"Mother," he repeated, "it's no use. It's like this here Destiny, as the books call it."

The great fortune that Tomlinson, the Wizard of Finance, was trying his best to lose had come to him with wonderful suddenness. As yet it was hardly six months old. As to how it had originated, there were all sorts of stories afloat in the weekly illustrated press. They agreed mostly on the general basis that Tomlinson had made his vast fortune by his own indomitable pluck and dogged industry. Some said that he had been at one time a mere farm hand who, by sheer doggedness, had fought his way from the hay-mow to the control of the produce market of seventeen states. Others had it that he had been a lumber-jack who, by sheer doggedness, had got possession of the whole lumber forest of the Lake district. Others said that he had been a miner in a Lake Superior copper mine who had, by the doggedness of his character, got a practical monopoly of the copper supply. These Saturday articles, at any rate, made the Saturday reader rigid with sympathetic doggedness himself, which was all that the editor (who was doggedly trying to make the paper pay) wanted to effect.

But in reality the making of Tomlinson's fortune was very simple. The recipe for it is open to anyone. It is only necessary to own a hillside farm beside Lake Erie where the uncleared bush and the broken fields go straggling down to the lake, and to have running through it a creek, such as that called Tomlinson's, brawling among the stones and willows, and to discover in the bed of a creek – a gold mine.

That is all.

Nor is it necessary in these well-ordered days to discover the gold for one's self. One might have lived a lifetime on the farm, as Tomlinson's father had, and never discover it for one's self. For that indeed the best medium of destiny is a geologist, let us say the senior professor of geology at Plutoria University.

That was how it happened.

The senior professor, so it chanced, was spending his vacation near by on the shores of the lake, and his time was mostly passed – for how better can a man spend a month of pleasure? – in looking for outcroppings of Devonian rock of the post-tertiary period. For which purpose he carried a vacation hammer in his pocket, and made from time to time a note or two as he went along, or filled his pockets with the chippings of vacation rocks.

So it chanced that he came to Tomlinson's Creek at the very point where a great slab of Devonian rock bursts through the clay of the bank. When the senior professor of geology saw it and noticed a stripe like a mark on a tiger's back – a fault he called it – that ran over the face of the block, he was at it in an instant, beating off fragments with his little hammer.

Tomlinson and his boy Fred were logging in the under-
brush near by with a long chain and yoke of oxen, but the
geologist was so excited that he did not see them till the
sound of his eager hammer had brought them to his side.
They took him up to the frame house in the clearing, where
the chatelaine was hoeing a potato patch with a man's hat
on her head, and they gave him buttermilk and soda cakes,
but his hand shook so that he could hardly eat them.

The geologist left Cahoga station that night for the City
with a newspaper full of specimens inside his suit-case, and
he knew that if any person or persons would put up money
enough to tear that block of rock away and follow the
fissure down, there would be found there something to
astonish humanity, geologists and all.

After that point in the launching of a gold mine the rest is
easy. Generous, warm-hearted men, interested in geology,
were soon found. There was no stint of money. The great
rock was torn sideways from its place, and from beneath it
the crumbled, glittering rock-dust that sparkled in the sun
was sent in little boxes to the testing laboratories of Plutoria University. There the senior professor of geology had
sat up with it far into the night in a darkened laboratory,
with little blue flames playing underneath crucibles, as in a
magician's cavern, and with the door locked. And as each
sample that he tested was set aside and tied in a cardboard
box by itself, he labelled it "aur. p. 75," and the pen shook
in his hand as he marked it. For to professors of geology
those symbols mean "this is seventy-five per cent pure
gold." So it was no wonder that the senior professor of
geology working far into the night among the blue flames
shook with excitement; not, of course, for the gold's sake as
money (he had no time to think of that), but because if this
thing was true it meant that an auriferous vein had been
found in what was Devonian rock of the post-tertiary
stratification, and if that was so it upset enough geology to
spoil a text-book. It would mean that the professor could

read a paper at the next Pan-Geological Conference that would turn the whole assembly into a bedlam.

It pleased him, too, to know that the men he was dealing with were generous. They had asked him to name his own price for the tests that he made, and when he had said two dollars per sample they had told him to go right ahead. The professor was not, I suppose, a mercenary man, but it pleased him to think that he could clean up sixteen dollars in a single evening in his laboratory. It showed, at any rate, that business men put science at its proper value. Strangest of all was the fact that the men had told him that even this ore was apparently nothing to what there was; it had all come out of one single spot in the creek, not the hundredth part of the whole claim. Lower down, where they had thrown the big dam across to make the bed dry, they were taking out this same stuff and even better, so they said, in cartloads. The hydraulic dredges were tearing it from the bed of the creek all day, and at night a great circuit of arc lights gleamed and sputtered over the roaring labour of the friends of geological research.

Thus had the Erie Auriferous Consolidated broken in a tidal wave over financial circles. On the Stock Exchange, in the downtown offices, and among the palm-trees of the Mausoleum Club they talked of nothing else. And so great was the power of the wave that it washed Tomlinson and his wife along on the crest of it, and landed them fifty feet up in their thousand-dollar suite in the Grand Palaver. And as a result of it "mother" wore a beetle-back jacket, and Tomlinson received a hundred telegrams a day, and Fred quit school and ate chocolates.

But in the business world the most amazing thing about it was the wonderful shrewdness of Tomlinson.

The first sign of it had been that he had utterly refused to allow the Erie Auriferous Consolidated (as the friends of geology called themselves) to take over the top half of the Tomlinson farm. For the bottom part he let them give him one-half of the preferred stock in the company in return for their supply of development capital. This was their own proposition; in fact, they reckoned that in doing this they were trading about two hundred thousand dollars' worth of machinery for, say ten million dollars of gold. But it frightened them when Tomlinson said "Yes" to the offer, and when he said that as to common stock they might keep it, it was no use to him, they were alarmed and uneasy till they made him take a block of it for the sake of market confidence.

But the top end of the farm he refused to surrender, and the friends of applied geology knew that there must be something pretty large behind this refusal; the more so as the reason that Tomlinson gave was such a simple one. He said that he didn't want to part with the top end of the place because his father was buried on it beside the creek, and so he didn't want the dam higher up, not for any consideration.

This was regarded in business circles as a piece of great shrewdness. "Says his father is buried there, eh? Devilish shrewd that!"

It was so long since any of the members of the Exchange or the Mausoleum Club had wandered into such places as Cahoga County that they did not know that there was nothing strange in what Tomlinson said. His father was buried there, on the farm itself, in a grave overgrown with raspberry bushes, and with a wooden headstone encompassed by a square of cedar rails, and slept as many another pioneer of Cahoga is sleeping.

"Devilish smart idea!" they said; and forthwith half the financial men of the city buried their fathers, or professed to have done so, in likely places – along the prospective right-of-way of a suburban railway, for example; in fact, in any place that marked them out for the joyous resurrection of an expropriation purchase.

Thus the astounding shrewdness of Tomlinson rapidly became a legend, the more so as he turned everything he touched to gold.

They narrated little stories of him in the whiskey-and-soda corners of the Mausoleum Club.

"I put it to him in a casual way," related, for example, Mr. Lucullus Fyshe, "casually, but quite frankly. I said, 'See here, this is just a bagatelle to you, no doubt, but to me it might be of some use. T.C. bonds,' I said, 'have risen twenty-two and a half in a week. You know as well as I do that they are only collateral trust, and that the stock underneath never could and never can earn a par dividend. Now,' I said, 'Mr. Tomlinson, tell me what all that means?' Would you believe it, the fellow looked me right in the face in that queer way he has and he said, 'I don't know!' "

"He said he didn't know!" repeated the listener, in a tone of amazement and respect. "By Jove! eh? he said he didn't know! The man's a wizard!"

"And he looked as if he didn't!" went on Mr. Fyshe. "That's the deuce of it. That man when he wants to can put on a look, sir, that simply means nothing, absolutely nothing."

In this way Tomlinson had earned his name of the Wizard of American Finance.

And meantime Tomlinson and his wife, within their suite at the Grand Palaver, had long since reached their decision. For there was one aspect and only one in which Tomlinson was really and truly a wizard. He saw clearly that for himself and his wife the vast fortune that had fallen to them was of no manner of use. What did it bring them? The noise and roar of the City in place of the silence of the farm and the racket of the great rotunda to drown the remembered murmur of the waters of the creek.

So Tomlinson had decided to rid himself of his new wealth, save only such as might be needed to make his son a different kind of man from himself.

"For Fred, of course," he said, "it's different. But out of such a lot as that it'll be easy to keep enough for him. It'll be a grand thing for Fred, this money. He won't have to grow up like you and me. He'll have opportunities we never got."

He was getting them already. The opportunity to wear seven-dollar patent leather shoes and a bell-shaped overcoat with a silk collar, to lounge into moving picture shows

and eat chocolates and smoke cigarettes – all these opportunities he was gathering immediately. Presently, when he
learned his way round a little, he would get still bigger ones.

"He's improving fast," said mother. She was thinking of
his patent leather shoes.

"He's popular," said his father. "I notice it downstairs.
He sasses any of them just as he likes; and no matter how
busy they are, as soon as they see it's Fred the're all ready to
have a laugh with him."

Certainly they were, as any hotel clerk with plastered
hair is ready to laugh with the son of a multimillionaire. It's
a certain sense of humour that they develop.

"But for us, mother," said the Wizard, "we'll be rid of it.
The gold is there. It's not right to keep it back. But we'll just
find a way to pass it on to folks that need it worse than we
do."

For a time they had thought of giving away the fortune.
But how? Who did they know that would take it?

It had crossed their minds – for who could live in the City
a month without observing the imposing buildings of Plutoria University, as fine as any departmental store in town?
– that they might give it to the college.

But there, it seemed, the way was blocked.

"You see, mother," said the puzzled Wizard, "we're not
known. We're strangers. I'd look fine going up there to the
college and saying, 'I want to give you people a million
dollars.' They'd laugh at me!"

"But don't one read it in the papers," his wife had
protested, "where Mr. Carnegie gives ever so much to the
colleges, more than all we've got, and they take it?"

"That's different," said the Wizard. "He's in with them.
They all know him. Why, he's a sort of chairman of different boards of colleges, and he knows all the heads of the
schools, and the professors, so it's no wonder that if he
offers to give a pension, or anything, they take it. Just think
of me going up to one of the professors up there in the
middle of his teaching and saying, 'I'd like to give you a
pension for life!' Imagine it! Think what he'd say!"

But the Tomlinsons couldn't imagine it, which was just as well.

So it came about that they had embarked on their system. Mother, who knew most arithmetic, was the leading spirit. She tracked out all the stocks and bonds in the front page of the *Financial Undertone*, and on her recommendation the Wizard bought. They knew the stocks only by their letters, but this itself gave a touch of high finance to their deliberations.

"I'd buy some of this R.O.P. if I was you," said mother; "it's gone down from 127 to 107 in two days, and I reckon it'll be all gone in ten days or so."

"Wouldn't 'G.G. deb.' be better? It goes down quicker."

"Well, it's a quick one," she assented, "but it don't go down so steady. You can't rely on it. You take ones like R.O.P. and T.R.R. pfd.; they go down all the time and you know where you are."

As a result of which Tomlinson would send his instructions. He did it all from the rotunda in a way of his own that he had evolved with a telegraph clerk who told him the names of brokers, and he dealt thus through brokers whom he never saw. As a result of this, the sluggish R.O.P. and T.R.R. would take as sudden a leap into the air as might a mule with a galvanic shock applied to its tail. At once the word was whispered that the "Tomlinson interests" were after the R.O.P. to reorganise it, and the whole floor of the Exchange scrambled for the stock.

And so it was that after a month or two of these operations the Wizard of Finance saw himself beaten.

"It's no good, mother," he repeated, "it's just a kind of Destiny."

Destiny perhaps it was.

But, if the Wizard of Finance had known it, at this very moment when he sat with the Aladdin's palace of his golden fortune reared so strangely about him, Destiny was preparing for him still stranger things.

Destiny, so it would seem, was devising its own ways and means of dealing with Tomlinson's fortune. As one of the ways and means, Destiny was sending at this moment as its special emissaries two huge, portly figures, wearing gigantic goloshes, and striding downwards from the halls of Plutoria University to the Grand Palaver Hotel. And one of these was the gigantic Dr. Boomer, the president of the college, and the other was his professor of Greek, almost as gigantic as himself. And they carried in their capacious pockets bundles of pamphlets on "Archaeological Remains of Mitylene," and the "Use of the Greek Pluperfect," and little treatises such as "Education and Philanthropy," by Dr. Boomer, and "The Excavation of Mitylene: An Estimate of Cost," by Dr. Boyster, "Boomer on the Foundation and Maintenance of Chairs," etc.

Many a man in city finance who had seen Dr. Boomer enter his office with a bundle of these monographs and a fighting glitter in his eyes had sunk back in his chair in dismay. For it meant that Dr. Boomer had tracked him out for a benefaction to the University, and that all resistance was hopeless.

When Dr. Boomer once laid upon a capitalist's desk his famous pamphlet on the "Use of the Greek Pluperfect," it was as if an Arabian sultan had sent the fatal bow-string to a condemned pasha, or Morgan the buccaneer had served the death-sign on a shuddering pirate.

So they came nearer and nearer, shouldering the passersby. The sound of them as they talked was like the roaring of the sea as Homer heard it. Never did Castor and Pollux come surging into battle as Dr. Boomer and Dr. Boyster bore down upon the Grand Palaver Hotel.

Tomlinson, the Wizard of Finance, had hesitated about going to the university. The university was coming to him. As for those millions of his, he could take his choice – dormitories, apparatus, campuses, buildings, endowment, anything he liked – but choose he must. And if he feared that after all his fortune was too vast even for such a disposal, Dr. Boomer would show him how he might use it in digging up ancient Mitylene, or modern Smyrna, or the lost cities of the Plain of Pactolus. If the size of the fortune troubled him Dr. Boomer would dig him up the whole African Sahara from Alexandria to Morocco, and ask for more.

But if Destiny held all this for Tomlinson in its outstretched palm before it, it concealed stranger things still beneath the folds of its toga.

There were enough surprises there to turn the faces of the whole directorate of the Erie Auriferous Consolidated as yellow as the gold that they mined.

For at this very moment, while the president of Plutoria University drew nearer and nearer to the Grand Palaver Hotel, the senior professor of geology was working again beside the blue flames in his darkened laboratory. And this time there was no shaking excitement over him. Nor were the labels that he marked, as sample followed sample in the tests, the same as those of the previous marking. Not by any means.

And his grave face as he worked in silence was as still as the stones of the post-tertiary period.

THREE

The Arrested Philanthropy of Mr. Tomlinson

"THIS, MR. TOMLINSON, is our campus," said President Boomer as they passed through the iron gates of Plutoria University.

"For camping?" said the Wizard.

"Not exactly," answered the president, "though it would, of course, suit for that. *Nihil humanum alienum*, eh?" and he broke into a loud, explosive laugh, while his spectacles irradiated that peculiar form of glee derived from a Latin quotation by those able to enjoy it. Dr. Boyster, walking on the other side of Mr. Tomlinson, joined in the laugh in a deep, reverberating chorus.

The two had the Wizard of Finance between them, and they were marching him up to the University. He was taken along much as is an arrested man who has promised to go quietly. They kept their hands off him, but they watched him sideways through their spectacles. At the least sign of restlessness they doused him with Latin. The Wizard of Finance, having been marked out by Dr. Boomer and Dr. Boyster as a prospective benefactor, was having Latin poured over him to reduce him to the proper degree of plasticity.

They had already put him through the first stage. They had, three days ago, called on him at the Grand Palaver and served him with a pamphlet on "The Excavation of Mitylene" as a sort of writ. Tomlinson and his wife had looked at the pictures of the ruins, and from the appearance of them

52

they judged that Mitylene was in Mexico, and they said that it was a shame to see it in that state and that the United States ought to intervene.

As the second stage on the path of philanthropy, the Wizard of Finance was now being taken to look at the university. Dr. Boomer knew by experience that no rich man could look at it without wanting to give it money.

And here the president had found that there is no better method of dealing with business men than to use Latin on them. For other purposes the president used other things. For example at a friendly dinner at the Mausoleum Club where light conversation was in order, Dr. Boomer chatted, as has been seen, on the archaeological remains of the Navajos. In the same way, at Mrs. Rasselyer-Brown's Dante luncheons, he generally talked of the Italian *cinque-centisti* and whether Gian Gobbo della Scala had left a greater name than Can Grande della Spiggiola. But such talk as that was naturally only for women. Business men are much too shrewd for that kind of thing; in fact, so shrewd are they, as President Boomer had long since discovered, that nothing pleases them so much as the quiet, firm assumption that they know Latin. It is like writing them up an asset. So it was that Dr. Boomer would greet a business acquaintance with a roaring salutation of, "*Terque quaterque beatus*," or stand wringing his hand off to the tune of "*Oh et presidium et dulce decus meum.*"

This caught them every time.

"You don't," said Tomlinson the Wizard in a hesitating tone as he looked at the smooth grass of the campus, "I suppose, raise anything on it?"

"No, no; this is only for field sports," said the president; "*sunt quos curriculo –*"

To which Dr. Boyster on the other side added, like a chorus, "*pulverem Olympicum.*"

This was their favourite quotation. It always gave President Boomer a chance to speak of the final letter "m" in Latin poetry, and to say that in his opinion the so-called elision of the final "m" was more properly a dropping of the vowel with a repercussion of the two last consonants. He supported this by quoting Ammianus, at which Dr. Boyster exclaimed, "Pooh! Ammianus: more dog Latin!" and appealed to Mr. Tomlinson as to whether any rational man nowadays cared what Ammianus thought?

To all of which Tomlinson answered never a word, but looked steadily first at one and then at the other. Dr. Boomer said afterwards that the penetration of Tomlinson was wonderful, and that it was excellent to see how Boyster tried in vain to draw him; and Boyster said afterwards that the way in which Tomlinson quietly refused to be led on by Boomer was delicious, and that it was a pity that Aristophanes was not there to do it justice.

All of which was happening as they went in at the iron gates and up the elm avenue of Plutoria University.

The university, as everyone knows, stands with its great gates on Plutoria Avenue, and with its largest buildings, those of the faculties of industrial and mechanical science, fronting full upon the street.

These buildings are exceptionally fine, standing fifteen stories high and comparing favourably with the best departmental stores or factories in the City. Indeed, after nightfall, when they are all lighted up for the evening technical classes and when their testing machinery is in full swing and there are students going in and out in overall suits, people have often mistaken the university, or this newer part of it, for a factory. A foreign visitor once said that the students looked like plumbers, and President Boomer was so proud of it that he put the phrase into his next Commencement address; and from there the newspapers got it and the Associated Press took it up and sent it all over the United States with the heading, "Have Appearance of Plumbers; Plutoria University Congratulated on Character of Students," and it was a proud day indeed for the heads of the Industrial Science faculty.

But the older part of the university stands so quietly and modestly at the top end of the elm avenue, so hidden by the leaves of it, that no one could mistake it for a factory. This indeed was once the whole university, and had stood there since colonial days under the name Concordia College. It had been filled with generations of presidents and professors of the older type with long white beards and rusty black clothes, and salaries of fifteen hundred dollars.

But the change both of name and of character from Concordia College to Plutoria University was the work of President Boomer. He had changed it from an old-fashioned college of the by-gone type to a university in the true modern sense. At Plutoria they now taught everything. Concordia College, for example, had no teaching of religion except lectures on the Bible. Now they had lectures also on Confucianism, Mohammedanism, Buddhism, with an optional course on atheism for students in the final year.

And, of course, they had long since admitted women, and there were now beautiful creatures with Cléo de Mérode hair studying astronomy at oaken desks and looking up at the teacher with eyes like comets. The university taught everything and did everything. It had whirling machines on the top of it that measured the speed of the wind, and deep in its basements it measured earthquakes with a seismograph; it held classes on forestry and dentistry and palmistry; it sent life classes into the slums, and death classes to the city morgue. It offered such a vast variety of themes, topics, and subjects to the students, that there was nothing that a student was compelled to learn, while from its own presses in its own press-building it sent out a shower of bulletins and monographs like driven snow from a rotary plough.

In fact, it had become, as President Boomer told all the business men in town, not merely a university, but a *universitas* in the true sense, and every one of its faculties was now a *facultas* in the real acceptance of the word, and its studies properly and truly *studia*; indeed, if the business men would only build a few more dormitories and put up enough money to form an adequate *fondatum* or *fundum* then the good work might be looked upon as complete.

As the three walked up the elm avenue there met them a

little stream of students with college books, and female students with winged-victory hats, and professors with last year's overcoats. And some went past with a smile and others with a shiver.

"That's Professor Withers," said the president in a sympathetic voice as one of the shivering figures went past; "poor Withers," and he sighed.

"What's wrong with him?" said the Wizard; "is he sick?"

"No, not sick," said the president quietly and sadly, "merely inefficient."

"Inefficient?"

"Unfortunately so. Mind you, I don't mean 'inefficient' in every sense. By no means. If anyone were to come to me and say, 'Boomer, can you put your hand for me on a first-class botanist?' I'd say, 'Take Withers.' I'd say it in a minute."

This was true. He would have. In fact, if anyone had made this kind of rash speech, Dr. Boomer would have given away half the professoriate.

"Well, what's wrong with him?" repeated Tomlinson. "I suppose he ain't quite up to the mark in some ways, eh?"

"Precisely," said the president, "not quite up to the mark – a very happy way of putting it. *Capax imperii nisi imperasset*, as no doubt you are thinking to yourself. The fact is that Withers, though an excellent fellow, can't manage large classes. With small classes he is all right, but with large classes the man is lost. He can't handle them."

"He can't, eh?" said the Wizard.

"No. But what can I do? There he is. I can't dismiss him, I can't pension him. I've no money for it."

Here the president slackened a little in his walk and looked sideways at the prospective benefactor. But Tomlinson gave no sign.

A second professorial figure passed them on the other side.

"There again," said the president, "that's another case

of inefficiency – Professor Shottat, our senior professor of English."

"What's wrong with *him*?" asked the Wizard.

"He can't handle *small* classes," said the president. "With large classes he is really excellent, but with small ones the man is simply hopeless."

In this fashion, before Mr. Tomlinson had measured the length of the avenue, he had had ample opportunity to judge of the crying need of money at Plutoria University, and of the perplexity of its president. He was shown professors who could handle the first year, but were powerless with the second; others who were all right with the second but broke down with the third, while others could handle the third but collapsed with the fourth. There were professors who were all right in their own subject, but perfectly impossible outside of it; others who were so occupied outside of their own subject that they were useless inside of it; others who knew their subject, but couldn't lecture; and others again who lectured admirably, but didn't know their subject.

In short it was clear – as it was meant to be – that the need of the moment was a sum of money sufficient to enable the president to dismiss everybody but himself and Dr. Boyster. The latter stood in a class all by himself. He had known the president for forty-five years, ever since he was a fat little boy with spectacles in a classical academy, stuffing himself on irregular Greek verbs as readily as if on oysters.

But it soon appeared that the need for dismissing the professors was only part of the trouble. There were the buildings to consider.

"This, I am ashamed to say," said Dr. Boomer, as they passed the imitation Greek portico of the old Concordia College building, "is our original home, the *fons et origo* of our studies, our faculty of arts."

It was indeed a dilapidated building, yet there was a certain majesty about it, too, especially when one reflected that it had been standing there looking much the same at the time when its students had trooped off in a flock to join the army of the Potomac, and much the same indeed three generations before that, when the classes were closed and the students clapped three-cornered hats on their heads and were off to enlist as minute men with flintlock muskets under General Washington.

But Dr. Boomer's one idea was to knock the building down and to build on its site a real *facultas* ten stories high, with elevators in it.

Tomlinson looked about him humbly as he stood in the main hall. The atmosphere of the place awed him. There were bulletins and time-tables and notices stuck on the walls that gave evidence of the activity of the place. "Professor Slithers will be unable to meet his classes to-day," ran one of them, and another, "Professor Withers will not meet his classes this week," and another, "Owing to illness, Professor Shottat will not lecture this month," while still another announced, "Owing to the indisposition of Professor Podge, all botanical classes are suspended, but Professor Podge hopes to be able to join in the Botanical Picnic Excursion to Loon Lake on Saturday afternoon." You could judge of the grinding routine of the work from the nature of these notices. Anyone familiar with the work of colleges would not heed it, but it shocked Tomlinson to think how often the professors of the college were stricken down by overwork.

Here and there in the hall, set into niches, were bronze busts of men with Roman faces and bare necks, and the edge of a toga cast over each shoulder.

"Who would these be?" asked Tomlinson, pointing at them.

"Some of the chief founders and benefactors of the faculty," answered the president, and at this the hopes of Tomlinson sank in his heart. For he realised the class of man one had to belong to in order to be accepted as a university benefactor.

"A splendid group of men, are they not?" said the president. "We owe them much. This is the late Mr. Hogworth, a man of singularly large heart." Here he pointed to a bronze figure wearing a wreath of laurel and inscribed "Gulielmus Hogworth, Litt. Doc." "He had made a great fortune in the produce business, and wishing to mark his gratitude to the community, he erected the anemometer, the wind-measure, on the roof of the building, attaching to it no other condition than that his name should be printed in the weekly reports immediately beside the velocity of the wind. The figure beside him is the late Mr. Underbugg, who founded our lectures on the Four Gospels on the sole stipulation that henceforth any reference of ours to the four gospels should be coupled with his name."

"What's that after his name?" asked Tomlinson.

"Litt. Doc.?" said the president. "Doctor of Letters, our honorary degree. We are always happy to grant it to our benefactors by a vote of the faculty."

Here Dr. Boomer and Dr. Boyster wheeled half round and looked quietly and steadily at the Wizard of Finance. To both their minds it was perfectly plain that an honourable bargain was being struck.

"Yes, Mr. Tomlinson," said the president, as they emerged from the building, "no doubt you begin to realise our unhappy position. Money, money, money," he repeated half musingly. "If I had the money I'd have that whole building down and dismantled in a fortnight."

From the central building the three passed to the museum building, where Tomlinson was shown a vast skeleton of a Diplodocus Maximus, and was specially warned not to confuse it with the Dinosaurus Perfectus, whose bones, however, could be bought if anyone, any man of large heart, would come to the university and say straight out, "Gentlemen, what can I do for you?" Better still, it appeared the whole museum, which was hopelessly antiquated, being twenty-five years old, could be entirely knocked down if a sufficient sum was forthcoming; and its curator, who was as ancient as the Dinosaurus itself, could be dismissed on half-pay if any man had a heart large enough for the dismissal.

From the museum they passed to the library, where there were full-length portraits of more founders and benefactors in long red robes, holding scrolls of paper, and others sitting holding pens and writing on parchment, with a Greek temple and a thunderstorm in the background.

And here again it appeared that the crying need of the moment was for someone to come to the university and say, "Gentlemen, what can I do for you?" On which the whole library, for it was twenty years old and out of date, might be blown up with dynamite and carted away.

But at all this the hopes of Tomlinson sank lower and lower. The red robes and the scrolls were too much for him.

From the library they passed to the tall buildings that housed the faculty of industrial and mechanical science. And here again the same pitiful lack of money was everywhere apparent. For example, in the physical science department there was a mass of apparatus for which the university was unable to afford suitable premises, and in the chemical department there were vast premises for which the university was unable to buy apparatus, and so on. Indeed, it was part of Dr. Boomer's method to get himself endowed first with premises too big for the apparatus, and then by appealing to public spirit to call for enough apparatus to more than fill the premises, by means of which system industrial science at Plutoria University advanced with increasing and gigantic strides.

But most of all the electric department interested the Wizard of Finance. And this time his voice lost its hesitating tone and he looked straight at Dr. Boomer as he began,

"I have a boy –"

"Ah!" said Dr. Boomer, with a huge ejaculation of surprise and relief; "you have a boy!"

There were volumes in his tone. What it meant was, "Now, indeed we have got you where we want you," and he exchanged a meaning look with the professor of Greek.

Within five minutes the president and Tomlinson and Dr. Boyster were gravely discussing on what terms and in what way Fred might be admitted to study in the faculty of industrial science. The president, on learning that Fred had put in four years in Cahoga County Section No. 3 School, and had been head of his class in ciphering, nodded his head gravely and said it would simply be a matter of a *pro tanto*; that, in fact, he felt sure that Fred might be admitted *ad eundem*. But the real condition on which they meant to admit him was, of course, not mentioned.

One door only in the faculty of industrial and mechanical science they did not pass, a heavy oak door at the end of a corridor bearing the painted inscription, "Geological and Metallurgical Laboratories." Stuck in the door was a card with the words (they were conceived in the courteous phrases of mechanical science, which is almost a branch of business in the real sense), "Busy – keep out."

Dr. Boomer looked at the card. "Ah, yes," he said, "Gildas is no doubt busy with his tests. We won't disturb him." The president was always proud to find a professor busy; it looked well.

But if Dr. Boomer had known what was going on behind the oaken door of the Department of Geology and Metallurgy, he would have felt considerably disturbed himself.

For here again Gildas, senior professor of geology, was working among his blue flames at a final test on which depended the fate of the Erie Auriferous Consolidated and all connected with it.

Before him there were some twenty or thirty packets of crumpled dust and splintered ore that glittered on the testing table. It had been taken up from the creek along its whole length, at even spaces twenty yards apart, by an expert sent down in haste by the directorate, after Gildas's second report, and heavily bribed to keep his mouth shut.

And as Professor Gildas stood and worked at the samples and tied them up after analysis in little white cardboard boxes, he marked each one very carefully and neatly with the words, "Pyrites: worthless."

Beside the professor worked a young demonstrator of last year's graduation class. It was he, in fact, who had written the polite notice on the card.

"What is the stuff, anyway?" he asked.

"A sulphuret of iron," said the professor, "or iron pyrites. In colour and appearance it is practically identical with gold. Indeed, in all ages," he went on, dropping at once into the class-room tone and adopting the professorial habit of jumping backwards twenty centuries in order to explain anything properly, "it has been readily mistaken for the precious metal. The ancients called it 'fool's gold.' Martin Frobisher brought back four shiploads of it from Baffin Land thinking that he had discovered an Eldorado. There are large deposits of it in the mines of Cornwall, and it is just possible," here the professor measured his words as if speaking of something that he wouldn't promise, "that the Cassiterides of the Phoenicians contained deposits of the same sulphuret. Indeed, I defy anyone," he continued, for he was piqued in his scientific pride, "to distinguish it from gold without a laboratory test. In large quantities, I concede, its lack of weight would betray it to a trained hand, but without testing its solubility in nitric acid, or the fact of its burning with a blue flame under the blow-pipe, it cannot be detected. In short, when crystallised in dode-cahedrons –"

"Is it any good?" broke in the demonstrator.

"Good?" said the professor. "Oh, you mean commer-cially? Not in the slightest. Much less valuable than, let us say, ordinary mud or clay. In fact, it is absolutely good for nothing."

They were silent for a moment, watching the blue flames above the brazier.

Then Gildas spoke again. "Oddly enough," he said, "the first set of samples were undoubtedly pure gold – not the faintest doubt of that. That is the really interesting part of the matter. These gentlemen concerned in the enterprise will, of course, lose their money, and I shall therefore decline to accept the very handsome fee which they had offered me for my services. But the main feature, the real point of interest in this matter remains. Here we have undoubtedly a sporadic deposit, – what miners call a pocket, – of pure gold in a Devonian formation of the post-tertiary period. This once established, we must revise our entire theory of the distribution of igneous and aqueous rocks. In fact, I am already getting notes together for a paper for the Pan-Geological under the heading, 'Auriferous Excretions in the Devonian Strata: a Working Hypothesis.' I hope to read it at the next meeting."

The young demonstrator looked at the professor with one eye half closed.

"I don't think I would if I were you," he said.

Now this young demonstrator knew nothing, or practically nothing, of geology, because he came of one of the richest and best families in town and didn't need to. But he was a smart young man, dressed in the latest fashion, with brown boots and a crosswise tie, and he knew more about money and business and the stock exchange in five minutes than Professor Gildas in his whole existence.

"Why not?" said the professor.

"Why, don't you see what's happened?"

"Eh?" said Gildas.

"What happened to those first samples? When that bunch got interested and planned to float the company? Don't you see? Somebody salted them on you."

"*Salted* them on me?" repeated the professor, mystified.

"Yes, salted them. Somebody got wise to what they were and swopped them on you for the real thing, so as to get your certified report that the stuff was gold."

"I begin to see," muttered the professor. "Somebody exchanged the samples, some person no doubt desirous of establishing the theory that a sporadic outcropping of the sort might be found in a post-tertiary formation. I see, I see. No doubt he intended to prepare a paper on it, and prove his thesis by these tests. I see it all!"

The demonstrator looked at the professor with a sort of pity.

"You're on!" he said, and he laughed softly to himself.

"Well," said Dr. Boomer, after Tomlinson had left the university, "what do you make of him?" The president had taken Dr. Boyster over to his house beside the campus, and there in his study had given him a cigar as big as a rope and taken another himself. This was a sign that Dr. Boomer wanted Dr. Boyster's opinion in plain English, without any Latin about it.

"Remarkable man," said the professor of Greek; "wonderful penetration, and a man of very few words. Of course his game is clear enough?"

"Entirely so," asserted Dr. Boomer.

"It's clear enough that he means to give the money on two conditions."

"Exactly," said the president.

"First that we admit his son, who is quite unqualified, to the senior studies in electrical science, and second that we grant him the degree of Doctor of Letters. Those are his terms."

"Can we meet them?"

"Oh, certainly. As to the son, there is no difficulty, of course; as to the degree, it's only a question of getting the faculty to vote it. I think we can manage it."

Vote it they did that very afternoon. True, if the members of the faculty had known the things that were being whispered, and more than whispered, in the City about Tomlinson and his fortune, no degree would ever have been conferred on him. But it so happened that at that moment the whole professoriate was absorbed in one of those great educational crises which from time to time shake a university to its base. The meeting of the faculty that day bid fair to lose all vestige of decorum in the excitement of the moment. For, as Dean Elderberry Foible, the head of the faculty, said, the motion that they had before them amounted practically to a revolution. The proposal was nothing less than the permission of the use of lead-pencils instead of pen and ink in the sessional examinations of the university. Anyone conversant with the inner life of a college will realise that to many of the professoriate this was nothing less than a last wild onslaught of socialistic democracy against the solid bulwarks of society. They must fight it back or die on the walls. To others it was one more step in the splendid progress of democratic education, comparable only to such epoch-making things as the abandonment of the cap and gown, and the omission of the word "sir" in speaking to a professor.

No wonder that the fight raged. Elderberry Foible, his fluffed white hair almost on end, beat in vain with his gavel for order. Finally, Chang of Physiology, who was a perfect dynamo of energy and was known frequently to work for three or four hours at a stretch, proposed that the faculty should adjourn the question and meet for its further discussion on the following Saturday morning. This revolutionary suggestion, involving work on Saturday, reduced the meeting to a mere turmoil, in the midst of which Elderberry Foible proposed that the whole question of the use of lead-pencils should be adjourned till that day six months, and that meantime a new special committee of seventeen professors, with power to add to their number, to call witnesses and, if need be, to hear them, should report on the entire matter *de novo*. This motion, after the striking out of the words *de novo* and the insertion of *ab initio*, was finally carried, after which the faculty sank back completely exhausted into its chair, the need of afternoon tea and toast stamped on every face.

And it was at this moment that President Boomer, who understood faculties as few men have done, quietly entered the room, laid his silk hat on a volume of Demosthenes, and proposed the vote of a degree of Doctor of Letters for Edward Tomlinson. He said that there was no need to remind the faculty of Tomlinson's services to the nation; they knew them. Of the members of the faculty, indeed, some thought that he meant the Tomlinson who wrote the famous monologue on the Iota Subscript, while others supposed that he referred to the celebrated philosopher

Tomlinson, whose new book on the Indivisibility of the Inseparable was just then maddening the entire world. In any case, they voted the degree without a word, still faint with exhaustion.

But while the university was conferring on Tomlinson the degree of Doctor of Letters, all over the City in business circles they were conferring on him far other titles. "Idiot," "Scoundrel," "Swindler," were the least of them. Every stock and share with which his name was known to be connected was coming down with a run, wiping out the accumulated profits of the Wizard at the rate of a thousand dollars a minute.

They not only questioned his honesty, but they went further and questioned his business capacity.

"The man," said Mr. Lucullus Fyshe, sitting in the Mausoleum Club and breathing freely at last after having disposed of all his holdings in the Erie Auriferous, "is an ignoramus. I asked him only the other day, quite casually, a perfectly simple business question. I said to him, 'T.C. Bonds have risen twenty-two and half in a week. You know and I know that they are only collateral trust, and that the stock underneath never could and never would earn a par dividend. Now,' I said, for I wanted to test the fellow, 'tell me what that means?' Would you believe me, he looked me right in the face in that stupid way of his, and he said, 'I don't know!'"

"He said he didn't know!" repeated the listener contemptuously; "the man is a damn fool!"

The reason of all this was that the results of the researches of the professor of geology were being whispered among the directorate of the Erie Auriferous. And the directors and chief shareholders were busily performing the interesting process called unloading. Nor did ever a farmer of Cahoga County in haying time, with a thunderstorm threatening, unload with greater rapidity than did the major shareholders of the Auriferous. Mr. Lucullus Fyshe traded off a quarter of his stock to an unwary member of the Mausoleum Club at a drop of thirty per cent., and being too prudent to hold the rest on any terms he conveyed it at once as a benefaction in trust to the Plutorian Orphans' and Foundlings' Home; while the purchaser of Mr. Fyshe's stock, learning too late of his folly, rushed for his lawyers to have the shares conveyed as a gift to the Home for Incurables.

Mr. Asmodeus Boulder transferred his entire holdings to the Imbeciles' Relief Society, and Mr. Furlong, senior, passed his over to a Chinese mission as fast as pen could traverse paper.

Down at the office of Skinyer and Beatem, the lawyers of the company, they were working overtime drawing up deeds and conveyances and trusts in perpetuity, with hardly time to put them into typewriting. Within twenty-four hours the entire stock of the company bid fair to be in the hands of Idiots, Orphans, Protestants, Foundlings, Imbeciles, Missionaries, Chinese, and other unfinancial people, with Tomlinson the Wizard of Finance as the senior shareholder and majority control. And whether the gentle Wizard, as he sat with mother planning his vast benefaction to Plutoria University, would have felt more at home with his new group of fellow-shareholders than his old, it were hard indeed to say.

But meantime at the office of Skinyer and Beatem all was activity. For not only were they drafting the conveyances of the perpetual trusts as fast as legal brains working overtime could do it, but in another part of the office a section of the firm were busily making their preparations against the expected actions for fraud and warrants of distraint and injunctions against disposal of assets and the whole battery of artillery which might open on them at any moment. And they worked like a corps of military engineers fortifying an escarpment, with the joy of battle in their faces.

The storm might break at any moment. Already at the

office of the *Financial Undertone* the type was set for a special extra with a heading three inches high:

COLLAPSE
OF THE ERIE CONSOLIDATED

ARREST OF THE MAN TOMLINSON
EXPECTED THIS AFTERNOON

Skinyer and Beatem had paid the editor, who was crooked, two thousand dollars cash to hold back that extra for twenty-four hours; and the editor had paid the reporting staff, who were crooked, twenty-five dollars each to keep the news quiet, and the compositors, who were also crooked, ten dollars per man to hold their mouths shut till the morning, with the result that from editors and sub-editors and reporters and compositors the news went seething forth in a flood that the Erie Auriferous Consolidated was going to shatter into fragments like the bursting of a dynamite bomb. It rushed with a thousand whispering tongues from street to street, till it filled the corridors of the law-courts and the lobbies of the offices, and till every honest man that held a share of the stock shivered in his tracks and reached out to give, sell, or destroy it. Only the unwinking Idiots, and the mild Orphans, and the calm Deaf-mutes, and the impassive Chinese held tight to what they had. So gathered the storm, till all the town, like the great rotunda of the Grand Palaver, was filled with a silent "call for Mr. Tomlinson," voiceless and ominous.

And while all this was happening, and while at Skinyer and Beatem's they worked with frantic pens and clattering type, there came a knock at the door, hesitant and uncertain, and before the eyes of the astounded office there stood in his wide-awake hat and long black coat the figure of 'the man Tomlinson' himself.

And Skinyer, the senior partner, no sooner heard what Tomlinson wanted than he dashed across the outer office to his partner's room with his hyena face all excitement as he said:

"Beatem, Beatem, come over to my room. This man is

absolutely the biggest thing in America. For sheer calmness and nerve I never heard of anything to approach him. What do you think he wants to do?"

"What?" said Beatem.

"Why, he's giving his entire fortune to the university."

"By Gad!" ejaculated Beatem, and the two lawyers looked at one another, lost in admiration of the marvellous genius and assurance of Tomlinson.

Yet what had happened was very simple.

Tomlinson had come back from the university filled with mingled hope and hesitation. The university, he saw, needed the money, and he hoped to give it his entire fortune, to put Dr. Boomer in a position to practically destroy the whole place. But, like many a modest man, he lacked the assurance to speak out. He felt that up to the present the benefactors of the university had been men of an entirely different class from himself.

It was mother who solved the situation for him.

"Well, father," she said, "there's one thing I've learned already since we've had money. If you want to get a thing done you can always find people to do it for you if you pay them. Why not go to those lawyers that manage things for the company and get them to arrange it all for you with the college?"

As a result, Tomlinson had turned up at the door of the Skinyer and Beatem office.

"Quite so, Mr. Tomlinson," said Skinyer, with his pen already dipped in the ink, "a perfectly simple matter. I can draw up a draft of conveyance with a few strokes of the pen. In fact, we can do it on the spot."

What he meant was, "In fact, we can do it so fast that I can pocket a fee of five hundred dollars right here and now while you have the money to pay me."

"Now then," he continued, "let us see how it is to run."

"Well," said Tomlinson, "I want you to put it that I give all my stock in the company to the university."

"All of it?" said Skinyer, with a quiet smile to Beatem.

"Every cent of it, sir," said Tomlinson; "just write down that I give all of it to the college."

"Very good," said Skinyer, and he began to write, "I, so-and-so, and so-and-so, of the county of so-and-so – Cahoga, I think you said, Mr. Tomlinson?"

"Yes, sir," said the Wizard, "I was raised there."

"– do hereby give, assign, devise, transfer, and the transfer is hereby given, devised and assigned, all those stocks, shares, hereditaments, etc., which I hold in the etc., etc., all, several and whatever – you will observe, Mr. Tomlinson, I am expressing myself with as great brevity as possible – to that institution, academy, college, school, university, now known and reputed to be Plutoria University, of the city of etc., etc."

He paused a moment. "Now what special objects or purposes shall I indicate?" he asked.

Whereupon Tomlinson explained as best he could, and Skinyer, working with great rapidity, indicated that the benefaction was to include a Demolition Fund for the removal of buildings, a Retirement Fund for the removal of professors, an Apparatus Fund for the destruction of apparatus, and a General Sinking Fund for the obliteration of anything not otherwise mentioned.

"And I'd like to do something, if I could, for Mr. Boomer himself, just as man to man," said Tomlinson.

"All right," said Beatem, and he could hardly keep his face straight. "Give him a chunk of the stock – give him half a million."

"I will," said Tomlinson; "he deserves it."

"Undoubtedly," said Mr. Skinyer.

And within a few minutes the whole transaction was done, and Tomlinson, filled with joy, was wringing the hands of Skinyer and Beatem, and telling them to name their own fee.

They had meant to, anyway.

"Is that legal, do you suppose?" said Beatem to Skinyer, after the Wizard had gone. "Will it hold water?"

"Oh, I don't think so," said Skinyer, "not for a minute. In fact, rather the other way. If they make an arrest for fraudulent flotation, this conveyance, I should think, would help to send him to the penitentiary. But I very much doubt if they can arrest him. Mind you, the fellow is devilish shrewd. *You* know, and I know, that he planned this whole flotation with a full knowledge of the fraud. *You* and *I* know it – very good – but we know it more from our trained instinct in such things than by any proof. The fellow has managed to surround himself with such an air of good faith from start to finish that it will be deuced hard to get at him."

"What will he do now?" said Beatem.

"I tell you what he'll do. Mark my words. Within twenty-four hours he'll clear out and be out of the state, and if they want to get him they'll have to extradite. I tell you he's a man of extraordinary capacity. The rest of us are nowhere beside him."

In which, perhaps, there was some truth.

"Well, mother," said the Wizard, when he reached the thousand-dollar suite, after his interview with Skinyer and Beatem, his face irradiated with simple joy, "it's done. I've put the college now in a position it never was in before, nor any other college; the lawyers say so themselves."

"That's good," said mother.

"Yes, and it's a good thing I didn't lose the money when I tried to. You see, mother, what I hadn't realised was the good that could be done with all that money if a man put his heart into it. They can start in as soon as they like and tear down those buildings. My! but it's just wonderful what you can do with money. I'm glad I didn't lose it."

So they talked far into the evening. That night they slept in an Aladdin's palace filled with golden fancies.

And in the morning the palace and all its visions fell tumbling about their heads in sudden and awful catastrophe. For with Tomlinson's first descent to the rotunda it broke. The whole great space seemed filled with the bulletins and the broadside sheets of the morning papers, the crowd surging to and fro buying the papers, men reading them as they stood, and everywhere in great letters there met his eye:

COLLAPSE

OF THE ERIE AURIFEROUS

THE GREAT GOLD SWINDLE

ARREST OF THE MAN TOMLINSON
EXPECTED THIS MORNING

So stood the Wizard of Finance beside a pillar, the paper fluttering in his hand, his eyes fixed, while about him a thousand eager eyes and rushing tongues sent shame into his stricken heart.

And there his boy Fred, sent from upstairs, found him; and at the sight of the seething crowd and his father's stricken face, aged as it seemed all in a moment, the boy's soul woke within him. What had happened he could not tell, only that his father stood there, dazed, beaten, and staring at him on every side in giant letters:

ARREST OF THE MAN TOMLINSON

"Come, father, come upstairs," he said, and took him by the arm, dragging him through the crowd.

In the next half-hour as they sat and waited for the arrest in the false grandeur of the thousand-dollar suite, – Tomlinson, his wife, and Fred, – the boy learnt more than all the teaching of the industrial faculty of Plutoria University could have taught him in a decade. Adversity laid its hand upon him, and at its touch his adolescent heart turned to finer stuff than the salted gold of the Erie Auriferous. As he looked upon his father's broken figure waiting meekly for arrest, and his mother's blubbered face, a great wrath burned itself into his soul.

"When the sheriff comes –" said Tomlinson, and his lip trembled as he spoke. He had no other picture of arrest than that.

"They can't arrest you, father," broke out the boy. "You've done nothing. You never swindled them. I tell you, if they try to arrest you, I'll –" and his voice broke and stopped upon a sob, and his hands clenched in passion.

"You stay here, you and mother. I'll go down. Give me your money and I'll go and pay them and we'll get out of this and go home. They can't stop us; there's nothing to arrest you for."

Nor was there. Fred paid the bill unmolested, save for the prying eyes and babbling tongues of the rotunda.

And a few hours from that, while the town was still ringing with news of his downfall, the Wizard with his wife and son walked down from their thousand-dollar suite into the corridor, their hands burdened with their satchels. A waiter, with something between a sneer and an obsequious smile upon his face, reached out for the valises, wondering if it was still worth while.

"You get to hell out of that!" said Fred. He had put on again his rough store suit in which he had come from Cahoga County, and there was a dangerous look about his big shoulders and his set jaw. And the waiter slunk back.

So did they pass, unarrested and unhindered, through corridor and rotunda to the outer portals of the great hotel.

Beside the door of the Palaver as they passed out was a tall official with a uniform and a round hat. He was called by the authorities a *chasseur* or a *commissionaire*, or some foreign name to mean that he did nothing.

At the sight of him the Wizard's face flushed for a moment, with a look of his old perplexity.

"I wonder," he began to murmur, "how much I ought –"

"Not a damn cent, father," said Fred, as he shouldered past the magnificent *chasseur*; "let him work."

With which admirable doctrine the Wizard and his son passed from the portals of the Grand Palaver.

Nor was there any arrest either then or later. In spite of the expectations of the rotunda and the announcements of the *Financial Undertone*, the "man Tomlinson" was *not* arrested, neither as he left the Grand Palaver nor as he stood waiting at the railroad station with Fred and mother for the outgoing train for Cahoga County.

There was nothing to arrest him for. That was not the least strange part of the career of the Wizard of Finance. For when all the affairs of the Erie Auriferous Consolidated were presently calculated up by the labours of Skinyer and Beatem and the legal representatives of the Orphans and the Idiots and the Deaf-mutes, they resolved themselves into the most beautiful and complete cipher conceivable. The salted gold about paid for the cost of the incorporation certificate: the development capital had disappeared, and those who lost most preferred to say the least about it; and as for Tomlinson, if one added up his gains on the stock market before the fall and subtracted his bill at the Grand Palaver and the thousand dollars which he gave to Skinyer and Beatem to recover his freehold on the lower half of his farm, and the cost of three tickets to Cahoga station, the debit and credit account balanced to a hair.

Thus did the whole fortune of Tomlinson vanish in a night, even as the golden palace seen in the mirage of a desert sunset may fade before the eyes of the beholder, and leave no trace behind.

It was some months after the collapse of the Erie Auriferous that the university conferred upon Tomlinson the degree of Doctor of Letters *in absentia*. A university must keep its word, and Dean Elderberry Foible, who was honesty itself, had stubbornly maintained that a vote of the faculty of arts once taken and written in the minute book became as irrefragable as the Devonian rock itself.

So the degree was conferred. And Dean Elderberry Foible, standing in a long red gown before Dr. Boomer, seated in a long blue gown, read out after the ancient custom of the college the Latin statement of the award of the degree of Doctor of Letters, "Eduardus Tomlinsonius, vir clarissimus, doctissimus, praestissimus," and a great many other things all ending in *issimus*.

But the recipient was not there to receive. He stood at that moment with his boy Fred on a windy hill-side beside Lake Erie, where Tomlinson's Creek ran again untrammelled to the lake. Nor was the scene altered to the eye, for Tomlinson and his son had long since broken a hole in the dam with pickaxe and crowbar, and day by day the angry water carried down the vestiges of the embankment till all were gone. The cedar poles of the electric lights had been cut into fence-rails; the wooden shanties of the Italian gang of Auriferous workers had been torn down and split into firewood; and where they had stood, the burdocks and the thistles of the luxuriant summer conspired to hide the traces of their shame. Nature reached out its hand and drew its coverlet of green over the grave of the vanished Eldorado.

And as the Wizard and his son stood upon the hill-side, they saw nothing but the land sloping to the lake and the creek murmuring again to the willows, while the off-shore wind rippled the rushes of the shallow water.

FOUR

The Yahi-Bahi Oriental Society of Mrs.

Rasselyer-Brown

Mrs. RASSELYER-BROWN lived on Plutoria Avenue in a vast sandstone palace, in which she held those fashionable entertainments which have made the name of Rasselyer-Brown what it is. Mr. Rasselyer-Brown lived there also.

The exterior of the house was more or less a model of the façade of an Italian palazzo of the sixteenth century. If one questioned Mrs. Rasselyer-Brown at dinner in regard to this (which was only a fair return for drinking five-dollar champagne) she answered that the façade was cinquecentisti, but that it reproduced also the Saracenic mullioned window of the Siennese School. But if the guest said later in the evening to Mr. Rasselyer-Brown that he understood that his house was cinquecentisti, he answered that he guessed it was. After which remark and an interval of silence Mr. Rasselyer-Brown would probably ask the guest if he was dry.

So from that one can tell exactly the sort of people the Rasselyer-Browns were.

In other words, Mr. Rasselyer-Brown was a severe handicap to Mrs. Rasselyer-Brown. He was more than that; the word isn't strong enough. He was, as Mrs. Rasselyer-Brown herself confessed to her confidential circle of three hundred friends, a drag. He was also a tie, and a weight, and a burden, and in Mrs. Rasselyer-Brown's religious moments a crucifix. Even in the early years of their married life, some twenty or twenty-five years ago, her husband had been a drag on her by being in the coal and wood business. It is hard for a woman to have to realise that her husband is making a fortune out of coal and wood and that people know it. It ties one down. What a woman wants most of all – this, of course, is merely a quotation from Mrs. Rasselyer-Brown's own thoughts as expressed to her three hundred friends – is room to expand, to grow. The hardest thing in the world is to be stifled: and there is nothing more stifling than a husband who doesn't know a Giotto from a Carlo Dolci, but who can distinguish nut coal from egg and is never asked to dinner without talking about the furnace.

These, of course, were early trials. They had passed to some extent, or were, at any rate, garlanded with the roses of time.

But the drag remained.

Even when the retail coal and wood stage was long since over, it was hard to have to put up with a husband who owned a coal mine and who bought pulp forests instead of illuminated missals of the twelfth century. A coal mine is a dreadful thing at a dinner-table. It humbles one so before one's guests.

It wouldn't have been so bad – this Mrs. Rasselyer-Brown herself admitted – if Mr. Rasselyer-Brown *did* anything. This phrase should be clearly understood. It meant if there was any one thing that he *did*. For instance if he had only *collected* anything. Thus, there was Mr. Lucullus Fyshe, who made soda-water, but at the same time everybody knew that he had the best collection of broken Italian furniture on the continent; there wasn't a sound piece among the lot.

And there was the similar example of old Mr. Feathertop. He didn't exactly *collect* things; he repudiated the name. He was wont to say, "Don't call me a collector, I'm *not*. I simply pick things up. Just where I happen to be, Rome, Warsaw, Bucharest, anywhere" – and it is to be noted what fine places these are to happen to be. And to think that Mr. Rasselyer-Brown would never put his foot outside of the United States! Whereas Mr. Feathertop would come back from what he called a run to Europe, and everybody would learn in a week that he had picked up the back of a violin in Dresden (actually discovered it in a violin shop), and the lid of a Etruscan kettle (he had lighted on it, by pure chance, in a kettle shop in Etruria), and Mrs. Rasselyer-Brown would feel faint with despair at the non-entity of her husband.

So one can understand how heavy her burden was.

"My dear," she often said to her bosom friend, Miss Snagg, "I shouldn't mind things so much" (the things she wouldn't mind were, let us say, the two million dollars of standing timber which Brown Limited, the ominous business name of Mr. Rasselyer-Brown, were buying that year) "if Mr. Rasselyer-Brown *did* anything. But he does *nothing*. Every morning after breakfast off to his wretched office, and never back till dinner, and in the evening nothing but his club, or some business meeting. One would think he would have more ambition. How I wish I had been a man."

It was certainly a shame.

So it came that, in almost everything she undertook Mrs. Rasselyer-Brown had to act without the least help from her husband. Every Wednesday, for instance, when the Dante Club met at her house (they selected four lines each week to meditate on, and then discussed them at lunch), Mrs. Rasselyer-Brown had to carry the whole burden of it – her very phrase, "the whole burden" – alone. Anyone who has carried four lines of Dante through a Moselle lunch knows what a weight it is.

In all these things her husband was useless, quite useless. It is not right to be ashamed of one's husband. And to do her justice, Mrs. Rasselyer-Brown always explained to her three hundred intimates that she was *not* ashamed of him; in fact, that she *refused* to be. But it was hard to see him brought into comparison at their own table with superior men. Put him, for instance, beside Mr. Sikleigh Snoop, the sex-poet, and where was he? Nowhere. He couldn't even understand what Mr. Snoop was saying. And when Mr. Snoop would stand on the hearth-rug with a cup of tea balanced in his hand, and discuss whether sex was or was not the dominant note in Botticelli, Mr. Rasselyer-Brown would be skulking in a corner in his ill-fitting dress-suit. His wife would often catch with an agonised ear such scraps of talk as, "When I was first in the coal and wood business," or, "It's a coal that burns quicker than egg, but it hasn't the heating power of nut," or even in a low undertone the words, "If you're feeling *dry* while he's reading –" And this at a time when everybody in the room ought to have been listening to Mr. Snoop.

Nor was even this the whole burden of Mrs. Rasselyer-Brown. There was another part of it which was perhaps more *real*, though Mrs. Rasselyer-Brown herself never put it into words. In fact, of this part of her burden she never spoke, even to her bosom friend Miss Snagg; nor did she talk about it to the ladies of the Dante Club, nor did she make speeches on it to the members of the Women's After-noon Art Society, nor to the Monday Bridge Club.

But the members of the Bridge Club and the Art Society and the Dante Club all talked about it among themselves.

Stated very simply, it was this: Mr. Rasselyer-Brown drank.

It was not meant that he was a drunkard or that he drank too much, or anything of that sort. He drank. That was all.

There was no excess about it. Mr. Rasselyer-Brown, of course, began the day with an eye-opener – and after all, what alert man does not wish his eyes well open in the morning? He followed it usually just before breakfast with a bracer – and what wiser precaution can a business man take than to brace his breakfast? On his way to business he generally had his motor stopped at the Grand Palaver for a moment, if it was a raw day, and dropped in and took something to keep out the damp. If it was a cold day he took something to keep out the cold, and if it was one of those clear, sunny days that are so dangerous to the system he took whatever the bar-tender (a recognised health expert) suggested to tone the system up. After which he could sit down in his office and transact more business, and bigger business, in coal, charcoal, wood, pulp, pulp-wood, and wood-pulp, in two hours than any other man in the business could in a week. Naturally so. For he was braced, and propped, and toned up, and his eyes had been opened, and his brain cleared, till outside of very big business indeed few men were on a footing with him.

In fact, it was business itself which had compelled Mr. Rasselyer-Brown to drink. It is all very well for a junior clerk on twenty dollars a week to do his work on sandwiches and malted milk. In big business it is not possible. When a man begins to rise in business, as Mr. Rasselyer-Brown had begun twenty-five years ago, he finds that if he wants to succeed he must cut malted milk clear out. In any position of responsibility a man has got to drink. No really big deal can be put through without it. If two keen men, sharp as flint, get together to make a deal in which each intends to outdo the other, the only way to succeed is for them to adjourn to some such place as the luncheon-room of the Mausoleum Club and both get partially drunk. This is what is called the personal element in business. And, beside it, plodding industry is nowhere.

Most of all do these principles hold true in such manly out-of-door enterprises as the forest and timber business, where one deals constantly with chief rangers, and pathfinders, and wood-stalkers, whose very names seem to suggest a horn of whiskey under a hemlock-tree.

But, – let it be repeated and carefully understood, – there was no excess about Mr. Rasselyer-Brown's drinking. Indeed, whatever he might be compelled to take during the day, and at the Mausoleum Club in the evening, after his return from his club at night Mr. Rasselyer-Brown made it a fixed rule to take nothing. He might, perhaps, as he passed into the house, step into the dining-room and take a very small drink at the sideboard. But this he counted as part of the return itself, and not after it. And he might, if his brain were over-fatigued, drop down later in the night in his pajamas and dressing-gown when the house was quiet, and compose his mind with a brandy and water, or something suitable to the stillness of the hour. But this was not really a drink. Mr. Rasselyer-Brown called it a *nip*; and of course any man may need a *nip* at a time when he would scorn a drink.

But after all, a woman may find herself again in her daughter. There, at least, is consolation. For, as Mrs. Rasselyer-Brown herself admitted, her daughter Dulphemia was herself again. There were, of course, differences, certain differences of face and appearance. Mr. Snoop had expressed this fact exquisitely when he said that it was the difference between a Burne-Jones and a Dante Gabriel Rossetti. But even at that the mother and daughter were so alike that people, certain people, were constantly mistaking them on the street. And as everybody that mistook them was apt to be asked to dine on five-dollar champagne there was plenty of temptation towards error.

There is no doubt that Dulphemia Rasselyer-Brown was a girl of remarkable character and intellect. So is any girl who has beautiful golden hair parted in thick bands on her forehead, and deep blue eyes soft as an Italian sky.

Even the oldest and most serious men in town admitted that in talking to her they were aware of a grasp, a reach, a depth that surprised them. Thus old Judge Longerstill, who talked to her at dinner for an hour on the jurisdiction of the Interstate Commerce Commission, felt sure from the way in which she looked up in his face at intervals and said, "How interesting!" that she had the mind of a lawyer. And Mr. Brace, the consulting engineer, who showed her on the table-cloth at dessert with three forks and a spoon the method in which the overflow of the spillway of the Gatun Dam is regulated, felt assured, from the way she leaned her face on her hand sideways and said, "How extraordinary!" that she had the brain of an engineer. Similarly foreign visitors to the social circles of the city were delighted with her. Viscount FitzThistle, who explained to Dulphemia for half an hour the intricacies of the Irish situation, was captivated at the quick grasp she showed by asking him at the end, without a second's hesitation, "And which are the Nationalists?"

This kind of thing represents female intellect in its best form. Every man that is really a man is willing to recognise it at once.

As to the young men, of course they flocked to the Rasselyer-Brown residence in shoals. There were batches of them every Sunday afternoon at five o'clock, encased in long black frockcoats, sitting very rigidly in upright chairs, trying to drink tea with one hand. One might see athletic young college men of the football team trying hard to talk about Italian music; and Italian tenors from the Grand Opera doing their best to talk about college football. There were young men in business talking about art, and young men in art talking about religion, and young clergymen talking about business. Because, of course, the Rasselyer-Brown residence was the kind of cultivated home where people of education and taste are at liberty to talk about things they don't know, and to utter freely ideas that they haven't got. It was only now and again, when one of the professors from the college across the avenue came booming into the room, that the whole conversation was pulverised into dust under the hammer of accurate knowledge.

This whole process was what was called, by those who understood such things a *salon*. Many people said that Mrs. Rasselyer-Brown's afternoons at home were exactly like the delightful *salons* of the eighteenth century: and whether the gatherings were or were not *salons* of the eighteenth century, there is no doubt that Mr. Rasselyer-Brown, under whose care certain favoured guests dropped quietly into the back alcove of the dining-room, did his best to put the gathering on a par with the best saloons of the twentieth.

Now it so happened that there had come a singularly

slack moment in the social life of the City. The Grand Opera had sung itself into a huge deficit and closed. There remained nothing of it except the efforts of a committee of ladies to raise enough money to enable Signor Puffi to leave town, and the generous attempt of another committee to gather funds in order to keep Signor Pasti in the City. Beyond this, opera was dead, though the fact that the deficit was nearly twice as large as it had been the year before showed that public interest in music was increasing. It was indeed a singularly trying time of the year. It was too early to go to Europe, and too late to go to Bermuda. It was too warm to go south, and yet still too cold to go north. In fact, one was almost compelled to stay at home – which was dreadful.

As a result Mrs. Rasselyer-Brown and her three hundred friends moved backward and forward on Plutoria Avenue, seeking novelty in vain. They washed in waves of silk from tango teas to bridge afternoons. They poured in liquid avalanches of colour into crowded receptions, and they sat in glittering rows and listened to lectures on the enfranchisement of the female sex. But for the moment all was weariness.

Now it happened, whether by accident or design, that just at this moment of general *ennui* Mrs. Rasselyer-Brown and her three hundred friends first heard of the presence in the city of Mr. Yahi-Bahi, the celebrated Oriental mystic. He was so celebrated that nobody even thought of asking who he was or where he came from. They merely told one another, and repeated it, that he was *the* celebrated Yahi-Bahi. They added for those who needed the knowledge that the name was pronounced Yahhy-Bahhy, and that the doctrine taught by Mr. Yahi-Bahi was Boohooism. This latter, if anyone inquired further, was explained to be a form of Shoodooism, only rather more intense. In fact, it was esoteric – on receipt of which information everybody remarked at once how infinitely superior the Oriental peoples are to ourselves.

Now as Mrs. Rasselyer-Brown was always a leader in

everything that was done in the best circles on Plutoria Avenue, she was naturally among the first to visit Mr. Yahi-Bahi.

"My dear," she said, in describing afterwards her experience to her bosom friend, Miss Snagg, "it was *most* interesting. We drove away down to the queerest part of the City, and went to the strangest little house imaginable, up the narrowest stairs one ever saw – quite Eastern, in fact, just like a scene out of the Koran."

"How fascinating!" said Miss Snagg. But as a matter of fact, if Mr. Yahi-Bahi's house had been inhabited, as it might have been, by a street-car conductor or a railway brakesman, Mrs. Rasselyer-Brown wouldn't have thought it in any way peculiar or fascinating.

"It was all hung with curtains inside," she went on, "with figures of snakes and Indian gods, perfectly weird."

"And did you see Mr. Yahi-Bahi?" asked Miss Snagg.

"Oh no, my dear. I only saw his assistant, Mr. Ram Spudd; such a queer little round man, a Bengalee, I believe. He put his back against a curtain and spread out his arms sideways and wouldn't let me pass. He said that Mr. Yahi-Bahi was in meditation and mustn't be disturbed."

"How delightful!" echoed Miss Snagg.

But in reality Mr. Yahi-Bahi was sitting behind the curtain eating a ten-cent can of pork and beans.

"What I like most about eastern people," went on Mrs. Rasselyer-Brown, "is their wonderful delicacy of feeling. After I had explained about my invitation to Mr. Yahi-Bahi to come and speak to us on Boohooism, and was going away, I took a dollar bill out of my purse and laid it on the table. You should have seen the way Mr. Ram Spudd took it. He made the deepest salaam and said, 'Isis guard you, beautiful lady.' Such perfect courtesy, and yet with the air of scorning the money. As I passed out I couldn't help slipping another dollar into his hand, and he took it as if utterly unaware of it, and muttered, 'Osiris keep you, O flower of women!' And as I got into the motor I gave him another dollar and he said, 'Osis and Osiris both prolong your existence, O lily of the rice-field'; and after he had said it he stood beside the door of the motor and waited without moving till I left. He had such a strange, rapt look, as if he were still expecting something!"

"How exquisite!" murmured Miss Snagg. It was her business in life to murmur such things as this for Mrs. Rasselyer-Brown. On the whole, reckoning Grand Opera tickets and dinners, she did very well out of it.

"Is it not?" said Mrs. Rasselyer-Brown. "So different from our men. I felt so ashamed of my chauffeur, our new man, you know; he seemed such a contrast beside Ram Spudd. The rude way in which he opened the door, and the rude way in which he climbed on to his own seat, and the *rudeness* with which he turned on the power – I felt positively ashamed. And he so managed it – I am sure he did it on purpose – that the car splashed a lot of mud over Mr. Spudd as it started."

Yet, oddly enough, the opinion of other people on this new chauffeur, that of Miss Dulphemia Rasselyer-Brown herself, for example, to whose service he was specially attached, was very different.

The great recommendation of him in the eyes of Miss Dulphemia and her friends, and the thing that give him a touch of mystery was – and what higher qualification can a chauffeur want? – that he didn't look like a chauffeur at all.

"My dear Dulphie," whispered Miss Philippa Furlong, the rector's sister (who was at that moment Dulphemia's second self), as they sat behind the new chauffeur, "don't tell me that he is a chauffeur, because he *isn't*. He can chauffe, of course, but that's nothing."

For the new chauffeur had a bronzed face, hard as metal, and a stern eye; and when he put on a chauffeur's overcoat somehow it seemed to turn into a military greatcoat; and even when he put on the round cloth cap of his profession it was converted straightway into a military shako. And by Miss Dulphemia and her friends it was presently reported – or was invented? – that he had served in the Philippines; which explained at once the scar upon his forehead, which

must have been received at Iloilo, or Huila-Huila, or some
other suitable place.

But what affected Miss Dulphemia Brown herself was
the splendid rudeness of the chauffeur's manner. It was so
different from that of the young men of the *salon*. Thus,
when Mr. Sikleigh Snoop handed her into the car at any
time he would dance about saying, "Allow me," and, "Permit me," and would dive forward to arrange the robes. But
the Philippine chauffeur merely swung the door open and
said to Dulphemia, "Get in," and then slammed it.

This, of course, sent a thrill up the spine and through the
imagination of Miss Dulphemia Rasselyer-Brown, because
it showed that the chauffeur was a gentleman in disguise.
She thought it very probable that he was a British noble-
man, a younger son, very wild, of a ducal family; and she
had her own theories as to why he had entered the service
of the Rasselyer-Browns. To be quite candid about it, she
expected that the Philippine chauffeur meant to elope with
her, and every time he drove her from a dinner or a dance
she sat back luxuriously, wishing and expecting the elope-
ment to begin.

But for the time being the interest of Dulphemia, as of
everybody else that was anybody at all, centred round Mr.
Yahi-Bahi and the new cult of Boohooism.

After the visit of Mrs. Rasselyer-Brown a great number
of ladies, also in motors, drove down to the house of Mr.
Yahi-Bahi. And all of them, whether they saw Mr. Yahi-
Bahi himself or his Bengalee assistant, Mr. Ram Spudd,
came back delighted.

"Such exquisite tact!" said one. "Such delicacy! As I
was about to go I laid a five-dollar gold piece on the edge of
the little table. Mr. Spudd scarcely seemed to see it. He
murmured, 'Osiris help you!' and pointed to the ceiling. I
raised my eyes instinctively, and when I lowered them the
money had disappeared. I think he must have caused it to
vanish."

"Oh, I'm sure he did," said the listener.

Others came back with wonderful stories of Mr. Yahi-Bahi's occult powers, especially his marvellous gift of reading the future.

Mrs. Buncomhearst, who had just lost her third husband – by divorce – had received from Mr. Yahi-Bahi a glimpse into the future that was almost uncanny in its exactness. She had asked for a divination, and Mr. Yahi-Bahi had effected one by causing her to lay six ten-dollar pieces on the table arranged in the form of a mystic serpent. Over these he had bent and peered deeply, as if seeking to unravel their meaning, and finally he had given her the prophecy, "Many things are yet to happen before others begin."

"How *does* he do it?" asked everybody.

As a result of all this it naturally came about that Mr. Yahi-Bahi and Mr. Ram Spudd were invited to appear at the residence of Mrs. Rasselyer-Brown; and it was understood that steps would be taken to form a special society, to be known as the Yahi-Bahi Oriental Society.

Mr. Sikleigh Snoop, the sex-poet, was the leading spirit in the organisation. He had a special fitness for the task: he had actually resided in India. In fact, he had spent six weeks there on a stop-over ticket of a round-the-world 635 dollar steamship pilgrimage; and he knew the whole country from Jehumbapore in Bhootal to Jehumbalabad in the Carnatic. So he was looked upon as a great authority on India, China, Mongolia, and all such places, by the ladies of Plutoria Avenue.

Next in importance was Mrs. Buncomhearst, who became later, by a perfectly natural process, the president of the society. She was already president of the Daughters of the Revolution, a society confined exclusively to the descendants of Washington's officers and others; she was also president of the Sisters of England, an organisation limited exclusively to women born in England and elsewhere; of the Daughters of Kossuth, made up solely of Hungarians and friends of Hungary and other nations; and of the Circle of Franz Joseph, which was composed exclusively of the partisans, and others, of Austria. In fact, ever since she had lost her third husband, Mrs. Buncomhearst had thrown herself – that was her phrase – into outside activities. Her one wish was, on her own statement, to lose herself. So very naturally Mrs. Rasselyer-Brown looked at once to Mrs. Buncomhearst to preside over the meetings of the new society.

The large dining-room at the Rasselyer-Browns' had been cleared out as a sort of auditorium, and in it some fifty or sixty of Mrs. Rasselyer-Brown's more intimate friends had gathered. The whole meeting was composed of ladies, except for the presence of one or two men who represented special cases. There was, of course, little Mr. Spillikins, with his vacuous face and football hair, who was there, as everybody knew, on account of Dulphemia; and there was old Judge Longerstill, who sat leaning on a gold-headed stick with his head sideways, trying to hear some fraction of what was being said. He came to the gathering in the hope that it would prove a likely place for seconding a vote of thanks and saying a few words – half an hour's talk, perhaps – on the constitution of the United States. Failing that, he felt sure that at least someone would call him "this eminent old gentleman," and even that was better than staying at home.

But for the most part the audience was composed of women, and they sat in a little buzz of conversation waiting for Mr. Yahi-Bahi.

"I wonder," called Mrs. Buncomhearst from the chair, "if some lady would be good enough to write minutes? Miss Snagg, I wonder if you would be kind enough to write minutes? Could you?"

"I shall be delighted," said Miss Snagg, "but I'm afraid there's hardly time to write them before we begin, is there?"

"Oh, but it would be all right to write them *afterwards*," chorussed several ladies who understood such things; "it's quite often done that way."

"And I should like to move that we vote a constitution," said a stout lady with a double eye-glass.

"Is that carried?" said Mrs. Buncomhearst. "All those in favour please signify."

Nobody stirred.

"Carried," said the president. "And perhaps you would be good enough, Mrs. Fyshe," she said, turning towards the stout lady, "to *write* the constitution."

"Do you think it necessary to *write* it?" said Mrs. Fyshe. "I should like to move, if I may, that I almost wonder whether it is necessary to write the constitution – unless, of course, anybody thinks that we really ought to."

"Ladies," said the president, "you have heard the motion. All those against it –"

There was no sign.

"All those in favour of it –"

There was still no sign.

"Lost," she said.

Then, looking across at the clock on the mantel-piece, and realising that Mr. Yahi-Bahi must have been delayed and that something must be done, she said:

"And now, ladies, as we have in our midst a most eminent gentleman who probably has thought more deeply about constitutions than –"

All eyes turned at once towards Judge Longerstill, but as fortune had it at this very moment Mr. Sikleigh Snoop entered, followed by Mr. Yahi-Bahi and Mr. Ram Spudd.

Mr. Yahi-Bahi was tall. His drooping Oriental costume made him taller still. He had a long brown face and liquid brown eyes of such depth that when he turned them full upon the ladies before him a shiver of interest and apprehension followed in the track of his glance.

"My dear," said Miss Snagg afterwards, "he seemed simply to see right through us."

This was correct. He did.

Mr Ram Spudd presented a contrast to his superior. He was short and round, with a dimpled mahogany face and eyes that twinkled in it like little puddles of molasses. His head was bound in a turban and his body was swathed in so many bands and sashes that he looked almost circular. The clothes of both Mr. Yahi-Bahi and Ram Spudd were covered with the mystic signs of Buddha and the seven serpents of Vishnu.

It was impossible, of course, for Mr. Yahi-Bahi or Mr. Ram Spudd to address the audience. Their knowledge of English was known to be too slight for that. Their communications were expressed entirely through the medium of Mr. Snoop, and even he explained afterwards that it was very difficult. The only languages of India which he was able to speak, he said, with any fluency were Gargamic and Gumaic, both of these being old Dravidian dialects with only two hundred and three words in each, and hence in themselves very difficult to converse in. Mr. Yahi-Bahi answered in what Mr. Snoop understood to be the Iramic of the Vedas, a very rich language, but one which unfortunately he did not understand. The dilemma is one familiar to all Oriental scholars.

All of this Mr. Snoop explained in the opening speech which he proceeded to make. And after this he went on to disclose, amid deep interest, the general nature of the cult of Boohooism. He said that they could best understand it if he told them that its central doctrine was that of Bahee. Indeed, the first aim of all followers of the cult was to attain to Bahee. Anybody who could spend a certain number of hours each day, say sixteen, in silent meditation on Boohooism would find his mind gradually reaching a condition of Bahee. The chief aim of Bahee itself was sacrifice: a true follower of the cult must be willing to sacrifice his friends, or his relatives, and even strangers, in order to reach Bahee. In this way one was able fully to realise oneself and enter into the Higher Indifference. Beyond this, further meditation and fasting – by which was meant living solely on fish, fruit, wine, and meat – one presently attained to complete

Swaraj or Control of Self, and might in time pass into the absolute Nirvana, or the Negation of Emptiness, the supreme goal of Boohooism.

As a first step to all this, Mr. Snoop explained, each neophyte or candidate for holiness must, after searching his own heart, send ten dollars to Mr. Yahi-Bahi. Gold, it appeared, was recognised in the cult of Boohooism as typifying the three chief virtues, whereas silver or paper money did not; even national bank-notes were only regarded as *dô*, or a half-way palliation; and outside currencies such as Canadian or Mexican bills were looked upon as entirely *boo*, or contemptible. The Oriental view of money, said Mr. Snoop, was far superior to our own, but it also might be attained by deep thought, and, as a beginning, by sending ten dollars to Mr. Yahi-Bahi.

After this Mr. Snoop, in conclusion, read a very beautiful Hindu poem, translating it as he went along. It began, "O cow, standing beside the Ganges, and apparently without visible occupation," and it was voted exquisite by all who heard it. The absence of rhyme and the entire removal of ideas marked it as far beyond anything reached as yet by Occidental culture.

When Mr. Snoop had concluded the president called upon Judge Longerstill for a few words of thanks, which he gave, followed by a brief talk on the constitution of the United States.

After this the society was declared constituted, Mr. Yahi-Bahi made four salaams, one to each point of the compass, and the meeting dispersed.

And that evening, over fifty dinner tables, everybody discussed the nature of Bahee, and tried in vain to explain it to men too stupid to understand.

Now it so happened that on the very afternoon of this meeting at Mrs. Rasselyer-Brown's, the Philippine chauffeur did a strange and peculiar thing. He first asked Mr. Rasselyer-Brown for a few hours' leave of absence to attend

the funeral of his mother-in-law. This was a request which
Mr. Rasselyer-Brown, on principle, never refused to a man-
servant.

Whereupon, the Philippine chauffeur, no longer attired
as one, visited the residence of Mr. Yahi-Bahi. He let
himself in with a marvellous little key which he produced
from a very wonderful bunch of such. He was in the house
for nearly half an hour, and when he emerged the notebook
in his breast pocket, had there been an eye to read it, would
have been seen to be filled with stranger details in regard to
Oriental mysticism than even Mr. Yahi-Bahi had given to
the world. So strange were they that before the Philippine
chauffeur returned to the Rasselyer-Brown residence he
telegraphed certain and sundry parts of them to New York.
But why he should have addressed them to the head of a
detective bureau instead of to a college of Oriental research
it passes the imagination to conceive. But as the chauffeur
duly reappeared at motor-time in the evening the incident
passed unnoticed.

It is beyond the scope of the present narrative to trace the
progress of Boohooism during the splendid but brief career
of the Yahi-Bahi Oriental Society. There could be no doubt
of its success. Its principles appealed with great strength to
all the more cultivated among the ladies of Plutoria
Avenue. There was something in the Oriental mysticism of
its doctrines which rendered previous belief stale and puer-
ile. The practice of the sacred rites began at once. The
ladies' counters of the Plutorian banks were inundated with
requests for ten-dollar pieces in exchange for bank-notes.
At dinner in the best houses nothing was eaten except a thin
soup (or brû), followed by fish, succeeded by meat or by
game, especially such birds as are particularly pleasing to
Buddha, as the partridge, the pheasant, and the woodcock.
After this, except for fruits and wine, the principle of
Swaraj, or denial of self, was rigidly imposed. Special
Oriental dinners of this sort were given, followed by listen-

ing to the reading of Oriental poetry, with closed eyes and with the mind as far as possible in a state of Stoj, or Negation of Thought.

By this means the general doctrine of Boohooism spread rapidly. Indeed, a great many of the members of the society soon attained to a stage of Bahee, or the Higher Indifference, that it would have been hard to equal outside of Juggapore or Jumbumbabad. For example, when Mrs. Buncomhearst learned of the remarriage of her second husband – she had lost him three years before, owing to a difference of opinion on the emancipation of women – she shewed the most complete Bahee possible. And when Miss Snagg learned that her brother in Venezuela had died – a very sudden death brought on by drinking rum for seventeen years – and had left her ten thousand dollars, the Bahee which she exhibited almost amounted to Nirvana.

In fact, the very general dissemination of the Oriental idea became more and more noticeable with each week that passed. Some members attained to so complete a Bahee, or Higher Indifference, that they even ceased to attend the meetings of the society; others reached a Swaraj, or Control of Self, so great that they no longer read its pamphlets; while others again actually passed into Nirvana, to a Complete Negation of Self, so rapidly that they did not even pay their subscriptions.

But features of this sort, of course, are familiar wherever a successful occult creed makes its way against the prejudices of the multitude.

The really notable part of the whole experience was the marvellous demonstration of occult power which attended the final séance of the society, the true nature of which is still wrapped in mystery.

For some weeks it had been rumoured that a very special feat or demonstration of power by Mr. Yahi-Bahi was under contemplation. In fact, the rapid spread of Swaraj and of Nirvana among the members rendered such a feat highly desirable. Just what form the demonstration would take was for some time a matter of doubt. It was whispered at first that Mr. Yahi-Bahi would attempt the mysterious eastern rite of burying Ram Spudd alive in the garden of the Rasselyer-Brown residence and leaving him there in a state of Stoj, or Suspended Inanition, for eight days. But this project was abandoned, owing to some doubt, apparently, in the mind of Mr. Ram Spudd as to his astral fitness for the high state of Stoj necessitated by the experiment.

At last it became known to the members of the Poosh, or Inner Circle, under the seal of confidence, that Mr. Yahi-Bahi would attempt nothing less than the supreme feat of occultism, namely, a reincarnation, or more correctly a reastralisation of Buddha.

The members of the Inner Circle shivered with a luxurious sense of mystery when they heard of it.

"Has it ever been done before?" they asked of Mr. Snoop.

"Only a few times," he said; "once, I believe, by Jambum, the famous Yogi of the Carnatic; once, perhaps twice, by Boohoo, the founder of the sect. But it is looked upon as extremely rare. Mr. Yahi tells me that the great danger is that, if the slightest part of the formula is incorrectly observed, the person attempting the astralisation is swallowed up into nothingness. However, he declares himself willing to try."

The séance was to take place at Mrs. Rasselyer-Brown's residence, and was to be at midnight.

"At midnight!" said each member in surprise. And the answer was, "Yes, at midnight. You see, midnight here is exactly midday in Allahabad in India."

This explanation was, of course, ample. "Midnight," repeated everybody to everybody else, "is exactly midday in Allahabad." That made things perfectly clear. Whereas if midnight had been midday in Timbuctoo the whole situation would have been different.

Each of the ladies was requested to bring to the séance some ornament of gold; but it must be plain gold, without any setting of stones.

It was known already that, according to the cult of Boohooism, gold, plain gold, is the seat of the three virtues – beauty, wisdom, and grace. Therefore, according to the creed of Boohooism, anyone who has enough gold, plain gold, is endowed with these virtues and is all right. All that is needed is to have enough of it; the virtues follow as a consequence.

But for the great experiment the gold used must not be set with stones, with the one exception of rubies, which are known to be endowed with the three attributes of Hindu worship – modesty, loquacity, and pomposity.

In the present case it was found that as a number of ladies had nothing but gold ornaments set with diamonds, a second exception was made; especially as Mr. Yahi-Bahi, on appeal, decided that diamonds, though less pleasing to Buddha than rubies, possessed the secondary Hindu virtues of divisibility, movability, and disposability.

On the evening in question the residence of Mrs. Rasselyer-Brown might have been observed at midnight wrapped in utter darkness. No lights were shown. A single taper, brought by Ram Spudd from the Taj Mohal, and resembling in its outer texture those sold at the five-and-ten store near Mr. Spudd's residence, burned on a small table in the vast dining-room. The servants had been sent upstairs and expressly enjoined to retire at half past ten. Moreover, Mr. Rasselyer-Brown had had to attend that evening, at the Mausoleum Club, a meeting of the trustees of the Church of St. Asaph, and he had come home at eleven o'clock, as he always did after diocesan work of this sort, quite used up; in fact, so fatigued that he had gone upstairs to his own suite of rooms sideways, his knees bending under him. So utterly used up was he with his church work that, as far as any interest in what might be going on in his own residence, he had attained to a state of Bahee, or Higher Indifference, that even Buddha might have envied.

The guests, as had been arranged, arrived noiselessly and on foot. All motors were left at least a block away. They made their way up the steps of the darkened house, and were admitted without ringing, the door opening silently in front of them. Mr. Yahi-Bahi and Mr. Ram Spudd, who had arrived on foot carrying a large parcel, were already there, and were behind a screen in the darkened room, reported to be in meditation.

At a whispered word from Mr. Snoop, who did duty at the door, all furs and wraps were discarded in the hall and laid in a pile. Then the guests passed silently into the great dining-room. There was no light in it except the dim taper which stood on a little table. On this table each guest, as instructed, laid on ornament of gold, and at the same time was uttered in a low voice the word "Ksvoo." This means, "O Buddha, I herewith lay my unworthy offering at thy feet; take it and keep it for ever." It was explained that this was only a form.

"What is he doing?" whispered the assembled guests as they saw Mr. Yahi-Bahi pass across the darkened room and stand in front of the sideboard.

"Hush!" said Mr. Snoop; "he's laying the propitiatory offering for Buddha."

"It's an Indian rite," whispered Mrs. Rasselyer-Brown.

Mr. Yahi-Bahi could be seen dimly moving to and fro in front of the sideboard. There was a faint clinking of glass.

"He has to set out a glass of Burmese brandy, powdered over with nutmeg and aromatics," whispered Mrs. Rasselyer-Brown. "I had the greatest hunt to get it all for him. He said that nothing but Burmese brandy would do, because in the Hindu religion the god can only be invoked with Burmese brandy, or, failing that, Hennessy's with three stars, which is not entirely displeasing to Buddha."

"The aromatics," whispered Mr. Snoop, "are supposed to waft a perfume or incense to reach the nostrils of the god. The glass of propitiatory wine and the aromatic spices are mentioned in the Vishnu-Buddayat."

Mr. Yahi-Bahi, his preparations completed, was now seen to stand in front of the sideboard bowing deeply four

times in an Oriental salaam. The light of the single taper
had by this time burned so dim that his movements were
vague and uncertain. His body cast great flickering shad-
ows on the half-seen wall. From his throat there issued a
low wail in which the word wah! wah! could be
distinguished.

The excitement was intense.

"What does 'wah' mean?" whispered Mr. Spillikins.

"Hush!" said Mr. Snoop; "it means, 'O Buddha, wherever thou art in thy lofty Nirvana, descend yet once in astral
form before our eyes!'"

Mr. Yahi-Bahi rose. He was seen to place one finger on
his lips and then, silently moving across the room, he
disappeared behind the screen. Of what Mr. Ram Spudd
was doing during this period there is no record. It was
presumed that he was still praying.

The stillness was now absolute.

"We must wait in perfect silence," whispered Mr. Snoop
from the extreme tips of his lips.

Everybody sat in strained intensity, silent, looking
towards the vague outline of the sideboard.

The minutes passed. No one moved. All were spellbound
in expectancy.

Still the minutes passed. The taper had flickered down
till the great room was almost in darkness.

Could it be that by some neglect in the preparations, the
substitution perhaps of the wrong brandy, the astralisation
could not be effected?

But no.

Quite suddenly, it seemed, everybody in the darkened
room was aware of a *presence*. That was the word as
afterwards repeated in a hundred confidential discussions.
A *presence*. One couldn't call it a body. It wasn't. It was a
figure, an astral form, a presence.

"Buddha!" they gasped as they looked at it.

Just how the figure entered the room, the spectators
could never afterwards agree. Some thought it appeared
through the wall, deliberately astralising itself as it passed

through the bricks. Others seemed to have seen it pass in at the further door of the room, as if it had astralised itself at the foot of the stairs in the back of the hall outside.

Be that as it may, there it stood before them, the astralised shape of the Indian deity, so that to every lip there rose the half-articulated word, "Buddha"; or at least to every lip except that of Mrs. Rasselyer-Brown. From her there came no sound.

The figure as afterwards described was attired in a long *shirâk*, such as is worn by the Grand Llama of Tibet, and resembling, if the comparison were not profane, a modern dressing-gown. The legs, if one might so call them, of the apparition were enwrapped in loose punjahamas, a word which is said to be the origin of the modern pyjamas; while the feet, if they were feet, were encased in loose slippers.

Buddha moved slowly across the room. Arrived at the sideboard the astral figure paused, and even in the uncertain light Buddha was seen to raise and drink the propitiatory offering. That much was perfectly clear. Whether Buddha spoke or not is doubtful. Certain of the spectators thought that he said, "*Must a fagotnit*," which is Hindustanee for "Blessings on this house." To Mrs. Rasselyer-Brown's distracted mind it seemed as if Buddha said, "I must have forgotten it." But this wild fancy she never breathed to a soul.

Silently Buddha recrossed the room, slowly wiping one arm across his mouth after the Hindu gesture of farewell.

For perhaps a full minute after the disappearance of Buddha not a soul moved. Then quite suddenly Mrs. Rasselyer-Brown, unable to stand the tension any longer, pressed an electric switch and the whole room was flooded with light.

There sat the affrighted guests staring at one another with pale faces.

But, to the amazement and horror of all, the little table in the centre stood empty – not a single gem, not a fraction of the gold that had lain upon it was left. All had disappeared.

The truth seemed to burst upon everyone at once. There was no doubt of what had happened.

The gold and the jewels had been deastralised. Under the occult power of the vision they had been demonetised, engulfed into the astral plane along with the vanishing Buddha.

Filled with the sense of horror still to come, somebody pulled aside the little screen. They fully expected to find the lifeless bodies of Mr. Yahi-Bahi and the faithful Ram Spudd. What they saw before them was more dreadful still. The outer Oriental garments of the two devotees lay strewn upon the floor. The long sash of Yahi-Bahi and the thick turban of Ram Spudd were side by side near them; almost sickening in its repulsive realism was the thick black head of hair of the junior devotee, apparently torn from his scalp as if by lightning and bearing a horrible resemblance to the cast-off wig of an actor.

The truth was too plain.

"They are engulfed!" cried a dozen voices at once.

It was realised in a flash that Yahi-Bahi and Ram Spudd had paid the penalty of their daring with their lives. Through some fatal neglect, against which they had fairly warned the participants of the séance, the two Orientals had been carried bodily in the astral plane.

"How dreadful!" murmured Mr. Snoop. "We must have made some awful error."

"Are they deastralised?" murmured Mrs. Buncomhearst.

"Not a doubt of it," said Mr. Snoop.

And then another voice in the group was heard to say, "We must hush it up. We *can't* have it known!"

On which a chorus of voices joined in, everybody urging that it must be hushed up.

"Couldn't you try to reastralise them?" said somebody to Mr. Snoop.

"No, no," said Mr. Snoop, still shaking. "Better not try to. We must hush it up if we can."

And the general assent to this sentiment shewed that after all the principles of Bahee, or Indifference to Others, had taken a real root in the society.

"Hush it up," cried everybody, and there was a general move towards the hall.

"Good Heavens!" exclaimed Mrs. Buncomhearst; "our wraps!"

"Deastralised!" said the guests.

There was a moment of further consternation as everybody gazed at the spot where the ill-fated pile of furs and wraps had lain.

"Never mind," said everybody, "let's go without them – don't stay. Just think if the police should –"

And at the word police, all of a sudden there was heard in the street the clanging of a bell and the racing gallop of the horses of the police patrol waggon.

"The police!" cried everybody. "Hush it up! Hush it up!"

For of course the principles of Bahee are not known to the police.

In another moment the door bell of the house rang with a long and violent peal, and in a second as it seemed, the whole hall was filled with bulky figures uniformed in blue.

"It's all right, Mrs. Rasselyer-Brown," cried a loud, firm voice from the sidewalk. "We have them both. Everything is here. We got them before they'd gone a block. But if you don't mind, the police must get a couple of names for witnesses in the warrant."

It was the Philippine chauffeur. But he was no longer attired as such. He wore the uniform of an inspector of police, and there was the metal badge of the Detective Department now ostentatiously outside his coat.

And beside him, one on each side of him, there stood the deastralised forms of Yahi-Bahi and Ram Spudd. They wore long overcoats, doubtless the contents of the magic parcels, and the Philippine chauffeur had a grip of iron on the neck of each as they stood. Mr. Spudd had lost his Oriental hair, and the face of Mr. Yahi-Bahi, perhaps in the struggle which had taken place, had been scraped white in patches.

They were making no attempt to break away. Indeed, Mr. Spudd, with that complete Bahee, or Submission to Fate, which is attained only by long services in state penitentiaries, was smiling and smoking a cigarette.

"We were waiting for them," explained a tall police officer to the two or three ladies who now gathered round him with a return of courage. "They had the stuff in a hand-cart and were pushing it away. The chief caught them at the corner, and rang the patrol from there. You'll find everything all right, I think, ladies," he added, as a burly assistant was seen carrying an armload of furs up the steps.

Somehow many of the ladies realised at the moment what cheery, safe, reliable people policemen in blue are, and what a friendly, familiar shelter they offer against the wiles of Oriental occultism.

"Are they old criminals?" someone asked.

"Yes, ma'am. They've worked this same thing in four cities already, and both of them have done time, and lots of it. They've only been out six months. No need to worry over them," he concluded with a shrug of the shoulders.

So the furs were restored and the gold and the jewels parcelled out among the owners, and in due course Mr. Yahi-Bahi and Mr. Ram Spudd were lifted up into the patrol waggon, where they seated themselves with a composure worthy of the best traditions of Jehumbabah and Bahoolapore. In fact, Mr. Spudd was heard to address the police as "boys," and to remark that they had "got them good" that time.

So the séance ended and the guests vanished, and the Yahi-Bahi Society terminated itself without even a vote of dissolution.

And in all the later confidential discussions of the episode only one point of mysticism remained. After they had time really to reflect on it, free from all danger of arrest, the members of the society realised that on one point the police were entirely off the truth of things. For Mr. Yahi-Bahi, whether a thief or not, and whether he came from the Orient, or, as the police said, from Missouri, had actually succeeded in reastralising Buddha.

Nor was anyone more emphatic on this point than Mrs. Rasselyer-Brown herself.

"For after all," she said, "if it was not Buddha, who was it?"

And the question was never answered.

FIVE

The Love Story of Mr. Peter Spillikins

ALMOST any day, on Plutoria Avenue or thereabouts, you may see little Mr. Spillikins out walking with his four tall sons, who are practically as old as himself.

To be exact, Mr. Spillikins is twenty-four, and Bob, the oldest of the boys, must be at least twenty. Their exact ages are no longer known, because, by a dreadful accident, their mother forgot them. This was at a time when the boys were all at Mr. Wackem's Academy for Exceptional Youths in the foothills of Tennessee, and while their mother, Mrs. Everleigh, was spending the winter on the Riviera and felt that for their own sake she must not allow herself to have the boys with her.

But now, of course, since Mrs. Everleigh has remarried and become Mrs. Everleigh-Spillikins there is no need to keep them at Mr. Wackem's any longer. Mr. Spillikins is able to look after them.

Mr. Spillikins generally wears a little top hat and an English morning coat. The boys are in Eton jackets and black trousers, which, at their mother's wish, are kept just a little too short for them. This is because Mrs. Everleigh-Spillikins feels that the day will come some day – say fifteen years hence, – when the boys will no longer be children, and meantime it is so nice to feel that they are still mere boys. Bob is the eldest, but Sib the youngest is the tallest, whereas Willie the third boy is the dullest, although this has often been denied by those who claim that Gib the second boy is just a trifle duller. Thus at any rate there is a certain equality and good fellowship all round.

Mrs. Everleigh-Spillikins is not to be seen walking with them. She is probably at the race-meet, being taken there by Captain Cormorant of the United States navy, which Mr. Spillikins considers very handsome of him. Every now and then the captain, being in the navy, is compelled to be at sea for perhaps a whole afternoon or even several days; in which case Mrs. Everleigh-Spillikins is very generally taken to the Hunt Club or the Country Club by Lieutenant Hawk, which Mr. Spillikins regards as awfully thoughtful of him. Or if Lieutenant Hawk is also out of town for the day, as he sometimes has to be, because he is in the United States army, Mrs. Everleigh-Spillikins is taken out by old Colonel Shake, who is in the State militia and who is at leisure all the time.

During their walks on Plutoria Avenue one may hear the four boys addressing Mr. Spillikins as "father" and "dad" in deep bull-frog voices.

"Say, dad," drawls Bob, "couldn't we all go to the ball game?"

"No, say, dad," says Gib, "let's all go back to the house and play five-cent pool in the billiard-room?"

"All right, boys," says Mr. Spillikins. And a few minutes later one may see them all hustling up the steps of the Everleigh-Spillikins's mansion, quite eager at the prospect, and all talking together.

Now the whole of this daily panorama, to the eye that can read it, represents the outcome of the tangled love story of Mr. Spillikins, which culminated during the summer house-party at Castel Casteggio, the woodland retreat of Mr. and Mrs. Newberry.

But to understand the story one must turn back a year or so to the time when Mr. Peter Spillikins used to walk on

Plutoria Avenue alone, or sit in the Mausoleum Club listening to the advice of people who told him that he really ought to get married.

In those days the first thing that one noticed about Mr. Peter Spillikins was his exalted view of the other sex. Every time he passed a beautiful woman in the street he said to himself, "I say!" Even when he met a moderately beautiful one he murmured, "By Jove!" When an Easter hat went sailing past, or a group of summer parasols stood talking on a leafy corner, Mr. Spillikins ejaculated, "My word!" At the opera and at tango teas his projecting blue eyes almost popped out of his head.

Similarly, if he happened to be with one of his friends, he would murmur, "I say, *do* look at that beautiful girl," or would exclaim, "I say, don't look, but isn't that an awfully pretty girl across the street?" or at the opera, "Old man, don't let her see you looking, but do you see that lovely girl in the box opposite?"

One must add to this that Mr. Spillikins, in spite of his large and bulging blue eyes, enjoyed the heavenly gift of short sight. As a consequence he lived in a world of amazingly beautiful women. And as his mind was focussed in the same way as his eyes he endowed them with all the virtues and graces which ought to adhere to fifty-dollar flowered hats and cerise parasols with ivory handles.

Nor, to do him justice, did Mr. Spillikins confine this attitude to his view of women alone. He brought it to bear on everything. Every time he went to the opera he would come away enthusiastic, saying, "By Jove, isn't it simply splendid! Of course, I haven't the ear to appreciate it – I'm not musical, you know – but even with the little that I know, it's great; it absolutely puts me to sleep." And of each new novel that he bought he said, "It's a perfectly wonderful book! Of course I haven't the head to understand it, so I didn't finish it, but it's simply thrilling." Similarly with painting, "It's one of the most marvellous pictures I ever saw," he would say. "Of course I've no eye for pictures, and I couldn't see anything in it, but it's wonderful!"

The career of Mr. Spillikins up to the point of which we are speaking had hitherto not been very satisfactory, or at least not from the point of view of Mr. Boulder, who was his uncle and trustee. Mr. Boulder's first idea had been to have Mr. Spillikins attend the university. Dr. Boomer, the president, had done his best to spread abroad the idea that a university education was perfectly suitable even for the rich; that it didn't follow that because a man was a university graduate he need either work or pursue his studies any further; that what the university aimed to do was merely to put a certain stamp upon a man. That was all. And this stamp, according to the tenor of the president's convocation addresses, was perfectly harmless. No one ought to be afraid of it. As a result, a great many of the very best young men in the City, who had no need for education at all, were beginning to attend college. "It marked," said Dr. Boomer, "a revolution."

Mr. Spillikins himself was fascinated with his studies. The professors seemed to him living wonders.

"By Jove!" he said, "the professor of mathematics is a marvel. You ought to see him explaining trigonometry on the blackboard. You can't understand a word of it." He hardly knew which of his studies he liked best. "Physics," he said, "is a wonderful study. I got five per cent. in it. But, by Jove! I had to work for it. I'd go in for it altogether if they'd let me."

But that was just the trouble – they wouldn't. And so in course of time Mr. Spillikins was compelled, for academic reasons, to abandon his life-work. His last words about it were, "Gad! I nearly passed in trigonometry!" and he always said afterwards that he had got a tremendous lot out of the university.

After that, as he had to leave the university, his trustee, Mr. Boulder, put Mr. Spillikins into business. It was, of course, his own business, one of the many enterprises for which Mr. Spillikins, ever since he was twenty-one, had already been signing documents and countersigning cheques. So Mr. Spillikins found himself in a mahogany office selling wholesale oil. And he liked it. He said that business sharpened one up tremendously.

"I'm afraid, Mr. Spillikins," a caller in the mahogany office would say, "that we can't meet you at five dollars. Four seventy is the best we can do on the present market."

"My dear chap," said Mr. Spillikins, "that's all right. After all, thirty cents isn't much, eh what? Dash it, old man, we won't fight about thirty cents. How much do you want?"

"Well, at four seventy we'll take twenty thousand barrels."

"By Jove!" said Mr. Spillikins; "twenty thousand barrels. Gad! you want a lot, don't you? Pretty big sale, eh, for a beginner like me? I guess uncle'll be tickled to death."

So tickled was he that after a few weeks of oil selling Mr. Boulder urged Mr. Spillikins to retire, and wrote off many thousand dollars from the capital value of his estate.

So after this there was only one thing for Mr. Spillikins to do, and everybody told him so – namely, to get married.

"Spillikins," said his friends at the club after they had taken all his loose money over the card table, "you ought to get married."

"Think so?" said Mr. Spillikins.

Goodness knows he was willing enough. In fact, up to this point Mr. Spillikins's whole existence had been one long aspiring sigh directed towards the joys of matrimony.

In his brief college days his timid glances had wandered by an irresistible attraction towards the seats on the right-hand side of the classroom, where the girls of the first year sat, with golden pigtails down their backs, doing trigonometry.

He would have married any of them. But when a girl can work out trigonometry at sight, what use can she possibly have for marriage? None. Mr. Spillikins knew this and it kept him silent. And even when the most beautiful girl in the class married the demonstrator and thus terminated her studies in her second year, Spillikins realised that it was only because the man was, undeniably, a demonstrator and knew things.

Later on, when Spillikins went into business and into society, the same fate pursued him. He loved, for at least six months, Georgiana McTeague, the niece of the presbyterian minister of St. Osoph's. He loved her so well that for her sake he temporarily abandoned his pew at St. Asaph's, which was episcopalian, and listened to fourteen consecutive sermons on hell. But the affair got no further than that. Once or twice, indeed, Spillikins walked home with Georgiana from church and talked about hell with her; and once her uncle asked him into the manse for cold supper after evening service, and they had a long talk about hell all through the meal and upstairs in the sitting-room afterwards. But somehow Spillikins could get no further with it. He read up all he could about hell so as to be able to talk with Georgiana, but in the end it failed: a young minister fresh from college came and preached at St. Osoph's six special sermons on the absolute certainty of eternal punishment, and he married Miss McTeague as a result of it.

And meantime Mr. Spillikins had got engaged, or practically so, to Adelina Lightleigh; not that he had spoken to her, but he considered himself bound to her. For her sake he had given up hell altogether, and was dancing till two in the morning and studying auction bridge out of a book. For a time he felt so sure that she meant to have him that he began bringing his greatest friend, Edward Ruff, of the college football team, of whom Spillikins was very proud, up to the Lightleighs' residence. He specially wanted Adelina and Edward to be great friends, so that Adelina and he might ask Edward up to the house after he was married. And they got to be such great friends, and so quickly, that they were married in New York that autumn. After which Spillikins used to be invited up to the house by Edward and Adelina. They both used to tell him how much they owed him; and they too used to join in the chorus and say, "You know, Peter, you're awfully silly not to get married."

Now all this had happened and finished at about the time when the Yahi-Bahi Society ran its course. At its first meeting Mr. Spillikins had met Dulphemia Rasselyer-Brown. At the very sight of her he began reading up the life of Buddha and a translation of the Upanishads so as to fit himself to aspire to live with her. Even when the society ended in disaster Mr. Spillikins's love only burned the stronger. Consequently, as soon as he knew that Mr. and Mrs. Rasselyer-Brown were going away for the summer, and that Dulphemia was to go to stay with the Newberrys at Castel Casteggio, this latter place, the summer retreat of the Newberrys, became the one spot on earth for Mr. Peter Spillikins.

Naturally, therefore, Mr. Spillikins was presently transported to the seventh heaven when in due course of time he received a note which said, "We shall be so pleased if you can come out and spend a week or two with us here. We will send the car down to the Thursday train to meet you. We live here in the simplest fashion possible; in fact, as Mr. Newberry says, we are just roughing it, but I am sure you don't mind for a change. Dulphemia is with us, but we are quite a small party."

The note was signed "Margaret Newberry" and was written on heavy cream paper with a silver monogram such as people use when roughing it.

The Newberry's, like everybody else, went away from town in the summer-time. Mr. Newberry being still in business, after a fashion, it would not have looked well for him to remain in town throughout the year. It would have created a bad impression on the market as to how much he was making.

In fact, in the early summer everybody went out of town. The few who ever revisited the place in August reported that they hadn't seen a soul on the street.

It was a sort of longing for the simple life, for nature, that came over everybody. Some people sought it at the seaside, where nature had thrown out her broad plank walks and her long piers and her vaudeville shows. Others sought it in the heart of the country, where nature had spread her oiled motor roads and her wayside inns. Others, like the Newberrys, preferred to "rough it" in country residences of their own.

Some of the people, as already said, went for business reasons, to avoid the suspicion of having to work all the year round. Others went to Europe to avoid the reproach of living always in America. Others, perhaps most people, went for medical reasons, being sent away by their doctors. Not that they were ill; but the doctors of Plutoria Avenue, such as Doctor Slyder, always preferred to send all their patients out of town during the summer months. No well-to-do doctor cares to be bothered with them. And of course patients, even when they are anxious to go anywhere on their own account, much prefer to be sent there by their doctor.

"My dear madam," Dr. Slyder would say to a lady who, as he knew, was most anxious to go to Virginia, "there's really nothing I can do for you." Here he spoke the truth. "It's not a case of treatment. It's simply a matter of dropping everything and going away. Now why don't you go for a month or two to some quiet place, where you will simply *do nothing*?" (She never, as he knew, did anything, anyway.) "What do you say to Hot Springs, Virginia? – absolute quiet, good golf, not a soul there, plenty of tennis." Or else he would say, "My dear madam, you're simply *worn out*. Why don't you just drop everything and go to Canada? – perfectly quiet, not a soul there, and, I believe, nowadays quite fashionable."

Thus, after all the patients had been sent away, Dr. Slyder and his colleagues of Plutoria Avenue managed to slip away themselves for a month or two, heading straight for Paris and Vienna. There they were able, so they said, to keep in touch with what continental doctors were doing. They probably were.

Now it so happened that both the parents of Miss Dulphemia Rasselyer-Brown had been sent out of town in this fashion. Mrs. Rasselyer-Brown's distressing experience with Yahi-Bahi had left her in a condition in which she was utterly fit for nothing, except to go on a Mediterranean cruise, with about eighty other people also fit for nothing.

Mr. Rasselyer-Brown himself, though never exactly an invalid, had confessed that after all the fuss of the Yahi-Bahi business he needed bracing up, needed putting into shape, and had put himself into Dr. Slyder's hands. The doctor had examined him, questioned him searchingly as to what he drank, and ended by prescribing port wine to be taken firmly and unflinchingly during the evening, and for the daytime, at any moment of exhaustion, a light cordial such as rye whiskey, or rum and Vichy water. In addition to which Dr. Slyder had recommended Mr. Rasselyer-Brown to leave town.

"Why don't you go down to Nagahakett on the Atlantic?" he said.

"Is that in Maine?" said Mr. Rasselyer-Brown in horror.

"Oh, dear me, no!" answered the doctor reassuringly. "It's in New Brunswick, Canada; excellent place, most liberal license laws; first class cuisine and bar in the hotel. No tourists, no golf, too cold to swim – just the place to enjoy oneself."

So Mr. Rasselyer-Brown had gone away also, and as a result Dulphemia Rasselyer-Brown, at the particular moment of which we speak, was declared by the Boudoir and Society column of the *Plutorian Daily Dollar* to be staying with Mr. and Mrs. Newberry at their charming retreat, Castel Casteggio.

The Newberrys belonged to the class of people whose one aim in the summer is to lead the simple life. Mr. Newberry himself said that his one idea of a vacation was to get right out into the bush, and put on old clothes, and just eat when he felt like it.

This was why he had built Castel Casteggio. It stood about forty miles from the city, out among the wooded hills on the shore of a little lake. Except for the fifteen or twenty residences like it that dotted the sides of the lake, it was entirely isolated. The only way to reach it was by the motor road that wound its way among leafy hills from the railway station fifteen miles away. Every foot of the road was private property, as all nature ought to be. The whole country about Castel Casteggio was absolutely primeval, or at any rate as primeval as Scotch gardeners and French landscape artists could make it. The lake itself lay like a sparkling gem from nature's workshop – except that they had raised the level of it ten feet, stone-banked the sides, cleared out the brush, and put a motor road round it. Beyond that it was pure nature.

Castel Casteggio itself, a beautiful house of white brick with sweeping piazzas and glittering conservatories, standing among great trees with rolling lawns broken with flower-beds as the ground sloped to the lake, was perhaps the most beautiful house of all; at any rate, it was an ideal spot to wear old clothes in, to dine early (at 7.30) and, except for tennis parties, motor boat parties, lawn teas, and golf, to live absolutely to oneself.

It should be explained that the house was not called Castel Casteggio because the Newberrys were Italian: they were not; nor because they owned estates in Italy: they didn't; nor had travelled there: they hadn't. Indeed, for a time they had thought of giving it a Welsh name, or a Scotch. But the beautiful country residence of the Asterisk-Thomsons that stood close by in the same primeval country was already called Pennygw-rydd, and the woodland retreat of the Hyphen-Joneses just across the little lake was called Strathythan-na-Clee, and the charming châlet of the Wilson-Smiths was called Yodel-Dudel; so it seemed fairer to select an Italian name.

"By Jove! Miss Furlong, how awfully good of you to come down!"

The little suburban train – two cars only, both first class, for the train went nowhere except out into the primeval wilderness – had drawn up at the diminutive roadside station. Mr. Spillikins had alighted, and there was Miss Philippa Furlong sitting behind the chauffeur in the Newberrys' motor. She was looking as beautiful as only the younger sister of a High Church episcopalian rector can look, dressed in white, the colour of saintliness, on a beautiful morning in July.

There was no doubt about Philippa Furlong. Her beauty was of that peculiar and almost sacred kind found only in the immediate neighbourhood of the High Church clergy. It was admitted by all who envied or admired her that she could enter a church more gracefully, move more swimmingly up the aisle, and pray better than any girl on Plutoria Avenue.

Mr. Spillikins, as he gazed at her in her white summer dress and wide picture hat, with her parasol nodding above her head, realised that after all, religion, as embodied in the younger sisters of the High Church clergy, fills a great place in the world.

"By Jove!" he repeated, "how awfully good of you!"

"Not a bit," said Philippa. "Hop in. Dulphemia was coming, but she couldn't. Is that all you have with you?"

The last remark was ironical. It referred to the two quite large steamer trunks of Mr. Spillikins that were being loaded, together with his suit-case, tennis racket, and golf kit, on to the fore part of the motor. Mr. Spillikins, as a young man of social experience, had roughed it before. He knew what a lot of clothes one needs for it.

So the motor sped away, and went bowling noiselessly over the oiled road, and turning corners where the green boughs of the great trees almost swished in their faces, and rounding and twisting among curves of the hills as it carried Spillikins and Philippa away from the lower domain or ordinary fields and farms up into the enchanted country of private property and the magic castles of Casteggio and Pennygw-rydd.

Mr. Spillikins must have assured Philippa at least a

dozen times in starting off how awfully good it was of her to come down in the motor; and he was so pleased at her coming to meet him that Philippa never even hinted that the truth was that she had expected somebody else on the same train. For to a girl brought up in the principles of the High Church the truth is a very sacred thing. She keeps it to herself.

And naturally, with such a sympathetic listener, it was not long before Mr. Spillikins had begun to talk of Dulphemia and his hopes.

"I don't know whether she really cares for me or not," said Mr. Spillikins, "but I have pretty good hope. The other day, or at least about two months ago, at one of the Yahi-Bahi meetings – you were not in that, were you?" he said, breaking off.

"Only just at the beginning," said Philippa; "we went to Bermuda."

"Oh yes, I remember. Do you know, I thought it pretty rough at the end, especially on Ram Spudd. I liked him. I sent him two pounds of tobacco to the penitentiary last week; you can get it in to them, you know, if you know how."

"But what were you going to say?" asked Philippa.

"Oh yes," said Mr. Spillikins. And he realised that he had actually drifted off the topic of Dulphemia, a thing that had never happened to him before. "I was going to say that at one of the meetings, you know, I asked her if I might call her Dulphemia."

"And what did she say to that?" asked Philippa.

"She said she didn't care what I called her. So I think that looks pretty good, don't you?"

"Awfully good," said Philippa.

"And a little after that I took her slippers home from the Charity Ball at the Grand Palaver. Archie Jones took her home herself in his car, but I took her slippers. She'd forgotten them. I thought that a pretty good sign, wasn't it? You wouldn't let a chap carry round your slippers unless you knew him pretty well, would you, Miss Philippa?"

"Oh no, nobody would," said Philippa. This, of course, was a standing principle of the Anglican Church.

"And a little after that Dulphemia and Charlie Mostyn and I were walking to Mrs. Buncomhearst's musical, and we'd only just started along the street, when she stopped and sent me back for her music – me, mind you, not Charlie. That seems to me awfully significant."

"It seems to speak volumes," said Philippa.

"Doesn't it?" said Mr. Spillikins. "You don't mind my telling you all about this, Miss Philippa?" he added.

Incidentally Mr. Spillikins felt that it was all right to call her Miss Philippa, because she had a sister who was really Miss Furlong, so it would have been quite wrong, as Mr. Spillikins realised, to have called Miss Philippa by her surname. In any case, the beauty of the morning was against it.

"I don't mind a bit," said Philippa. "I think it's awfully nice of you to tell me about it."

She didn't add that she knew all about it already.

"You see," said Mr. Spillikins, "you're so awfully sympathetic. It makes it so easy to talk to you. With other girls, especially with clever ones, even with Dulphemia, I often feel a perfect jackass beside them. But I don't feel that way with you at all."

"Don't you really?" said Philippa, but the honest admiration in Mr. Spillikins's protruding blue eyes forbade a sarcastic answer.

"By Jove!" said Mr. Spillikins presently, with complete irrelevance, "I hope you don't mind my saying it, but you look awfully well in white – stunning." He felt that a man who was affianced, or practically so, was allowed the smaller liberty of paying honest compliments.

"Oh, this old thing," laughed Philippa, with a contemptuous shake of her dress. "But up here, you know, we just wear anything." She didn't say that this old thing was only two weeks old and had cost eighty dollars, or the equivalent of one person's pew rent at St. Asaph's for six months.

And after that they had only time, so it seemed to Mr.

Spillikins, for two or three remarks, and he had scarcely had leisure to reflect what a charming girl Philippa had grown to be since she went to Bermuda – the effect, no doubt, of the climate of those fortunate islands – when quite suddenly they rounded a curve into an avenue of nodding trees, and there were the great lawn and wide piazzas and the conservatories of Castel Casteggio right in front of them.

"Here we are," said Philippa, "and there's Mr. Newberry out on the lawn."

"Now, here," Mr. Newberry was saying a little later, waving his hand, "is where you get what I think the finest view of the place."

He was standing at the corner of the lawn where it sloped, dotted with great trees, to the banks of the little lake, and was showing Mr. Spillikins the beauties of Castel Casteggio.

Mr. Newberry wore on his short circular person the summer costume of a man taking his ease and careless of dress: plain white flannel trousers, not worth more than six dollars a leg, an ordinary white silk shirt with a rolled collar, that couldn't have cost more than fifteen dollars, and on his head an ordinary Panama hat, say forty dollars.

"By Jove!" said Mr. Spillikins, as he looked about him at the house and the beautiful lawn with its great trees, "it's a lovely place."

"Isn't it?" said Mr. Newberry. "But you ought to have seen it when I took hold of it. To make the motor road alone I had to dynamite out about a hundred yards of rock, and then I fetched up cement, tons and tons of it, and boulders to buttress the embankment."

"Did you really!" said Mr. Spillikins, looking at Mr. Newberry with great respect.

"Yes, and even that was nothing to the house itself. Do you know, I had to go at least forty feet for the foundations. First I went through about twenty feet of loose clay, after that I struck sand, and I'd no sooner got through that than, by George! I landed in eight feet of water. I had to pump it out; I think I took out a thousand gallons before I got clear down to the rock. Then I took my solid steel beams in fifty-foot lengths," here Mr. Newberry imitated with his arms the action of a man setting up a steel beam, "and set them upright and bolted them on the rock. After that I threw my steel girders across, clapped on my roof rafters, all steel, in sixty-foot pieces, and then just held it easily, just supported it a bit, and let it sink gradually to its place."

Mr. Newberry illustrated with his two arms the action of a huge house being allowed to sink slowly to a firm rest.

"You don't say so!" said Mr. Spillikins, lost in amazement at the wonderful physical strength that Mr. Newberry must have.

"Excuse me just a minute," broke off Mr. Newberry, "while I smooth out the gravel where you're standing. You've rather disturbed it, I'm afraid."

"Oh, I'm awfully sorry," said Mr. Spillikins.

"Oh, not at all, not at all," said his host. "I don't mind in the least. It's only on account of McAlister."

"Who?" asked Mr. Spillikins.

"My gardener. He doesn't care to have us walk on the gravel paths. It scuffs up the gravel so. But sometimes one forgets."

It should be said here, for the sake of clearness, that one of the chief glories of Castel Casteggio lay in its servants. All of them, it goes without saying, had been brought from Great Britain. The comfort they gave to Mr. and Mrs. Newberry was unspeakable. In fact, as they themselves admitted, servants of the kind are simply not to be found in America.

"Our Scotch gardener," Mrs. Newberry always explained, "is a perfect character. I don't know how we could get another like him. Do you know, my dear, he simply *won't allow* us to pick the roses; and if any of us walk across the grass he is furious. And he positively refuses to let us use the vegetables. He told me quite plainly that it we took any of his young peas or his early cucumbers he would leave. We are to have them later on when he's finished growing them."

"How delightful it is to have servants of that sort," the lady addressed would murmur; "so devoted and so different from servants on this side of the water. Just imagine, my dear, my chauffeur, when I was in Colorado, actually threatened to leave me merely because I wanted to reduce his wages. I think it's these wretched labour unions."

"I'm sure it is. Of course we have trouble with McAlister at times, but he's always very reasonable when we put things in the right light. Last week, for example, I was afraid that we had gone too far with him. He is always accustomed to have a quart of beer every morning at half-past ten – the maids are told to bring it out to him, and after that he goes to sleep in the little arbour beside the tulip bed. And the other day when he went there he found that one of our guests who hadn't been told, was actually sitting in there reading. Of course he was *furious*. I was afraid for the moment that he would give notice on the spot."

"What *would* you have done?"

"Positively, my dear, I don't know. But we explained to him at once that it was only an accident and that the person hadn't known and that of course it wouldn't occur again. After that he was softened a little, but he went off muttering to himself, and that evening he dug up all the new tulips and threw them over the fence. We saw him do it, but we didn't dare say anything."

"Oh no," echoed the other lady; "if you had you might have lost him."

"Exactly. And I don't think we could possibly get another man like him; at least, not on this side of the water."

"But come," said Mr. Newberry, after he had finished adjusting the gravel with his foot, "there are Mrs. Newberry and the girls on the verandah. Let's go and join them."

A few minutes later Mr. Spillikins was talking with Mrs. Newberry and Dulphemia Rasselyer-Brown, and telling Mrs. Newberry what a beautiful house she had. Beside them stood Philippa Furlong, and she had her arm around Dulphemia's waist; and the picture that they thus made, with their heads close together, Dulphemia's hair being golden and Philippa's chestnut-brown, was such that Mr. Spillikins had no eyes for Mrs. Newberry nor for Castel Casteggio nor for anything. So much so that he practically didn't see at all the little girl in green that stood unobtrusively on the further side of Mrs. Newberry. Indeed, though somebody had murmured her name in introduction, he couldn't have repeated it if asked two minutes afterwards. His eyes and his mind were elsewhere.

But hers were not.

For the Little Girl in Green looked at Mr. Spillikins with wide eyes, and when she looked at him she saw all at once such wonderful things about him as nobody had ever seen before.

For she could see from the poise of his head how awfully clever he was; and from the way he stood with his hands in his side pockets she could see how manly and brave he must be; and of course there was firmness and strength written all over him. In short, she saw as she looked such a Peter Spillikins as truly never existed, or could exist – or at least such a Peter Spillikins as no one else in the world had ever suspected before.

All in a moment she was ever so glad that she accepted Mrs. Newberry's invitation to Castel Casteggio and hadn't been afraid to come. For the Little Girl in Green, whose Christian name was Norah, was only what is called a poor relation of Mrs. Newberry, and her father was a person of no account whatever, who didn't belong to the Mausoleum Club or to any other club, and who lived, with Norah, on a street that nobody who was anybody lived upon. Norah had been asked up a few days before out of the City to give her air – which is the only thing that can be safely and freely given to poor relations. Thus she had arrived at Castel Casteggio with one diminutive trunk, so small and shabby that even the servants who carried it upstairs were ashamed of it. In it were a pair of brand new tennis shoes (at ninety cents reduced to seventy-five), and a white dress of the kind that is called "almost evening," and such few other things as poor relations might bring with fear and trembling to join in the simple rusticity of the rich.

Thus stood Norah looking at Mr. Spillikins.

As for him, such is the contrariety of human things, he had no eyes for her at all.

"What a perfectly charming house this is," Mr. Spillikins was saying. He always said this on such occasions, but it seemed to the Little Girl in Green that he spoke with wonderful social ease.

"I am so glad you think so," said Mrs. Newberry (this was what she always answered); "you've no idea what work it has been. This year we put in all this new glass in the east conservatory, over a thousand panes. Such a tremendous business!"

"I was just telling Mr. Spillikins," said Mr. Newberry, "about the work we had blasting out the motor road. You can see the gap where it lies better from here, I think, Spillikins. I must have exploded a ton and a half of dynamite on it."

"By Jove!" said Mr. Spillikins; "it must be dangerous work, eh? I wonder you aren't afraid of it."

"One simply gets used to it, that's all," said Newberry, shrugging his shoulders; "but of course it *is* dangerous. I blew up two Italians on the last job." He paused a minute and added musingly, "Hardy fellows, the Italians. I prefer them to any other people for the blasting."

"Did you blow them up yourself?" asked Mr. Spillikins.

"I wasn't here," answered Mr. Newberry. "In fact, I never care to be here when I'm blasting. We go to town. But I had to foot the bill for them all the same. Quite right, too.

The risk, of course, was mine, not theirs; that's the law, you know. They cost me two thousand each."

"But come," said Mrs. Newberry, "I think we must go and dress for dinner. Franklin will be frightfully put out if we're late. Franklin is our butler," she went on, seeing that Mr. Spillikins didn't understand the reference, "and as we brought him out from England we have to be rather careful. With a good man like Franklin one is always so afraid of losing him – and after last night we have to be doubly careful."

"Why last night?" asked Mr. Spillikins.

"Oh, it wasn't much," said Mrs. Newberry. "In fact, it was merely an accident. Only it just chanced that at dinner, quite late in the meal, when we had had nearly everything (we dine very simply here, Mr. Spillikins), Mr. Newberry, who was thirsty and who wasn't really thinking what he was saying, asked Franklin to give him a glass of hock. Franklin said at once, "I'm very sorry, sir, I don't care to serve my hock after the entrée!"

"And of course he was right," said Dulphemia with emphasis.

"Exactly; he was perfectly right. They know, you know. We were afraid that there might be trouble, but Mr. Newberry went and saw Franklin afterwards and he behaved very well over it. But suppose we go and dress? It's half-past six already and we've only an hour."

In this congenial company Mr. Spillikins spent the next three days.

Life at Castel Casteggio, as the Newberrys loved to explain, was conducted on the very simplest plan. Early breakfast, country fashion, at nine o'clock; after that nothing to eat till lunch, unless one cared to have lemonade or bottled ale sent out with a biscuit or a macaroon to the tennis court. Lunch itself was a perfectly plain midday meal, lasting till about 1.30, and consisting simply of cold meats (say four kinds) and salads, with perhaps a made dish or two, and, for anybody who cared for it, a hot steak or a chop, or both. After that one had coffee and cigarettes in the shade of the piazza and waited for afternoon tea. This latter was served at a wicker table in any part of the grounds that the gardener was not at that moment clipping, trimming, or otherwise using. Afternoon tea being over, one rested or walked on the lawn till it was time to dress for dinner.

This simple routine was broken only by irruptions of people in motors or motor boats from Pennygw-rydd or Yodel-Dudel Châlet.

The whole thing, from the point of view of Mr. Spillikins or Dulphemia or Philippa, represented rusticity itself.

To the Little Girl in Green it seemed as brilliant as the Court of Versailles; especially evening dinner – a plain home meal as the others thought it – when she had four glasses to drink out of and used to wonder over such problems as whether you were supposed, when Franklin poured out wine, to tell him to stop or to wait till he stopped without being told to stop; and other similar mysteries, such as many people before and after have meditated upon.

During all this time Mr. Spillikins was nerving himself to propose to Dulphemia Rasselyer-Brown. In fact, he spent part of his time walking up and down under the trees with Philippa Furlong and discussing with her the proposal that he meant to make, together with such topics as marriage in general and his own unworthiness.

He might have waited indefinitely had he not learned, on the third day of his visit, that Dulphemia was to go away in the morning to join her father at Nagahakett.

That evening he found the necessary nerve to speak, and the proposal in almost every aspect of it was most successful.

"By Jove!" Spillikins said to Philippa Furlong next morning, in explaining what had happened, "she was awfully nice about it. I think she must have guessed, in a way, don't you, what I was going to say? But at any rate she was awfully nice – let me say everything I wanted, and when

I explained what a fool I was, she said she didn't think I was half such a fool as people thought me. But it's all right. It turns out that she isn't thinking of getting married. I asked her if I might always go on thinking of her, and she said I might."

And that morning when Dulphemia was carried off in the motor to the station, Mr. Spillikins, without exactly being aware how he had done it, had somehow transferred himself to Philippa.

"Isn't she a splendid girl!" he said at least ten times a day to Norah, the Little Girl in Green. And Norah always agreed, because she really thought Philippa a perfectly wonderful creature.

There is no doubt that, but for a slight shift of circumstances, Mr. Spillikins would have proposed to Miss Furlong. Indeed, he spent a good part of his time rehearsing little speeches that began, "Of course I know I'm an awful ass in a way," or, "Of course I know that I'm not at all the sort of fellow," and so on.

But not one of them ever was delivered.

For it so happened that on the Thursday, one week after Mr. Spillikins's arrival, Philippa went again to the station in the motor. And when she came back there was another passenger with her, a tall young man in tweed, and they both began calling out to the Newberrys from a distance of at least a hundred yards.

And both the Newberrys suddenly exclaimed, "Why, it's Tom!" and rushed off to meet the motor. And there was such a laughing and jubilation as the two descended and carried Tom's valises to the verandah, that Mr. Spillikins felt as suddenly and completely out of it as the Little Girl in Green herself – especially as his ear had caught, among the first things said, the words, "Congratulate us, Mrs. Newberry, we're engaged."

After which Mr. Spillikins had the pleasure of sitting and listening while it was explained, in wicker chairs on the verandah, that Philippa and Tom had been engaged already for ever so long – in fact, nearly two weeks, only they had agreed not to say a word to anybody till Tom had gone to North Carolina and back, to see his people.

And as to who Tom was, or what was the relation between Tom and the Newberrys, Mr. Spillikins neither knew nor cared; nor did it interest him in the least that Philippa had met Tom in Bermuda, and that she hadn't known that he even knew the Newberrys, nor any other of the exuberant disclosures of the moment. In fact, if there was any one period rather than another when Mr. Spillikins felt corroborated in his private view of himself, it was at this moment.

So the next day Tom and Philippa vanished together.

"We shall be quite a small party now," said Mrs. Newberry; "in fact, quite by ourselves till Mrs. Everleigh comes, and she won't be here for a fortnight."

At which the heart of the Little Girl in Green was glad, because she had been afraid that other girls might be coming, whereas she knew that Mrs. Everleigh was a widow with four sons and must be ever so old, past forty.

The next few days were spent by Mr. Spillikins almost entirely in the society of Norah. He thought them on the whole rather pleasant days, but slow. To her they were an uninterrupted dream of happiness never to be forgotten.

The Newberrys left them to themselves; not with any intent; it was merely that they were perpetually busy walking about the grounds of Castel Casteggio, blowing up things with dynamite, throwing steel bridges over gullies, and hoisting heavy timber with derricks. Nor were they to blame for it. For it had not always been theirs to command dynamite and control the forces of nature. There had been a time, now long ago, when the two Newberrys had lived, both of them, on twenty dollars a week, and Mrs. Newberry had made her own dresses, and Mr. Newberry had spent vigorous evenings in making hand-made shelves for their sitting-room. That was long ago, and since then Mr. Newberry, like many other people of those earlier days, had risen to wealth and Castel Casteggio, while others, like Norah's father, had stayed just where they were.

So the Newberrys left Peter and Norah to themselves all day. Even after dinner, in the evening, Mr. Newberry was very apt to call to his wife in the dusk from some distant corner of the lawn:

"Margaret, come over here and tell me if you don't think we might cut down this elm, tear the stump out by the roots, and throw it into the ravine."

And the answer was, "One minute, Edward; just wait till I get a wrap."

Before they came back the dusk had grown to darkness, and they had redynamited half the estate.

During all of which time Mr. Spillikins sat with Norah on the piazza. He talked and she listened. He told her, for instance, all about his terrific experiences in the oil business, and about his exciting career at college; or presently they went indoors and Norah played the piano and Mr. Spillikins sat and smoked and listened. In such a house as the Newberrys', where dynamite and the greater explosives were everyday matters, a little thing like the use of tobacco in the drawing-room didn't count. As for the music, "Go right ahead," said Mr. Spillikins; "I'm not musical, but I don't mind music a bit."

In the daytime they played tennis. There was a court at one end of the lawn beneath the trees, all chequered with sunlight and mingled shadow; very beautiful, Norah thought, though Mr. Spillikins explained that the spotted light put him off his game. In fact, it was owing entirely to this bad light that Mr. Spillikins's fast drives, wonderful though they were, somehow never got inside the service court.

Norah, of course, thought Mr. Spillikins a wonderful player. She was glad – in fact, it suited them both – when he beat her six to nothing. She didn't know and didn't care that there was no one else in the world that Mr. Spillikins could beat like that. Once he even said to her,

"By Gad! you don't play half a bad game, you know. I think, you know, with practice you'd come on quite a lot."

After that the games were understood to be more or less

in the form of lessons, which put Mr. Spillikins on a pedestal of superiority, and allowed any bad strokes on his part to be viewed as a form of indulgence.

Also, as the tennis was viewed in this light, it was Norah's part to pick up the balls at the net and throw them back to Mr. Spillikins. He let her do this, not from rudeness, for it wasn't in him, but because in such a primeval place as Castel Casteggio the natural primitive relation of the sexes is bound to reassert itself.

But of love Mr. Spillikins never thought. He had viewed it so eagerly and so often from a distance that when it stood here modestly at his very elbow he did not recognise its presence. His mind had been fashioned, as it were, to connect love with something stunning and sensational, with Easter hats and harem skirts and the luxurious consciousness of the unattainable.

Even at that, there is no knowing what might have happened. Tennis, in the chequered light of sun and shadow cast by summer leaves, is a dangerous game. There came a day when they were standing one each side of the net and Mr. Spillikins was explaining to Norah the proper way to hold a racquet so as to be able to give those magnificent backhand sweeps of his, by which he generally drove the ball half-way to the lake; and explaining this involved putting his hand right over Norah's on the handle of the racquet, so that for just half a second her hand was clasped tight in his; and if that half-second had been lengthened out into a whole second it is quite possible that what was already subconscious in his mind would have broken its way triumphantly to the surface, and Norah's hand would have stayed in his – how willingly – ! for the rest of their two lives.

But just at that moment Mr. Spillikins looked up, and he said in quite an altered tone,

"By Jove! who's that awfully good-looking woman getting out of the motor?"

And their hands unclasped. Norah looked over towards the house and said,

"Why it's Mrs. Everleigh. I thought she wasn't coming for another week."

"I say," said Mr. Spillikins, straining his short sight to the uttermost, "what perfectly wonderful golden hair, eh?"

"Why, it's –" Norah began, and then she stopped. It didn't seem right to explain that Mrs. Everleigh's hair was dyed.

"And who's that tall chap standing beside her?" said Mr. Spillikins.

"I think it's Captain Cormorant, but I don't think he's going to stay. He's only brought her up in the motor from town."

"By Jove, how good of him!" said Spillikins; and this sentiment in regard to Captain Cormorant, though he didn't know it, was to become a keynote of his existence.

"I didn't know she was coming so soon," said Norah, and there was weariness already in her heart. Certainly she didn't know it; still less did she know, or anyone else, that the reason of Mrs. Everleigh's coming was because Mr. Spillikins was there. She came with a set purpose, and she sent Captain Cormorant directly back in the motor because she didn't want him on the premises.

"Oughtn't we to go up to the house?" said Norah.

"All right," said Mr. Spillikins with great alacrity, "let's go."

Now as this story began with the information that Mrs. Everleigh is at present Mrs. Everleigh-Spillikins, there is no need to pursue in detail the stages of Mr. Spillikins's wooing. Its course was swift and happy. Mr. Spillikins, having seen the back of Mrs. Everleigh's head, had decided instanter that she was the most beautiful woman in the world; and that impression is not easily corrected in the half-light of a shaded drawing-room; nor across a dinner-table lighted only with candles with deep red shades; nor even in the daytime through a veil. In any case, it is only fair to state that if Mrs. Everleigh was not and is not a singularly beautiful woman, Mr. Spillikins still doesn't know it. And in point of attraction the homage of such experts as

Captain Cormorant and Lieutenant Hawk speaks for itself.

So the course of Mr. Spillikins's love, for love it must have been, ran swiftly to its goal. Each stage of it was duly marked by his comments to Norah.

"She *is* a splendid woman," he said, "so sympathetic. She always seems to know just what one's going to say."

So she did, for she was making him say it.

"By Jove!" he said a day later, "Mrs. Everleigh's an awfully fine woman, isn't she? I was telling her about my having been in the oil business for a little while, and she thinks that I'd really be awfully good in money things. She said she wished she had me to manage her money for her."

This also was quite true, except that Mrs. Everleigh had not made it quite clear that the management of her money was of the form generally known as deficit financing. In fact, her money was, very crudely stated, non-existent, and it needed a lot of management.

A day or two later Mr. Spillikins was saying, "I think Mrs. Everleigh must have had great sorrow, don't you? Yesterday she was showing me a photograph of her little boy – she has a little boy, you know –"

"Yes, I know," said Norah. She didn't add that she knew that Mrs. Everleigh had four.

"– and she was saying how awfully rough it is having to have him always away from her at Dr. Something's academy where he is."

And very soon after that Mr. Spillikins was saying, with quite a quaver in his voice,

"By Jove! yes, I'm awfully lucky; I never thought for a moment that she'd have me, you know – a woman like her, with so much attention and everything. I can't imagine what she sees in me."

Which was just as well.

And then Mr. Spillikins checked himself, for he noticed – this was on the verandah in the morning – that Norah had a hat and jacket on and that the motor was rolling towards the door.

"I say," he said, "are you going away?"

"Yes, didn't you know?" Norah said. "I thought you heard them speaking of it at dinner last night. I have to go home; father's alone, you know."

"Oh, I'm awfully sorry," said Mr. Spillikins; "we shan't have any more tennis."

"Good-bye," said Norah, and as she said it and put out her hand there were tears brimming up into her eyes. But Mr. Spillikins, being short of sight, didn't see them.

"Good-bye," he said.

Then as the motor carried her away he stood for a moment in a sort of reverie. Perhaps certain things that might have been rose unformed and inarticulate before his mind. And then a voice called from the drawing-room within, in a measured and assured tone,

"Peter, darling, where are you?"

"Coming," cried Mr. Spillikins, and he came.

On the second day of the engagement Mrs. Everleigh showed to Peter a little photograph in a brooch.

"This is Gib, my second little boy," she said.

Mr. Spillikins started to say, "I didn't know –" and then checked himself and said, "By Gad! what a fine-looking little chap, eh? I'm awfully fond of boys."

"Dear little fellow, isn't he?" said Mrs. Everleigh. "He's really rather taller than that now, because this picture was taken a little while ago."

And the next day she said, "This is Willie, my third boy," and on the day after that she said, "This is Sib, my youngest boy; I'm sure you'll love him."

"I'm sure I shall," said Mr. Spillikins. He loved him already for being the youngest.

And so in the fulness of time – nor was it so very full either, in fact, only about five weeks – Peter Spillikins and Mrs.

Everleigh were married in St. Asaph's Church on Plutoria Avenue. And the wedding was one of the most beautiful and sumptuous of the weddings of the September season. There were flowers, and bridesmaids in long veils, and tall ushers in frock-coats, and awnings at the church door, and strings of motors with wedding-favours on imported chauffeurs, and all that goes to invest marriage on Plutoria Avenue with its peculiar sacredness. The face of the young rector, Mr. Fareforth Furlong, wore the added saintliness that springs from the five-hundred dollar fee. The whole town was there, or at least everybody that was anybody; and if there was one person absent, one who sat by herself in the darkened drawing-room of a dull little house on a shabby street, who knew or cared?

So after the ceremony the happy couple – for were they not so? – left for New York. There they spent their honeymoon. They had thought of going, – it was Mr. Spillikins's idea, – to the coast of Maine. But Mrs. Everleigh-Spillikins said that New York was much nicer, so restful, whereas, as everyone knows, the coast of Maine is frightfully noisy.

Moreover, it so happened that before the Everleigh-Spillikinses had been more than four or five days in New York the ship of Captain Cormorant dropped anchor in the Hudson; and when the anchor of that ship was once down it generally stayed there. So the captain was able to take the Everleigh-Spillikinses about in New York, and to give a tea for Mrs. Everleigh-Spillikins on the deck of his vessel so that she might meet the officers, and another tea in a private room of a restaurant on Fifth Avenue so that she might meet no one but himself.

And at this tea Captain Cormorant said, among other things, "Did he kick up rough at all when you told him about the money?"

And Mrs. Everleigh, now Mrs. Everleigh-Spillikins, said, "Not he! I think he is actually pleased to know that I haven't any. Do you know, Arthur, he's really an awfully good fellow," and as she said it she moved her hand away from under Captain Cormorant's on the tea-table.

"I say," said the Captain, "don't get sentimental over him."

So that is how it is that the Everleigh-Spillikinses came to reside on Plutoria Avenue in a beautiful stone house, with the billiard-room in an extension on the second floor. Through the windows of it one can almost hear the click of the billiard balls, and a voice saying, "Hold on, father, you had your shot."

SIX

The Rival Churches of

St. Asaph and St. Osoph

THE CHURCH of St. Asaph, more properly called St. Asaph's in the Fields, stands among the elm trees of Plutoria Avenue opposite the university, its tall spire pointing to the blue sky. Its rector is fond of saying that it seems to him to point, as it were, a warning against the sins of a commercial age. More particularly does he say this in his Lenten services at noonday, when the business men sit in front of him in rows, their bald heads uncovered and their faces stamped with contrition as they think of mergers that they should have made, and real estate that they failed to buy for lack of faith.

The ground on which St. Asaph's stands is worth seven dollars and a half a foot. The mortgagees, as they kneel in prayer in their long frock-coats, feel that they have built upon a rock. It is a beautifully appointed church. There are windows with priceless stained glass that were imported from Normandy, the rector himself swearing out the invoices to save the congregation the grievous burden of the customs duty. There is a pipe organ in the transept that cost ten thousand dollars to instal. The debenture-holders, as they join in the morning anthem, love to hear the dulcet notes of the great organ and to reflect that it is a good as new. Just behind the church is St. Asaph's Sunday School, with a ten-thousand dollar mortgage of its own. And below that again, on the side street, is the building of the Young Men's Guild, with a bowling-alley and a swimming-bath deep enough to drown two young men at a time, and a billiard-room with seven tables. It is the rector's boast that with a Guild House such as that there is no need for any young man of the congregation to frequent a saloon. Nor is there.

And on Sunday mornings, when the great organ plays, and the mortgagees and the bond-holders and the debenture-holders and the Sunday school teachers and the billiard-markers all lift up their voices together, there is emitted from St. Asaph's a volume of praise that is practically as fine and effective as paid professional work.

St. Asaph's is episcopal. As a consequence it has in it and about it all those things which go to make up the episcopal church – brass tablets let into its walls, blackbirds singing in the elm trees, parishioners who dine at eight o'clock, and a rector who wears a little crucifix and dances the tango.

On the other hand, there stands upon the same street, not a hundred yards away, the rival church of St. Osoph – presbyterian down to its very foundations in bed-rock, thirty feet below the level of the avenue. It has a short, squat tower – and a low roof, and its narrow windows are glazed with frosted glass. It has dark spruce trees instead of elms, crows instead of blackbirds, and a gloomy minister with a shovel hat who lectures on philosophy on week-days at the university. He loves to think that his congregation are made of the lowly and the meek in spirit, and to reflect that, lowly and meek as they are, there are men among them that could buy out half the congregation of St. Asaph's.

St. Osoph's is only presbyterian in a special sense. It is, in fact, too presbyterian to be any longer connected with any other body whatsoever. It seceded some forty years ago from the original body to which it belonged, and later on, with three other churches, it seceded from the group of seceding congregations. Still later it fell into a difference with the three other churches on the question of eternal punishment, the word "eternal" not appearing to the elders of St. Osoph's to designate a sufficiently long period. The dispute ended in a secession which left the church of St.

Osoph practically isolated in a world of sin whose approaching fate it neither denied nor deplored.

In one respect the rival churches of Plutoria Avenue had had a similar history. Each of them had moved up by successive stages from the lower and poorer parts of the city. Forty years ago St. Asaph's had been nothing more than a little frame church with a tin spire, away in the west of the slums, and St. Osoph's a square, diminutive building away in the east. But the site of St. Asaph's had been bought by a brewing company, and the trustees, shrewd men of business, themselves rising into wealth, had rebuilt it right in the track of the advancing tide of a real estate boom. The elders of St. Osoph, quiet men, but illumined by an inner light, had followed suit and moved their church right against the side of an expanding distillery. Thus both the churches, as decade followed decade, made their way up the slope of the City till St. Asaph's was presently gloriously expropriated by the street railway company, and planted its spire in triumph on Plutoria Avenue itself. But St. Osoph's followed. With each change of site it moved nearer and nearer to St. Asaph's. Its elders were shrewd men. With each move of their church they took careful thought in the rebuilding. In the manufacturing district it was built with sixteen windows on each side and was converted at a huge profit into a bicycle factory. On the residential street it was made long and deep and was sold to a moving picture company without the alteration of so much as a pew. As a last step a syndicate, formed among the members of the congregation themselves, bought ground on Plutoria Avenue, and sublet it to themselves as a site for the church, at a nominal interest of five per cent. per annum, payable nominally every three months and secured by a nominal mortgage.

As the two churches moved, their congregations, or at least all that was best of them – such members as were sharing in the rising fortunes of the City – moved also, and now for some six or seven years the two churches and the two congregations had confronted one another among the elm trees of the Avenue opposite to the university.

But at this point the fortunes of the churches had diverged. St. Asaph's was a brilliant success; St. Osoph's was a failure. Even its own trustees couldn't deny it. At a time when St. Asaph's was not only paying its interest but showing a handsome surplus on everything it undertook, the church of St. Osoph was moving steadily backwards.

There was no doubt, of course, as to the cause. Everybody knew it. It was simply a question of men, and, as everybody said, one had only to compare the two men conducting the churches to see why one succeeded and the other failed.

The Reverend Edward Fareforth Furlong of St. Asaph's was a man who threw his whole energy into his parish work. The subtleties of theological controversy he left to minds less active than his own. His creed was one of works rather than of words, and whatever he was doing he did it with his whole heart. Whether he was lunching at the Mausoleum Club with one of his churchwardens, or playing the flute, – which he played as only the episcopal clergy can play it – accompanied on the harp by one of the fairest of the ladies of his choir, or whether he was dancing the new episcopal tango with the younger daughters of the elder parishioners, he threw himself into it with all his might. He could drink tea more gracefully and play tennis better than any clergyman on this side of the Atlantic. He could stand beside the white stone font of St. Asaph's in his long white surplice holding a white-robed infant, worth half a million dollars, looking as beautifully innocent as the child itself, and drawing from every matron of the congregation with unmarried daughters the despairing cry, "What a pity that he has no children of his own!"

Equally sound was his theology. No man was known to preach shorter sermons or to explain away the book of Genesis more agreeably than the rector of St. Asaph's; and if he found it necessary to refer to the Deity he did so under the name of Jehovah or Jah, or even Yaweh, in a manner calculated not to hurt the sensitiveness of any of the parishioners. People who would shudder at brutal talk of the older fashion about the wrath of God listened with well-bred interest to a sermon on the personal characteristics of Jah. In the same way Mr. Furlong always referred to the devil, not as Satan but as Sû or Swâ, which took all the sting out of him. Beelzebub he spoke of as Behel-Zawbab, which rendered him perfectly harmless. The Garden of Eden he spoke of as the Paradeisos, which explained it entirely; the flood as the Diluvium, which cleared it up completely; and Jonah he named, after the correct fashion, Joh Nah, which put the whole situation (his being swallowed by Baloo, or the Great Lizard) on a perfectly satisfactory footing. Hell itself was spoken of as She-ol, and it appeared that it was not a place of burning, but rather of what one might describe as moral torment. This settled She-ol once and for all: nobody minds moral torment. In short, there was nothing in the theological system of Mr. Furlong that need have occasioned in any of his congregation a moment's discomfort. There could be no greater contrast with Mr. Fareforth Furlong than the minister of St. Osoph's, the Rev. Dr. McTeague, who was also honorary professor of philosophy at the university. The one was young, the other was old; the one could dance, the other could not; the one moved about at church picnics and lawn teas among the bevy of disciples in pink and blue sashes; the other moped around under the trees of the university campus, with blinking eyes that saw nothing and an abstracted mind that had spent fifty years in trying to reconcile Hegel with St. Paul, and was still busy with it. Mr. Furlong went forward with the times; Dr. McTeague slid quietly backwards with the centuries.

Dr. McTeague was a failure, and all his congregation knew it. "He is not up to date," they said. That was his crowning sin. "He don't go forward any," said the business members of the congregation. "That old man believes just exactly the same sort of stuff now that he did forty years ago. What's more, he *preaches* it. You can't run a church that way, can you?"

His trustees had done their best to meet the difficulty. They had offered Dr. McTeague a two-years' vacation to go and see the Holy Land. He refused; he said he could picture it. They reduced his salary by fifty per cent.; he never noticed it. They offered him an assistant; but he shook his head, saying that he didn't know where he could find a man to do just the work that he was doing. Meantime he mooned about among the trees concocting a mixture of St. Paul with Hegel, three parts to one, for his Sunday sermon, and one part to three for his Monday lecture.

No doubt it was his dual function that was to blame for his failure. And this, perhaps, was the fault of Dr. Boomer, the president of the university. Dr. Boomer, like all university presidents of to-day, belonged to the presbyterian church; or rather, to state it more correctly, he included presbyterianism within himself. He was, of course, a member of the board of management of St. Osoph's, and it was he who had urged, very strongly, the appointment of Dr. McTeague, then senior professor of philosophy, as minister.

"A saintly man," he said, "the very man for the post. If you should ask me whether he is entirely at home as a professor of philosophy on our staff at the university, I should be compelled to say no. We are forced to admit that as a lecturer he does not meet our views. He appears to find it difficult to keep religion out of his teaching. In fact, his lectures are suffused with a rather dangerous attempt at moral teaching which is apt to contaminate our students. But in the Church I should imagine that would be, if anything, an advantage. Indeed, if you were to come to me and say, 'Boomer, we wish to appoint Dr. McTeague as our minister,' I should say, quite frankly, 'Take him.'"

So Dr. McTeague had been appointed. Then, to the surprise of everybody, he refused to give up his lectures in philosophy. He said he felt a call to give them. The salary, he said, was of no consequence. He wrote to Mr. Furlong senior (the father of the episcopal rector, and honorary treasurer of the Plutoria University), and stated that he proposed to give his lectures for nothing. The trustees of the college protested; they urged that the case might set a dangerous precedent which other professors might follow. While fully admitting that Dr. McTeague's lectures were well worth giving for nothing, they begged him to reconsider his offer. But he refused; and from that day on, in spite of all offers that he should retire on double his salary, that he should visit the Holy Land, or Syria, or Armenia, where the dreadful massacres of Christians were taking place, Dr. McTeague clung to his post with a tenacity worthy of the best traditions of Scotland. His only internal perplexity was that he didn't see how, when the time came for him to die, twenty or thirty years hence, they would ever be able to replace him.

Such was the situation of the two churches on a certain beautiful morning in June, when an unforeseen event altered entirely the current of their fortunes.

"No, thank you, Juliana," said the young rector to his sister across the breakfast table, – and there was something as near to bitterness in his look as his saintly, smooth-shaven face was capable of reflecting, – "no, thank you, no more porridge. Prunes? no, no, thank you; I don't think I care for any. And, by the way," he added, "don't bother to keep any lunch for me. I have a great deal of business – that is, of work in the parish, – to see to, and I must just find time to get a bite of something to eat when and where I can."

In his own mind he was resolving that the place should be the Mausoleum Club and the time just as soon as the head waiter would serve him.

After which the Reverend Edward Fareforth Furlong bowed his head for a moment in a short, silent blessing, – the one prescribed by the episcopal church in America for a breakfast of porridge and prunes.

It was their first breakfast together, and it spoke volumes to the rector. He knew what it implied. It stood for his elder sister Juliana's views on the need of personal sacrifice as a means of grace. The rector sighed as he rose. He had never missed his younger sister Philippa, now married and departed, so keenly. Philippa had had opinions of her own on bacon and eggs and on lamb chops with watercress as a means of stimulating the soul. But Juliana was different. The rector understood now exactly why it was that his father had exclaimed, on the news of Philippa's engagement, without a second's hesitation, "Then, of course, Juliana must live with you! Nonsense, my dear boy, nonsense! It's my duty to spare her to you. After all, I can always eat at the club; they can give me a bite of something or other, surely. To a man of my age, Edward, food is really of no consequence. No, no; Juliana must move into the rectory at once."

The rector's elder sister rose. She looked tall and sallow and forbidding in the plain black dress that contrasted sadly with the charming clerical costumes of white and pink and the broad episcopal hats with flowers in them that Philippa used to wear for morning work in the parish.

"For what time shall I order dinner?" she asked. "You and Philippa used to have it at half-past seven, did you not? Don't you think that rather too late?"

"A trifle, perhaps," said the rector uneasily. He didn't care to explain to Juliana that it was impossible to get home any earlier from the kind of *thé dansant* that everybody was giving just now. "But don't trouble about dinner. I may be working very late. If I need anything to eat I shall get a biscuit and some tea at the Guild Rooms, or –"

He didn't finish the sentence, but in his mind he added, "or else a really first-class dinner at the Mausoleum Club, or at the Newberrys' or the Rasselyer-Browns' – anywhere except here."

"If you are going, then," said Juliana, "may I have the key of the church."

A look of pain passed over the rector's face. He knew perfectly well what Juliana wanted the key for. She meant to go into his church and pray in it.

The rector of St. Asaph's was, he trusted, as broad-minded a man as an Anglican clergyman ought to be. He had no objections to any reasonable use of his church – for a thanksgiving festival or for musical recitals, for example – but when it came to opening up the church and using it to pray in, the thing was going a little too far. What was more, he had an idea from the look of Juliana's face that she meant to pray for *him*. This, for a clergyman, was hard to bear. Philippa, like the good girl that she was, had prayed only for herself, and then only at the proper times and places, and in a proper praying costume. The rector began to realise what difficulties it might make for a clergyman to have a religious sister as his house-mate.

But he was never a man for unseemly argument. "It is hanging in my study," he said.

And with that the Rev. Fareforth Furlong passed into the hall, took up the simple silk hat, the stick and gloves of the working clergyman, and walked out on to the avenue to begin his day's work in the parish.

The rector's parish, viewed in its earthly aspect, was a singularly beautiful place. For it extended all along Plutoria Avenue, where the street is widest and the elm trees are at their leafiest and the motors at their very drowsiest. It lay up and down the shaded side streets of the residential district, darkened with great chestnuts and hushed in a stillness that was almost religion itself. There was not a house in the parish assessed at less than twenty-five thousand, and in the very heart of it the Mausoleum Club, with its smooth white stone and its Grecian architecture, carried one back to the ancient world and made one think of Athens and of Paul preaching on Mars Hill. It was, all considered, a splendid thing to fight sin in such a parish and to keep it out of it. For kept out it was. One might look the length and breadth of the broad avenue and see no sign of sin all along it. There was certainly none in the smooth faces of the chauffeurs trundling their drowsy motors; no sign of it in the expensive children paraded by imported nursemaids in the chequered light of the shaded street; least of all was there any sign of it in the Stock Exchange members of the congregation as they walked along side by side to their lunch at the Mausoleum Club, their silk hats nodding together in earnest colloquy on Shares Preferred, and Profits Undivided. So might have walked, so must have walked, the very Fathers of the Church themselves.

Whatever sin there was in the City was shoved sideways into the roaring streets of commerce where the elevated railway ran, and below that again into the slums. Here there must have been any quantity of sin. The rector of St. Asaph's was certain of it. Many of the richer of his parishioners had been down in parties late at night to look at it, and the ladies of his congregation were joined together into all sorts of guilds and societies and bands of endeavour for stamping it out and driving it under or putting it into jail till it surrendered.

But the slums lay outside the rector's parish. He had no right to interfere. They were under the charge of a special mission or auxiliary, a remnant of the St. Asaph's of the past, placed under the care of a divinity student, at four hundred dollars per annum. His charge included all the slums and three police-courts and two music-halls and the City jail. One Sunday afternoon in every three months the rector and several ladies went down and sang hymns for him in his mission-house. But his work was really very easy. A funeral, for example, at the mission, was a simple affair, meaning nothing more than the preparation of a plain coffin and a glassless hearse and the distribution of a few artificial everlasting flowers to women crying in their aprons; a thing easily done: whereas in St. Asaph's parish, where all the really important souls were, a funeral was a large event, requiring taste and tact, and a nice shading of delicacy in distinguishing mourners from beneficiaries, and private grief from business representation at the ceremony. A funeral with a plain coffin and a hearse was as nothing beside an interment, with a casket smothered in hot-house syringas, borne in a coach and followed by special reporters from the financial papers.

It appeared to the rector afterwards as almost a shocking coincidence that the first person whom he met upon the avenue should have been the Rev. Dr. McTeague himself. Mr. Furlong gave him the form of amiable "good morning" that the episcopal church always extends to those in error. But he did not hear it. The minister's head was bent low, his eyes gazed into vacancy, and from the movements of his lips and from the fact that he carried a leather case of notes, he was plainly on his way to his philosophical lecture. But the rector had no time to muse upon the abstracted appearance of his rival. For, as always happened to him, he was no sooner upon the street than his parish work of the day began. In fact, he had hardly taken a dozen steps after passing Dr. McTeague when he was brought up standing by two beautiful parishioners with pink parasols.

"Oh, Mr. Furlong," exclaimed one of them, "so fortunate to happen to catch you; we were just going into the rectory to consult you. Should the girls – for the lawn tea for the Guild on Friday, you know – wear white dresses with light blue sashes all the same, or do you think we might allow them to wear any coloured sashes that they like? What do you think?"

This was an important problem. In fact, there was a piece of parish work here that it took the Reverend Fareforth half an hour to attend to, standing the while in earnest colloquy with the two ladies under the shadow of the elm trees. But a clergyman must never be grudging of his time.

"Good-bye, then," they said at last. "Are you coming to the Browning Club this morning? Oh, so sorry! but we shall see you at the musicale this afternoon, shall we not?"

"Oh, I trust so," said the rector.

"How dreadfully hard he works," said the ladies to one another as they moved away.

Thus slowly and with many interruptions the rector made his progress along the avenue. At times he stopped to permit a pink-cheeked infant in a perambulator to beat him with a rattle while he inquired its age of an episcopal nurse, gay with flowing ribbons. He lifted his hat to the bright parasols of his parishioners passing in glistening motors, bowed to episcopalians, nodded amiably to presbyterians, and even acknowledged with his lifted hat the passing of persons of graver forms of error.

Thus he took his way along the avenue and down a side street towards the business district of the City, until just at the edge of it, where the trees were about to stop and the shops were about to begin, he found himself at the door of the Hymnal Supply Corporation, Limited. The premises as seen from the outside combined the idea of an office with an ecclesiastical appearance. The door was as that of a chancel or vestry; there was a large plate-glass window filled with Bibles and Testaments, all spread open and shewing every variety of language in their pages. These were marked, "Arabic," "Syriac," "Coptic," "Ojibway," "Irish" and so forth. On the window in small white lettering were the words, "Hymnal Supply Corporation," and below that "Hosanna Pipe and Steam Organ Incorporated," and still lower the legend, "Bible Society of the Good Shepherd Limited."

There was no doubt of the sacred character of the place.

Here laboured Mr. Furlong senior, the father of the Rev. Edward Fareforth. He was a man of many activities, president and managing director of the companies just mentioned, trustee and secretary of St. Asaph's, honorary treasurer of the university, etc.; and each of his occupations and offices was marked by something of a supramundane character, something higher than ordinary business. His different official positions naturally overlapped and brought him into contact with himself from a variety of angles. Thus he sold himself hymn books at a price per thousand, made as a business favour to himself, negotiated with himself the purchase of the ten thousand dollar organ (making a price on it to himself that he begged himself to regard as confidential), and as treasurer of the college he sent himself an informal note of enquiry asking if he knew of any sound investment for the annual deficit of the college funds, a matter of some sixty thousand dollars a year, which needed very careful handling. Any man – and there are many such – who has been concerned with business dealings of this sort with himself realises that they are more satisfactory than any other kind.

To what better person then could the rector of St. Asaph's bring the quarterly accounts and statements of his church than to Mr. Furlong senior.

The outer door was opened to the rector by a sanctified boy with such a face as is only found in the choirs of the episcopal church. In an outer office through which the rector passed were two sacred stenographers with hair as golden as the daffodils of Sheba, copying confidential letters on absolutely noiseless typewriters. They were making offers of Bibles in half-car-load lots at two and a half per cent. reduction, offering to reduce St. Mark by two cents on condition of immediate export, and to lay down St. John F.O.B. San Francisco for seven cents, while regretting that they could deliver fifteen thousand Rock of Ages in Missouri on no other terms than cash.

The sacred character of their work lent them a preoccupation beautiful to behold.

In the room beyond them was a white-haired confidential clerk, venerable as the Song of Solomon, and by him Mr. Fareforth Furlong was duly shown into the office of his father.

"Good-morning, Edward," said Mr. Furlong senior, as he shook hands. "I was expecting you. And while I think of it, I have just had a letter from Philippa. She and Tom will be home in two or three weeks. She writes from Egypt. She wishes me to tell you, as no doubt you have already anticipated, that she thinks she can hardly continue to be a member of the congregation when they come back. No doubt you felt this yourself?"

"Oh, entirely," said the rector. "Surely in matters of belief a wife must follow her husband."

"Exactly; especially as Tom's uncles occupy the position they do with regard to –" Mr. Furlong jerked his head backwards and pointed with his thumb over his shoulder in a way that his son knew was meant to indicate St. Osoph's Church.

The Overend brothers, who were Tom's uncles (his name being Tom Overend) were, as everybody knew, among the principal supporters of St. Osoph's. Not that they were, by origin, presbyterians. But they were self-made men, which put them once and for all out of sympathy with such a place as St. Asaph's. "We made ourselves," the two brothers used to repeat, in defiance of the catechism of the Anglican Church. They never wearied of explaining how Mr. Dick, the senior brother, had worked overtime by day to send Mr. George, the junior brother, to school by night, and how Mr. George had then worked overtime by night to send Mr. Dick to school by day. Thus they had come up the business ladder hand over hand, landing later on in life on the platform of success like two corpulent acrobats, panting with the strain of it. "For years," Mr. George would explain, "we had father and mother to keep as well; then they died, and Dick and me saw daylight." By which he meant no harm at all, but only stated a fact, and concealed the virtue of it.

And being self-made men they made it a point to do what they could to lessen the importance of such an institution as St. Asaph's Church. By the same contrariety of nature the two Overend brothers (their business name was Overend Brothers, Limited) were supporters of the dissentient Young Men's Guild, and the second or rival University Settlement, and of anything or everything that showed a likelihood of making trouble. On this principle they were warm supporters and friends of the Rev. Dr. McTeague.

The minister had even gone so far as to present to the brothers a copy of his philosophical work, "McTeague's Exposition of the Kantian Hypothesis," and the two brothers had read it through in the office, devoting each of them a whole morning to it. Mr. Dick, the senior brother, had said that he had never seen anything like it, and Mr. George, the junior, had declared that a man who could write that was capable of anything.

On the whole it was evident that the relations between the Overend family and the presbyterian religion were too intimate to allow Mrs. Tom Overend, formerly Miss Philippa Furlong, to sit anywhere else of a Sunday than under Dr. McTeague.

"Phillipa writes," continued Mr. Furlong, "that under the circumstances she and Tom would like to do something for your church. She would like – yes, I have the letter here – to give you, as a surprise, of course, either a new font or a carved pulpit; or perhaps a cheque; she wishes me on no account to mention it to you directly, but to ascertain indirectly from you, what would be the better surprise."

"Oh, a cheque, I think," said the rector; "one can do so much more with it, after all."

"Precisely," said his father; he was well aware of many things that can be done with a cheque that cannot possibly be done with a font.

"That's settled then," resumed Mr. Furlong; "and now I suppose you want me to run my eye over your quarterly statements, do you not, before we send them in to the trustees? That is what you've come for, is it not?"

"Yes," said the rector, drawing a bundle of blue and white papers from his pocket. "I have everything with me. Our shewing is, I believe, excellent, though I fear I fail to present it as clearly as it might be done."

Mr. Furlong senior spread the papers on the table before him and adjusted his spectacles to a more convenient angle. He smiled indulgently as he looked at the documents before him.

"I am afraid you would never make an accountant, Edward," he said.

"I fear not," said the rector.

"Your items," said his father, "are entered wrongly. Here, for example, in the general statement, you put down Distribution of Coals to the Poor to your credit. In the same way, Bibles and Prizes to the Sunday School you again mark to your credit. Why? Don't you see, my boy, that these things are debits? When you give out Bibles or distribute fuel to the poor you give out something for which you get no return. It is a debit. On the other hand, such items as Church Offertory, Scholars' Pennies, etc., are pure profit. Surely the principle is clear."

"I think I see it better now," said the Rev. Edward.

"Perfectly plain, isn't it?" his father went on. "And here again, Paupers' Burial Fund, a loss; enter it as such. Christmas Gift to Verger and Sexton, an absolute loss – you get nothing in return. Widow's Mite, Fines inflicted in Sunday School, etc., these are profit; write them down as such. By this method, you see, in ordinary business we can tell exactly where we stand: anything which we give out without return or reward we count as a debit; all that we take from others without giving in return we count as so much to our credit."

"Ah, yes," murmured the rector. "I begin to understand."

"Very good. But after all, Edward, I mustn't quarrel with the mere form of your accounts; the statement is really a splendid shewing. I see that not only is our mortgage and debenture interest all paid to date, but that a number of our enterprises are making a handsome return. I notice, for example, that the Girls' Friendly Society of the church not only pays for itself, but that you are able to take something out of its funds and transfer it to the Men's Book Club. Excellent! And I observe that you have been able to take a large portion of the Soup Kitchen Fund and put it into the Rector's Picnic Account. Very good indeed. In this respect your figures are a model for church accounts anywhere."

Mr. Furlong continued his scrutiny of the accounts. "Excellent," he murmured, "and on the whole an annual surplus, I see, of several thousands. But stop a bit," he continued, checking himself; "what's this? Are you aware, Edward, that you are losing money on your Foreign Missions Account?"

"I feared as much," said Edward.

"It's incontestable. Look at the figures for yourself: missionary's salary so much, clothes and books to converts so much – why, you're losing on it, Edward!" exclaimed Mr. Furlong, and he shook his head dubiously at the accounts before him.

"I thought," protested his son, "that in view of the character of the work itself –"

"Quite so," answered his father, "quite so. I fully admit the force of that. I am only asking you, is it worth it? Mind you, I am not speaking now as a Christian, but as a business man. Is it worth it?"

"I thought that perhaps, in view of the fact of our large surplus in other directions –"

"Exactly," said his father, "a heavy surplus. It is precisely on that point that I wished to speak to you this morning. You have at present a large annual surplus, and there is every prospect under Providence – in fact, I think in any case – of it continuing for years to come. If I may speak very frankly I should say that as long as our reverend friend Dr. McTeague continues in his charge of St. Osoph's – and I trust that he may be spared for many years to come – you are likely to enjoy the present prosperity of your church. Very good. The question arises, what disposition are we to make of our accumulating funds?"

"Yes," said the rector, hesitating.

"I am speaking to you now," said his father, "not as the secretary of your church, but as president of the Hymnal Supply Company which I represent here. Now please understand, Edward, I don't want in any way to force or control your judgment. I merely wish to shew you certain – shall I say certain opportunities that present themselves for the disposal of our funds? The matter can be taken up later, formally, by yourself and the trustees of the church. As a matter of fact, I have already written to myself as secretary in the matter, and I have received what I consider a quite encouraging answer. Let me explain what I propose."

Mr. Furlong senior rose, and opening the door of the office,

"Everett," he said to the ancient clerk, "kindly give me a Bible."

It was given to him.

Mr. Furlong stood with the Bible poised in his hand.

"Now we," he went on, "I mean the Hymnal Supply Corporation, have an idea for bringing out an entirely new Bible."

A look of dismay appeared on the saintly face of the rector.

"A new Bible!" he gasped.

"Precisely!" said his father, "a new Bible! This one – and we find it every day in our business – is all wrong".

"All wrong!" said the rector with horror in his face.

"My dear boy," exclaimed his father, "pray, pray, do not misunderstand me. Don't imagine for a moment that I mean wrong in a religious sense. Such a thought could never, I hope, enter my mind. All that I mean is that this Bible is badly made up."

"Badly made up!" repeated his son, as mystified as ever.

"I see that you do not understand me. What I mean is this. Let me try to make myself quite clear. For the market of to-day this Bible" – and he poised it again on his hand, as if to test its weight, "is too heavy. The people of to-day want something lighter, something easier to get hold of. Now if –"

But what Mr. Furlong was about to say was lost forever to the world.

For just at this juncture something occurred calculated to divert not only Mr. Furlong's sentence, but the fortunes and the surplus of St. Asaph's itself. At the very moment when Mr. Furlong was speaking a newspaper delivery man in the street outside handed to the sanctified boy the office copy of the noonday paper. And the boy had no sooner looked at its headlines than he said, "How dreadful!" Being sanctified, he had no stronger form of speech than that. But he handed the paper forthwith to one of the stenographers with hair like the daffodils of Sheba, and when she looked at it she exclaimed, "How awful!" And she knocked at once at the door of the ancient clerk and gave the paper to him; and when he looked at it and saw the headline the ancient clerk murmured, "Ah!" in the gentle tone in which very old people greet the news of catastrophe or sudden death.

But in his turn he opened Mr. Furlong's door and put down the paper, laying his finger on the column for a moment without a word.

Mr. Furlong stopped short in his sentence. "Dear me!" he said as his eyes caught the item of news. "How very dreadful!"

"What is it?" said the rector.

"Dr. McTeague," answered his father. "He has been stricken with paralysis!"

"How shocking!" said the rector, aghast. "But when? I saw him only this morning."

"It has just happened," said his father, following down the column of the newspaper as he spoke, "this morning at the university, in his classroom, at a lecture. Dear me, how dreadful! I must go and see the president at once."

Mr. Furlong was about to reach for his hat and stick when at that moment the aged clerk knocked at the door.

"Dr. Boomer," he announced in a tone of solemnity suited to the occasion.

Dr. Boomer entered, shook hands in silence and sat down.

"You have heard our sad news, I suppose?" he said. He used the word "our" as between the university president and his honorary treasurer.

"How did it happen?" asked Mr. Furlong.

"Most distressing," said the president. "Dr. McTeague,

it seems had just entered his ten o'clock class (the hour was about ten-twenty) and was about to open his lecture, when one of his students rose in his seat and asked a question. It is a practice," continued Dr. Boomer, "which, I need hardly say, we do not encourage; the young man, I believe, was a new-comer in the philosophy class. At any rate, he asked Dr. McTeague, quite suddenly it appears, how he could reconcile his theory of transcendental immaterialism with a scheme of rigid moral determinism. Dr. McTeague stared for a moment, his mouth, so the class assert, painfully open. The student repeated the question, and poor McTeague fell forward over his desk, paralysed."

"Is he dead?" gasped Mr. Furlong.

"No," said the president. "But we expect his death at any moment. Dr. Slyder, I may say, is with him now and is doing all he can."

"In any case, I suppose, he could hardly recover enough to continue his college duties," said the young rector.

"Out of the question," said the president. "I should not like to state that of itself mere paralysis need incapacitate a professor. Dr. Thrum, our professor of the theory of music, is, as you know, paralysed in his ears, and Mr. Slant, our professor of optics, is paralysed in his right eye. But this is a case of paralysis of the brain. I fear it is incompatible with professorial work."

"Then, I suppose," said Mr. Furlong senior, "we shall have to think of the question of a successor."

They had both *been* thinking of it for at least three minutes.

"We must," said the president. "For the moment I feel too stunned by the sad news to act. I have merely telegraphed to two or three leading colleges for a *locum tenens* and sent out a few advertisements announcing the chair as vacant. But it will be difficult to replace McTeague. He was a man," added Dr. Boomer, rehearsing in advance, unconsciously, no doubt, his forthcoming oration over Dr. McTeague's death, "of a singular grasp, a breadth of culture, and he was able, as few men are, to instil what I might call a spirit of religion into his teaching. His lectures, indeed, were suffused with moral instruction, and exercised over his students an influence second only to that of the pulpit itself."

He paused.

"Ah yes, the pulpit," said Mr. Furlong, "there indeed you will miss him."

"That," said Dr. Boomer very reverently, "is our real loss, deep, irreparable. I suppose, indeed I am certain, we shall never again see such a man in the pulpit of St. Osoph's. Which reminds me," he added more briskly, "I must ask the newspaper people to let it be known that there will be service as usual the day after to-morrow, and that Dr. McTeague's death will, of course, make no difference – that is to say – I must see the newspaper people at once."

That afternoon all the newspaper editors in the City were busy getting their obituary notices ready for the demise of Dr. McTeague.

"The death of Dr. McTeague," wrote the editor of the *Commercial and Financial Undertone*, a paper which had almost openly advocated the minister's dismissal for five years back, "comes upon us as an irreparable loss. His place will be difficult, nay, impossible, to fill. Whether as a philosopher or a divine he cannot be replaced."

"We have no hesitation in saying," so wrote the editor of the *Plutorian Times*, a three-cent morning paper, which was able to take a broad or three-cent point of view of men and things, "that the loss of Dr. McTeague will be just as much felt in Europe as in America. To Germany the news that the hand that penned 'McTeague's Shorter Exposition of the Kantian Hypothesis' has ceased to write will come with the shock of poignant anguish; while to France –"

The editor left the article unfinished at that point. After all, he was a ready writer, and he reflected that there would be time enough before actually going to press to consider from what particular angle the blow of McTeague's death would strike down the people of France.

So ran in speech and in writing, during two or three days, the requiem of Dr. McTeague.

Altogether there were more kind things said of him in the three days during which he was taken for dead, than in thirty years of his life – which seemed a pity.

And after it all, at the close of the third day, Dr. McTeague feebly opened his eyes.

But when he opened them the world had already passed on, and left him behind.

SEVEN

The Ministrations of the
Rev. Uttermust Dumfarthing

W ELL THEN, gentlemen, I think we have all agreed upon
our man?"

Mr. Dick Overend looked around the table as he spoke
at the managing trustees of St. Osoph's church. They were
assembled in an upper committee room of the Mausoleum
Club. Their official place of meeting was in a board room
off the vestry of the church. But they had felt a draught in it,
some four years ago, which had wafted them over to the
club as their place of assembly. In the club there were no
draughts.

Mr. Dick Overend sat at the head of the table, his
brother George beside him, and Dr. Boomer at the foot.
Beside them were Mr. Boulder, Mr. Skinyer (of Skinyer
and Beatem) and the rest of the trustees.

"You are agreed, then, on the Reverend Uttermust
Dumfarthing?"

"Quite agreed," murmured several trustees together.

"A most remarkable man," said Dr. Boomer. "I heard
him preach in his present church. He gave utterance to
thoughts that I have myself been thinking for years. I never
listened to anything so sound or so scholarly."

"I heard him the night he preached in New York," said
Mr. Boulder. "He preached a sermon to the poor. He told
them they were no good. I never heard, outside of a Scotch
pulpit, such splendid invective."

"Is he Scotch?" said one of the trustees.

"Of Scotch parentage," said the university president. "I believe he is one of the Dumfarthings of Dumferline, Dumfries."

Everybody said "Oh," and there was a pause.

"Is he married?" asked one of the trustees. "I understand," answered Dr. Boomer, "that he is a widower with one child, a little girl."

"Does he make any conditions?"

"None whatever," said the chairman, consulting a letter before him, "except that he is to have absolute control, and in regard to salary. These two points settled, he says, he places himself entirely in our hands."

"And the salary?" asked someone.

"Ten thousand dollars," said the chairman, "payable quarterly in advance."

A chorus of approval went round the table. "Good," "Excellent," "A first-class man," muttered the trustees, "just what we want."

"I am sure, gentlemen," said Mr. Dick Overend, voicing the sentiments of everybody, "we do *not* want a cheap man. Several of the candidates whose names have been under consideration here have been in many respects – in point of religious qualification, let us say – most desirable men. The name of Dr. McSkwirt, for example, has been mentioned with great favour by several of the trustees. But he's a cheap man. I feel we don't want him."

"What is Mr. Dumfarthing getting where he is?" asked Mr. Boulder.

"Nine thousand nine hundred," said the chairman.

"And Dr. McSkwirt?"

"Fourteen hundred dollars."

"Well, that settles it!" exclaimed everybody with a burst of enlightenment.

And so it was settled.

In fact, nothing could have been plainer.

"I suppose," said Mr. George Overend as they were

about to rise, "that we are quite justified in taking it for granted that Dr. McTeague will never be able to resume work?"

"Oh, absolutely for granted," said Dr. Boomer. "Poor McTeague! I hear from Slyder that he was making desperate efforts this morning to sit up in bed. His nurse with difficulty prevented him."

"Is his power of speech gone?" asked Mr. Boulder.

"Practically so; in any case, Dr. Slyder insists on his not using it. In fact, poor McTeague's mind is a wreck. His nurse was telling me that this morning he was reaching out his hand for the newspaper, and seemed to want to read one of the editorials. It was quite pathetic," concluded Dr. Boomer, shaking his head.

So the whole matter was settled, and next day all the town knew that St. Osoph's Church had extended a call to the Rev. Uttermust Dumfarthing, and that he had accepted it.

Within a few weeks of this date the Reverend Uttermust Dumfarthing moved into the manse of St. Osoph's and assumed his charge. And forthwith he became the sole topic of conversation on Plutoria Avenue. "Have you seen the new minister of St. Osoph's?" everybody asked. "Have you been to hear Dr. Dumfarthing?" "Were you at St. Osoph's Church on Sunday morning? Ah, you really should go! most striking sermon I ever listened to."

The effect of him was absolute and instantaneous; there was no doubt of it.

"My dear," said Mrs. Buncomhearst to one of her friends, in describing how she had met him, "I never saw a more striking man. Such power in his face! Mr. Boulder introduced him to me on the avenue, and he hardly seemed to see me at all, simply scowled! I was never so favourably impressed with any man."

On his very first Sunday he preached to his congregation on eternal punishment, leaning forward in his black gown and shaking his fist at them. Dr. McTeague had never shaken his fist in thirty years, and as for the Rev. Fareforth Furlong, he was incapable of it.

But the Rev. Uttermust Dumfarthing told his congregation that he was convinced that at least seventy per cent. of them were destined for eternal punishment; and he didn't call it by that name, but labelled it simply and forcibly "hell." The word had not been heard in any church in the better part of the City for a generation. The congregation was so swelled next Sunday that the minister raised the percentage to eighty-five, and everybody went away delighted. Young and old flocked to St. Osoph's. Before a month had passed the congregation at the evening service at St. Asaph's Church was so slender that the offertory, as Mr. Furlong senior himself calculated, was scarcely sufficient to pay the overhead charge of collecting it.

The presence of so many young men sitting in serried files close to the front was the only feature of his congregation that extorted from the Rev. Mr. Dumfarthing something like approval.

"It is joy to me to see," he remarked to several of his trustees, "that there are in the City so many godly young men, whatever the elders may be."

But there may have been a secondary cause at work, for among the godly young men of Plutoria Avenue the topic of conversation had not been, "Have you heard the new presbyterian minister?" but, "Have you seen his daughter? You *haven't*? Well, Say!"

For it turned out that the "child" of Dr. Uttermust Dumfarthing, so-called by the trustees, was the kind of child that wears a little round hat, straight from Paris, with an upright feather in it, and a silk dress in four sections, and shoes with high heels that would have broken the heart of John Calvin. Moreover, she had the distinction of being the only person on Plutoria Avenue who was not one whit afraid of the Reverend Uttermust Dumfarthing. She even amused herself, in violation of all rules, by attending evening service at St. Asaph's, where she sat listening to the

Reverend Edward, and feeling that she had never heard anything so sensible in her life.

"I'm simply dying to meet your brother," she said to Mrs. Tom Overend, otherwise Philippa; "he's such a complete contrast with father." She knew no higher form of praise. "Father's sermons are always so frightfully full of religion."

And Philippa promised that meet him she should.

But whatever may have been the effect of the presence of Catherine Dumfarthing, there is no doubt the greater part of the changed situation was due to Dr. Dumfarthing himself.

Everything he did was calculated to please. He preached sermons to the rich and told them they were mere cobwebs, and they like it; he preached a special sermon to the poor and warned them to be mighty careful; he gave a series of weekly talks to working men, and knocked them sideways; and in the Sunday School he gave the children so fierce a talk on charity and the need of giving freely and quickly, that such a stream of pennies and nickels poured into Catherine Dumfarthing's Sunday School Fund as hadn't been seen in the church in fifty years.

Nor was Mr. Dumfarthing different in his private walk of life. He was heard to speak openly of the Overend brothers as "men of wrath," and they were so pleased that they repeated it to half the town. It was the best business advertisement they had had for years.

Dr. Boomer was captivated with the man. "True scholarship," he murmured, as Dr. Dumfarthing poured undiluted Greek and Hebrew from the pulpit, scorning to translate a word of it. Under Dr. Boomer's charge the minister was taken over the length and breadth of Plutoria University, and reviled it from the foundations up.

"Our library," said the president, "two hundred thousand volumes!"

"Aye," said the minister, "a powerful heap of rubbish, I'll be bound!"

"The photograph of our last year's graduating class," said the president.

"A poor lot, to judge by the faces of them," said the minister.

"This, Dr. Dumfarthing, is our new radiographic laboratory; Mr. Spiff, our demonstrator, is preparing slides which, I believe, actually show the movements of the atom itself, do they not, Mr. Spiff?"

"Ah," said the minister, piercing Mr. Spiff from beneath his dark brows, "it will not avail you, young man."

Dr. Boomer was delighted. "Poor McTeague," he said – "and by the way, Boyster, I hear that McTeague is trying to walk again; a great error, it shouldn't be allowed! – poor McTeague knew nothing of science."

The students themselves shared in the enthusiasm, especially after Dr. Dumfarthing had given them a Sunday afternoon talk in which he shewed that their studies were absolutely futile. As soon as they knew this they went to work with a vigour that put new life into the college.

Meantime the handsome face of the Reverend Edward Fareforth Furlong began to wear a sad and weary look that had never been seen on it before. He watched his congregation drifting from St. Asaph's to St. Osoph's and was powerless to prevent it. His sadness reached its climax one bright afternoon in the late summer, when he noticed that even his episcopal blackbirds were leaving his elms and moving westward to the spruce trees of the manse.

He stood looking at them with melancholy on his face.

"Why, Edward," cried his sister Philippa, as her motor stopped beside him, "how doleful you look! Get into the car and come out into the country for a ride. Let the parish teas look after themselves for to-day."

Tom, Philippa's husband, was driving his own car – he was rich enough to be able to – and seated with Philippa in the car was an unknown person, as prettily dressed as

Philippa herself. To the rector she was presently introduced as Miss Catherine Something – he didn't hear the rest of it. Nor did he need to. It was quite plain that her surname, whatever it was, was a very temporary and transitory affair.

So they sped rapidly out the City and away out into the country, mile after mile, through cool, crisp air, and among woods with the touch of autumn bright already upon them, and with blue sky and great still clouds white overhead. And the afternoon was so beautiful and so bright that as they went along there was no talk about religion at all! nor was there any mention of Mothers' Auxiliaries, or Girls' Friendly Societies, nor any discussion of the poor. It was too glorious a day. But they spoke instead of the new dances, and whether they had come to stay, and of such sensible topics as that. Then presently, as they went on still further, Philippa leaned forward and talked to Tom over his shoulder and reminded him that this was the very road to Castel Casteggio, and asked him if he remembered coming up it with her to join the Newberrys ever so long ago. Whatever it was that Tom answered it is not recorded, but it is certain that it took so long in the saying that the Reverend Edward talked in *tête-à-tête* with Catherine for fifteen measured miles, and was unaware that it was more than five minutes. Among other things he said, and she agreed – or she said and he agreed – that for the new dances it was necessary to have always one and the same partner, and to keep that partner all the time. And somehow simple sentiments of that sort, when said direct into a pair of listening blue eyes behind a purple motor veil, acquire an infinite significance.

Then, not much after that, say three or four minutes, they were all of a sudden back in town again, running along Plutoria Avenue, and to the rector's surprise the motor was stopping outside the manse, and Catherine was saying, "Oh, thank you ever so much, Philippa; it was just heavenly!" which showed that the afternoon had had its religious features after all.

"What!" said the rector's sister, as they moved off again, "didn't you know? That's Catherine Dumfarthing!"

When the Rev. Fareforth Furlong arrived home at the rectory he spent an hour or so in the deepest of deep thought in an arm-chair in his study. Nor was it any ordinary parish problem that he was revolving in his mind. He was trying to think out some means by which his sister Juliana might be induced to commit the sin of calling on the daughter of a presbyterian minister.

The thing had to be represented as in some fashion or other an act of self-denial, a form of mortification of the flesh. Otherwise he knew Juliana would never do it. But to call on Miss Catherine Dumfarthing seemed to him such an altogether delightful and unspeakably blissful process that he hardly knew how to approach the topic. So when Juliana presently came home the rector could find no better way of introducing the subject than by putting it on the ground of Philippa's marriage to Miss Dumfarthing's father's trustee's nephew.

"Juliana," he said, "don't you think that perhaps, on account of Philippa and Tom, you ought – or at least it might be best – for you to call on Miss Dumfarthing?"

Juliana turned to her brother as she laid aside her bonnet and her black gloves.

"I've just been there this afternoon," she said.

There was something as near to a blush on her face as her brother had ever seen.

"But she was not there!" he said.

"No," answered Juliana, "but Mr. Dumfarthing was. I stayed and talked some time with him, waiting for her."

The rector gave a sort of whistle, or rather that blowing out of air which is the episcopal symbol for it.

"Didn't you find him pretty solemn?" he said.

"Solemn!" answered his sister. "Surely, Edward, a man in such a calling as his ought to be solemn."

"I don't mean that exactly," said the rector; "I mean – er – hard, bitter, so to speak."

"Edward!" exclaimed Juliana, "how can you speak so. Mr. Dumfarthing hard! Mr. Dumfarthing bitter! Why, Edward, the man is gentleness and kindness itself. I don't think I ever met anyone so full of sympathy, of compassion with suffering."

Juliana's face had flushed. It was quite plain that she saw things in the Reverend Uttermust Dumfarthing – as some one woman does in every man – that no one else could see.

The Reverend Edward was abashed. "I wasn't thinking of his character," he said. "I was thinking rather of his doctrines. Wait till you have heard him preach."

Juliana flushed more deeply still. "I heard him last Sunday evening," she said.

The rector was silent, and his sister, as if impelled to speak, went on.

"And I don't see, Edward, how anyone could think him a hard or bigoted man in his creed. He walked home with me to the gate just now, and he was speaking of all the sin in the world, and of how few, how very few people, can be saved, and how many will have to be burned as worthless; and he spoke so beautifully. He regrets it, Edward, regrets it deeply. It is a real grief to him."

On which Juliana, half in anger, withdrew, and her brother the rector sat back in his chair with smiles rippling all over his saintly face. For he had been wondering whether it would be possible, even remotely possible, to get his sister to invite the Dumfarthings to high tea at the rectory some day at six o'clock (evening dinner was out of the question), and now he knew within himself that the thing was as good as done.

While such things as these were happening and about to happen, there were many others of the congregation of St. Asaph's beside the rector to whom the growing situation gave cause for serious perplexities. Indeed, all who were interested in the church, the trustees and the mortgagees and the underlying debenture-holders, were feeling anxious. For some of them underlay the Sunday School, whose scholars' offerings had declined forty per cent. and others underlay the new organ, not yet paid for, while others were lying deeper still beneath the ground site of the church with seven dollars and a half a square foot resting on them.

"I don't like it," said Mr. Lucullus Fyshe to Mr. Newberry (they were both prominent members of the congregation). "I don't like the look of things. I took up a block of Furlong's bonds on his Guild building from what seemed at the time the best of motives. The interest appeared absolutely certain. Now it's a month overdue on the last quarter. I feel alarmed."

"Neither do I like it," said Mr. Newberry, shaking his head; "and I'm sorry for Fareforth Furlong. An excellent fellow, Fyshe, excellent. I keep wondering, Sunday after Sunday, if there isn't something I can do to help him out. One might do something further perhaps in the way of new buildings or alterations. I have, in fact, offered – by myself, I mean, and without other aid – to dynamite out the front of his church, underpin it, and put him in a Norman gateway; either that, or blast out the back of it where the choir sit, just as he likes. I was thinking about it last Sunday as they were singing the anthem, and realising what a lot one might do there with a few sticks of dynamite."

"I doubt it," said Mr. Fyshe. "In fact, Newberry, to speak very frankly, I begin to ask myself, Is Furlong the man for the post?"

"Oh, surely," said Mr. Newberry in protest.

"Personally a charming fellow," went on Mr. Fyshe; "but is he, all said and done, quite the man to conduct a church? In the *first* place, he is *not* a business man."

"No," said Mr. Newberry reluctantly, "that I admit."

"Very good. And, *secondly*, even in the matter of his religion itself, one always feels as if he were too little fixed, too unstable. He simply moves with the times. That, at least, is what people are beginning to say of him, that he is

perpetually moving with the times. It doesn't do, Newberry, it doesn't do."

Whereupon Mr. Newberry went away troubled and
wrote to Fareforth Furlong a confidential letter with a
signed cheque in it for the amount of Mr. Fyshe's interest,
and with such further offerings of dynamite, of underpin-
ning and blasting as his conscience prompted.

When the rector received and read the note and saw the
figures of the cheque, there arose such a thankfulness in his
spirit as he hadn't felt for months, and he may well have
murmured, for the repose of Mr. Newberry's soul, a prayer
not found in the rubric of King James.

All the more cause had he to feel light at heart, for as it
chanced it was on that same evening that the Dumfarthings, father and daughter, were to take tea at the rectory.
Indeed, a few minutes before six o'clock they might have
been seen making their way from the manse to the rectory.

On their way along the avenue the minister took occasion to reprove his daughter for the worldliness of her hat (it
was a little trifle from New York that she had bought out of
the Sunday School money, – a temporary loan); and a little
further on he spoke to her severely about the parasol she
carried; and further yet about the strange fashion, specially
condemned by the Old Testament, in which she wore her
hair. So Catherine knew in her heart from this that she
must be looking her very prettiest, and went into the rectory radiant.

The tea was, of course, an awkward meal at the best.
There was an initial difficulty about grace, not easily sur-
mounted. And when the Rev. Mr. Dumfarthing sternly
refused tea as a pernicious drink weakening to the system,
the Anglican rector was too ignorant of the presbyterian
system to know enough to give him Scotch whiskey.

But there were bright spots in the meal as well. The
rector was even able to ask Catherine, sideways as a personal question, if she played tennis; and she was able to
whisper behind her hand, "Not allowed," and to make a
face in the direction of her father, who was absorbed for the

moment in a theological question with Juliana. Indeed, before the conversation became general again the rector had contrived to make a rapid arrangement with Catherine whereby she was to come with him to the Newberrys' tennis court the day following and learn the game, with or without permission.

So the tea was perhaps a success in its way. And it is noteworthy that Juliana spent the days that followed it in reading Calvin's "Institutes" (specially loaned to her) and "Dumfarthing on the Certainty of Damnation" (a gift), and in praying for her brother – a task practically without hope. During which same time the rector in white flannels, and Catherine in a white duck skirt and blouse, were flying about on the green grass of the Newberrys' court, and calling, "love," "love all," to one another so gayly and so brazenly that even Mr. Newberry felt that there must be something in it.

But all these things came merely as interludes in the moving currents of greater events; for as the summer faded into autumn and autumn into winter the anxieties of the trustees of St. Asaph's began to call for action of some sort.

"Edward," said the rector's father on the occasion of their next quarterly discussion, "I cannot conceal from you that the position of things is very serious. Your statements show a falling off in every direction. Your interest is everywhere in arrears; your current account overdrawn to the limit. At this rate, you know, the end is inevitable. Your debenture and bondholders will decide to foreclose; and if they do, you know, there is no power that can stop them. Even with your limited knowledge of business you are probably aware that there is no higher power that can influence or control the holder of a first mortgage."

"I fear so," said the Rev. Edward very sadly.

"Do you not think perhaps that some of the shortcoming lies with yourself?" continued Mr. Furlong. "Is it not possible that as a preacher you fail somewhat, do not, as it were, deal sufficiently with fundamental things as others do? You leave untouched the truly vital issues, such things as the creation, death, and, if I may refer to it, the life beyond the grave."

As a result of which the Reverend Edward preached a series of special sermons on the creation, for which he made a special and arduous preparation in the library of Plutoria University. He said that it had taken a million, possibly a hundred million, years of quite difficult work to accomplish, and that though when we looked at it all was darkness still we could not be far astray if we accepted and held fast to the teachings of Sir Charles Lyell. The book of Genesis, he said, was not be taken as meaning a day when it said a day, but rather something other than a mere day; and the word "light" meant not exactly light, but possibly some sort of phosphorescence, and that the use of the word "darkness" was to be understood not as meaning darkness, but to be taken as simply indicating obscurity. And when he had quite finished, the congregation declared the whole sermon to be mere milk and water. It insulted their intelligence, they said. After which, a week later, the Rev. Dr. Dumfarthing took up the same subject, and with the aid of seven plain texts pulverised the rector into fragments.

One notable result of the controversy was that Juliana Furlong refused henceforth to attend her brother's church and sat, even at morning service, under the minister of St. Osoph's.

"The sermon was, I fear, a mistake," said Mr. Furlong senior; "perhaps you had better not dwell too much on such topics. We must look for aid in another direction. In fact, Edward, I may mention to you in confidence that certain of your trustees are already devising ways and means that may help us out of our dilemma."

Indeed, although the Reverend Edward did not know it, a certain idea, or plan, was already germinating in the minds of the most influential supporters of St. Asaph's.

Such was the situation of the rival churches of St. Asaph and St. Osoph as the autumn slowly faded into winter: during which time the elm trees on Plutoria Avenue shivered and dropped their leaves and the chauffeurs of the motors first turned blue in their faces and then, when the great snows came, were suddenly converted into liveried coachmen with tall bearskins and whiskers like Russian horseguards, changing back again to blue-nosed chauffeurs the very moment of a thaw. During this time also the congregation of the Reverend Fareforth Furlong was diminishing month by month, and that of the Reverend Uttermust Dumfarthing was so numerous that they filled up the aisles at the back of the church. Here the worshippers stood and froze, for the minister had abandoned the use of steam heat in St. Osoph's on the ground that he could find no warrant for it.

During this same period other momentous things were happening, such as that Juliana Furlong was reading, under the immediate guidance of Dr. Dumfarthing, the *History of the Progress of Disruption in the Churches of Scotland* in ten volumes; such also as that Catherine Dumfarthing was wearing a green and gold winter suit with Russian furs and a Balkan hat and a Circassian feather, which cut a wide swath of destruction among the young men on Plutoria Avenue every afternoon as she passed. Moreover by the strongest of coincidences she scarcely ever seemed to come along the snow-covered avenue without meeting the Reverend Edward, – a fact which elicited new exclamations of surprise from them both every day: and by an equally strange coincidence they generally seemed, although coming in different directions, to be bound for the same place; towards which they wandered together with such slow steps and in such oblivion of the passers-by that even the children on the avenue knew by instinct whither they were wandering.

It was noted also that the broken figure of Dr. McTeague had reappeared upon the street, leaning heavily upon a stick and greeting those he met with such a meek and willing affability, as if in apology for his stroke of paralysis, that all who talked with him agreed that McTeague's mind was a wreck.

"He stood and spoke to me about the children for at least a quarter of an hour," related one of his former parishioners, "asking after them by name, and whether they were going to school yet and a lot of questions like that. He never used to speak of such things. Poor old McTeague, I'm afraid he is getting soft in the head." "I know," said the person addressed. "His mind is no good. He stopped me the other day to say how sorry he was to hear about my brother's illness. I could see from the way he spoke that his brain is getting feeble. He's losing his grip. He was speaking of how kind people had been to him after his accident and there were tears in his eyes. I think he's getting batty."

Nor were even these things the most momentous happenings of the period. For as winter slowly changed to early spring it became known that something of great portent was under way. It was rumoured that the trustees of St. Asaph's Church were putting their heads together. This was striking news. The last time that the head of Mr. Lucullus Fyshe, for example, had been placed side by side with that of Mr. Newberry, there had resulted a merger of four soda-water companies, bringing what was called industrial peace over an area as big as Texas and raising the price of soda by three peaceful cents per bottle. And the last time that Mr. Furlong senior's head had been laid side by side with those of Mr. Rasselyer-Brown and Mr. Skinyer, they had practically saved the country from the horrors of a coal famine by the simple process of raising the price of nut coal seventy-five cents a ton and thus guaranteeing its abundance.

Naturally, therefore, when it became known that such redoubtable heads as those of the trustees and the underlying mortgagees of St. Asaph's were being put together, it was fully expected that some important development would follow. It was not accurately known from which of the assembled heads first proceeded the great idea which was presently to solve the difficulties of the church. It may well have come from that of Mr. Lucullus Fyshe. Certainly a head which had brought peace out of civil war in the hardware business by amalgamating ten rival stores and had saved the very lives of five hundred employees by reducing their wages fourteen per cent, was capable of it.

At any rate it was Mr. Fyshe who first gave the idea a definite utterance.

"It's the only thing, Furlong," he said, across the lunch table at the Mausoleum Club. "It's the one solution. The two churches can't live under the present conditions of competition. We have here practically the same situation as we had with the two rum distilleries, – the output is too large for the demand. One or both of the two concerns must go under. It's their turn just now, but these fellows are business men enough to know that it may be ours tomorrow. We'll offer them a business solution. We'll propose a merger."

"I've been thinking of it," said Mr. Furlong senior, "I suppose it's feasible?"

"Feasible!" exclaimed Mr. Fyshe. "Why look what's being done every day everywhere, from the Standard Oil Company downwards."

"You would hardly, I think," said Mr. Furlong, with a quiet smile, "compare the Standard Oil Company to a church?"

"Well, no, I suppose not," said Mr. Fyshe, and he too smiled, – in fact he almost laughed. The notion was too ridiculous. One could hardly compare a mere church to a thing of the magnitude and importance of the Standard Oil Company.

"But on a lesser scale," continued Mr. Fyshe, "it's the same sort of thing. As for the difficulties of it, I needn't remind you of the much greater difficulties we had to grapple with in the rum merger. There, you remember, a number of the women held out as a matter of principle. It was not mere business with them. Church union is different. In fact it is one of the ideas of the day and everyone admits that what is needed is the application of the ordinary business principles of harmonious combination, with a proper – er – restriction of output and general economy of operation."

"Very good," said Mr. Furlong, "I'm sure if you're willing to try, the rest of us are."

"All right," said Mr. Fyshe. "I thought of setting Skinyer, of Skinyer and Beatem, to work on the form of the organisation. As you know he is not only a deeply religious man but he has already handled the Tin Pot Combination and the United Hardware and the Associated Tanneries. He ought to find this quite simple."

Within a day or two Mr. Skinyer had already commenced his labours. "I must first," he said, "get an accurate idea of the existing legal organisation of the two churches."

For which purpose he approached the rector of St. Asaph's.

"I just want to ask you, Mr. Furlong," said the lawyer, "a question or two as to the exact constitution, the form so to speak, of your church. What is it? Is it a single corporate body?"

"I suppose," said the rector thoughtfully, "one would define it as an indivisible spiritual unit manifesting itself *on* earth."

"Quite so," interrupted Mr. Skinyer, "but I don't mean what it is in the religious sense: I mean, in the real sense." "I fail to understand," said Mr. Furlong.

"Let me put it very clearly," said the lawyer. "Where does it get its authority?"

"From above," said the rector reverently.

"Precisely," said Mr. Skinyer, "no doubt, but I mean its authority in the *exact* sense of the term."

"It was enjoined on St. Peter," began the rector, but Mr. Skinyer interrupted him.

"That I am aware of," he said, "but what I mean is, – where does your church get its power, for example, to hold property, to collect debts, to use distraint against the property of others, to foreclose its mortgages and to cause judgment to be executed against those who fail to pay their debts to it? You will say at once that it has these powers direct from Heaven. No doubt that is true and no religious person would deny it. But we lawyers are compelled to take a narrower, a less elevating point of view. Are these powers conferred on you by the state legislature or by some higher authority?"

"Oh by a higher authority, I hope," said the rector very fervently. Whereupon Mr. Skinyer left him without further questioning, the rector's brain being evidently unfit for the subject of corporation law.

On the other hand he got satisfaction from the Rev. Dr. Dumfarthing at once.

"The church of St. Osoph," said the minister, "is a perpetual trust, holding property as such under a general law of the state and able as such to be made the object of suit or distraint. I speak with some assurance as I had occasion to enquire into the matter at the time when I was looking for guidance in regard to the call I had received to come here."

"It's a quite simple matter," Mr. Skinyer presently reported to Mr. Fyshe. "One of the churches is a perpetual trust, the other practically a state corporation. Each has full control over its property provided nothing is done by either to infringe the purity of its doctrine."

"Just what does that mean?" asked Mr. Fyshe.

"It must maintain its doctrine absolutely pure. Otherwise if certain of its trustees remain pure and the rest do not, those who stay pure are entitled to take the whole of the property. This, I believe, happens every day in Scotland where, of course, there is great eagerness to remain pure in doctrine."

"And what do you define as *pure doctrine*?" asked Mr. Fyshe.

"If the trustees are in dispute," said Mr. Skinyer, "the

courts decide, but any doctrine is held to be a pure doctrine if *all* the trustees regard it as a pure doctrine."

"I see," said Mr. Fyshe thoughtfully, "it's the same thing as what we called 'permissible policy' on the part of directors in the Tin Pot Combination."

"Exactly," assented Mr. Skinyer, "and it means that for the merger we need nothing, – I state it very frankly, – except general consent.

The preliminary stages of the making of the merger followed along familiar business lines. The trustees of St. Asaph's went through the process known as 'approaching' the trustees of St. Osoph's. First of all, for example, Mr. Lucullus Fyshe invited Mr. Asmodeus Boulder of St. Osoph's to lunch with him at the Mausoleum Club; the cost of the lunch, as is usual in such cases, was charged to the general expense account of the church. Of course nothing whatever was said during the lunch about the churches or their finances or anything concerning them. Such discussion would have been a gross business impropriety. A few days later the two brothers Overend dined with Mr. Furlong senior, the dinner being charged directly to the contingencies account of St. Asaph's. After which Mr. Skinyer and his partner, Mr. Beatem, went to the spring races together on the Profit and Loss account of St. Osoph's, and Philippa Overend and Catherine Dumfarthing were taken (by the Unforeseen Disbursements Account) to the grand opera, followed by a midnight supper.

All of these things constituted what was called the promotion of the merger and were almost exactly identical with the successive stages of the making of the Amalgamated Distilleries and the Associated Tin Pot Corporation; which was considered a most hopeful sign.

"Do you think they'll go into it?" asked Mr. Newberry of Mr. Furlong senior, anxiously. "After all, what inducement have they?"

"Every inducement," said Mr. Furlong. "All said and done they've only one large asset, – Dr. Dumfarthing. We're really offering to buy up Dr. Dumfarthing by pooling our assets with theirs."

"And what does Dr. Dumfarthing himself say to it?"

"Ah, there I am not so sure," said Mr. Furlong; "that may be a difficulty. So far there hasn't been a word from him, and his trustees are absolutely silent about his views. However, we shall soon know all about it. Skinyer is asking us all to come together one evening next week to draw up the articles of agreement."

"Has he got the financial basis arranged then?"

"I believe so," said Mr. Furlong. "His idea is to form a new corporation to be known as the United Church Limited or by some similar name. All the present mortgagees will be converted into unified bondholders, the pew rents will be capitalised into preferred stock and the common stock, drawing its dividend from the offertory, will be distributed among all members in standing. Skinyer says that it is really an ideal form of church union, one that he thinks is likely to be widely adopted. It has the advantages of removing all questions of religion, which he says are practically the only remaining obstacle to a union of all the churches. In fact it puts the churches once and for all on a business basis."

"But what about the question of doctrine, of belief?" asked Mr. Newberry.

"Skinyer says he can settle it," answered Mr. Furlong.

About a week after the above conversation the united trustees of St. Asaph's and St. Osoph's were gathered about a huge egg-shaped table in the board room of the Mausoleum Club. They were seated in intermingled fashion after the precedent of the recent Tin Pot Amalgamation and were smoking huge black cigars specially kept by the club for the promotion of companies and chargeable to expenses of organisation at fifty cents a cigar. There was an air of deep peace brooding over the assembly, as among men who have accomplished a difficult and meritorious task.

"Well, then," said Mr. Skinyer, who was in the chair, with a pile of documents in front of him, "I think that our general basis of financial union may be viewed as settled."

A murmur of assent went round the meeting. "The terms are set forth in the memorandum before us, which you have already signed. Only one other point, – a minor one, – remains to be considered. I refer to the doctrines or the religious belief of the new amalgamation."

"Is it necessary to go into that?" asked Mr. Boulder.

"Not entirely, perhaps," said Mr. Skinyer. "Still there have been, as you all know, certain points, – I won't say of disagreement, – but let us say of friendly argument, – between the members of the different churches, – such things for example," here he consulted his papers, "as the theory of the creation, the salvation of the soul, and so forth, have been mentioned in this connection. I have a memorandum of them here, though the points escape me for the moment. These, you may say, are not matters of first importance, especially as compared with the intricate financial questions which we have already settled in a satisfactory manner. Still I think it might be well if I were permitted with your unanimous approval to jot down a memorandum or two to be afterwards embodied in our articles."

There was a general murmur of approval.

"Very good," said Mr. Skinyer, settling himself back in his chair. "Now, first, in regard to the creation," here he looked all round the meeting in a way to command attention, – "Is it your wish that we should leave that merely to a gentlemen's agreement or do you want an explicit clause?"

"I think it might be well," said Mr. Dick Overend, "to leave no doubt about the theory of the creation."

"Good," said Mr. Skinyer. "I am going to put it down then something after this fashion: 'On and after, let us say, August 1st proximo, the process of the creation shall be held, and is hereby held, to be such and such only as is acceptable to a majority of the holders of common and preferred stock voting pro rata. Is that agreed?"

"Carried," cried several at once.

"Carried," repeated Mr. Skinyer. "Now let us pass on," – here he consulted his notes, – "to item two, eternal punishment. I have made a memorandum as follows, 'Should any doubts arise, on or after August first proximo, as to the existence of eternal punishment they shall be settled absolutely and finally by a pro rata vote of all the holders of common and preferred stock.' Is that agreed?"

"One moment!" said Mr. Fyshe, "do you think that quite fair to the bondholders? After all, as the virtual holders of the property, they are the persons most interested. I should like to amend your clause and make it read, – I am not phrasing it exactly but merely giving the sense of it, – that eternal punishment should be reserved for the mortgagees and bondholders."

At this there was an outbreak of mingled approval and dissent, several persons speaking at once. In the opinion of some, the stockholders of the company, especially the preferred stockholders, had as good a right to eternal punishment as the bondholders. Presently Mr. Skinyer, who had been busily writing notes, held up his hand for silence.

"Gentlemen," he said, "will you accept this as a compromise? We will keep the original clause but merely add to it the words, 'but no form of eternal punishment shall be declared valid if displeasing to a three-fifths majority of the holders of bonds.'"

"Carried, carried," cried everybody.

"To which I think we need only add," said Mr. Skinyer, "a clause to the effect that all other points of doctrine, belief or religious principle may be freely altered, amended, reversed or entirely abolished at any general annual meeting!"

There was a renewed chorus of "Carried, carried," and the trustees rose from the table shaking hands with one another, and lighting fresh cigars as they passed out of the club into the night air.

"The only thing that I don't understand," said Mr. Newberry to Dr. Boomer as they went out from the club arm in arm (for they might now walk in that fashion with the same propriety as two of the principals in a distillery merger), "the only thing that I don't understand is why the Reverend Mr. Dumfarthing should be willing to consent to the amalgamation."

"Do you really not know?" said Dr. Boomer.

"No."

"You have heard nothing?"

"Not a word," said Mr. Newberry.

"Ah," rejoined the president, "I see that our men have kept it very quiet, – naturally so, in view of the circumstances. The truth is that the Reverend Mr. Dumfarthing is leaving us."

"Leaving St. Osoph's!" exclaimed Mr. Newberry in utter astonishment.

"To our great regret. He has had a call, – a most inviting field of work, he says, a splendid opportunity. They offered him ten thousand one hundred; we were only giving him ten thousand here, though of course that feature of the situation would not weigh at all with a man like Dumfarthing."

"Oh no, of course not," said Mr. Newberry.

"As soon as we heard of the call we offered him ten thousand three hundred, – not that that would make any difference to a man of his character. Indeed Dumfarthing was still waiting and looking for guidance when they offered him eleven thousand. We couldn't meet it. It was beyond us, though we had the consolation of knowing that with such a man as Dumfarthing the money made no difference."

"And he has accepted the call?"

"Yes. He accepted it to-day. He sent word to Mr. Dick Overend, our chairman, that he would remain in his manse, looking for light, until two thirty, after which, if we had not communicated with him by that hour, he would cease to look for it."

"Dear me," said Mr. Newberry, deep in reflection, "so that when your trustees came to the meeting –"

"Exactly," said Dr. Boomer, – and something like a smile passed across his features for a moment, – "Dr. Dumfarthing had already sent away his telegram of acceptance."

"Why, then," said Mr. Newberry, "at the time of our discussion to-night, you were in the position of having no minister."

"Not at all. We had already appointed a successor."

"A successor?"

"Certainly. It will be in to-morrow morning's papers. The fact is that we decided to ask Dr. McTeague to resume his charge."

"Dr. McTeague!" repeated Mr. Newberry in amazement. "But surely his mind is understood to be –"

"Oh, not at all," interrupted Dr. Boomer. His mind appears, if anything, to be clearer and stronger than ever. Dr. Slyder tells us that paralysis of the brain very frequently has this effect; it soothes the brain, – clears it, as it were, so that very often intellectual problems which occasioned the greatest perplexity before present no difficulty whatever afterward. Dr. McTeague, I believe, finds no trouble now in reconciling St. Paul's dialectic with Hegel as he used to. He says that as far as he can see they both mean the same thing."

"Well, well," said Mr. Newberry, "and will Dr. McTeague also resume his philosophical lectures at the university?"

"We think it wiser not," said the president. "While we feel that Dr. McTeague's mind is in admirable condition for clerical work we fear that professorial duties might strain it. In order to get the full value of his remarkable intelligence, we propose to elect him to the governing body of the university. There his brain will be safe from any shock. As a professor there would always be the fear that one of his students might raise a question in his class. This of course is not a difficulty that arises in the pulpit or among the governors of the university."

"Of course not," said Mr. Newberry.

Thus was constituted the famous union or merger of the churches of St. Asaph and St. Osoph, viewed by many of those who made it as the beginning of a new era in the history of the modern church.

There is no doubt that it has been in every way an eminent success.

Rivalry, competition and controversies over points of dogma have become unknown on Plutoria Avenue. The parishioners of the two churches may now attend either of them just as they like. As the trustees are fond of explaining it doesn't make the slightest difference. The entire receipts of the churches being now pooled are divided without reference to individual attendance. At each half year there is issued a printed statement which is addressed to the shareholders of the United Churches Limited and is hardly to be distinguished in style or material from the annual and semi-annual reports of the Tin Pot Amalgamation and the United Hardware and other quasi-religious bodies of the sort. "Your directors," the last of these documents states, "are happy to inform you that in spite of the prevailing industrial depression the gross receipts of the corporation have shown such an increase as to justify the distribution of a stock dividend of special Offertory Stock Cumulative, which will be offered at par to all holders of common or preferred shares. You will also be gratified to learn that the directors have voted unanimously in favour of a special presentation to the Rev. Uttermust Dumfarthing on the occasion of his approaching marriage. It was earnestly debated whether this gift should take the form, as at first suggested, of a cash presentation, or, as afterwards suggested, of a written testimonial in the form of an address. The latter course was finally adopted as being more fitting to the circumstances and the address has accordingly been prepared, setting forth to the Rev. Dr. Dumfarthing, in old English lettering and wording, the opinion which is held of him by his former parishioners."

The "approaching marriage" referred of course to Dr. Dumfarthing's betrothal to Juliana Furlong. It was not known that he had ever exactly proposed to her. But it was understood that before giving up his charge he drew her attention, in very severe terms, to the fact that, as his daughter was now leaving him, he must either have some-one else to look after his manse or else be compelled to incur the expense of a paid housekeeper. This latter alter-native, he said, was not one that he cared to contemplate. He also reminded her that she was now at a time of life when she could hardly expect to pick and choose and that her spiritual condition was one of at least great uncertainty. These combined statements are held, under the law of Scotland at any rate, to be equivalent to an offer of marriage.

Catherine Dumfarthing did not join her father in his new manse. She first remained behind him, as the guest of Philippa Overend for a few weeks while she was occupied in packing up her things. After that she stayed for another two or three weeks to unpack them. This had been rendered necessary by a conversation held with the Reverend Edward Fareforth Furlong, in a shaded corner of the Over-end's garden. After which, in due course of time, Catherine and Edward were married, the ceremony being performed by the Reverend Dr. McTeague, whose eyes filled with philosophical tears as he gave them his blessing.

So the two churches of St. Asaph and St. Osoph stand side by side united and at peace. Their bells call softly back and forward to one another on Sunday mornings and such is the harmony between them that even the episcopal rooks in the elm trees of St. Asaph's and the presbyterian crows in the spruce trees of St. Osoph's are known to exchange perches on alternate Sundays.

EIGHT

The Great Fight for Clean Government

A S TO THE government of this city," said Mr. Newberry, leaning back in a leather arm-chair at the Mausoleum Club and lighting a second cigar, "it's rotten, that's all."

"Absolutely rotten," assented Mr. Dick Overend, ringing the bell for a second whiskey and soda.

"Corrupt," said Mr. Newberry, between two puffs of his cigar.

"Full of graft," said Mr. Overend, flicking his ashes into the grate.

"Crooked aldermen," said Mr. Newberry.

"A bum city solicitor," said Mr. Overend, "and an infernal grafter for treasurer."

"Yes," assented Mr. Newberry, and then, leaning forward in his chair and looking carefully about the corridors of the club, he spoke behind his hand and said, "And the mayor's the biggest grafter of the lot. And what's more," he added, sinking his voice to a whisper, "the time has come to speak out about it fearlessly."

Mr. Overend nodded. "It's a tyranny," he said.

"Worse than Russia," rejoined Mr. Newberry.

They had been sitting in a quiet corner of the club – it was on a Sunday evening – and had fallen into talking, first of all of the present rottenness of the federal politics of the

United States, – not argumentatively or with any heat, but with the reflective sadness that steals over an elderly man when he sits in the leather arm-chair of a comfortable club smoking a good cigar and musing on the decadence of the present day. The rottenness of the federal government didn't anger them. It merely grieved them.

They could remember, – both of them, – how different everything was when they were young men just entering on life. When Mr. Newberry and Mr. Dick Overend were young, men went into congress from pure patriotism; there was no such thing as graft or crookedness, as they both admitted, in those days; and as for the United States Senate – here their voices were almost hushed in awe – why, when they were young, the United States Senate, –

But no, neither of them could find a phrase big enough for their meaning.

They merely repeated "as for the United States Senate" – and then shook their heads and took long drinks of whiskey and soda.

Then, naturally, speaking of the rottenness of the federal government had led them to talk of the rottenness of the state legislature. How different from the state legislatures that they remembered as young men! Not merely different in the matter of graft, but different, so Mr. Newberry said, in the calibre of the men. He recalled how he had been taken as a boy of twelve by his father to hear a debate. He would never forget it. Giants! he said, that was what they were. In fact, the thing was more like a Witenagemot than a legislature. He said he distinctly recalled a man, whose name he didn't recollect, speaking on a question, he didn't just remember what, either for or against he couldn't just recall which; it thrilled him. He would never forget it. It stayed in his memory as if it were yesterday.

But as for the present legislature, – here Mr. Dick Overend sadly nodded assent in advance to what he knew was coming – as for the present legislature – well, – Mr. Newberry had had, he said, occasion to visit the state capital a week before in connection with a railway bill that he was

trying to, – that is, that he was anxious to, – in short in
connection with a railway bill, and when he looked about
him at the men in the legislature, – positively he felt
ashamed; he could put it no other way than that, –
ashamed.

After which, from speaking of the crookedness of the
state government Mr. Newberry and Mr. Dick Overend
were led to talk of the crookedness of the city government!
And they both agreed, as above, that things were worse
than in Russia. What secretly irritated them both most was
that they had lived and done business under this infernal
corruption for thirty or forty years and hadn't noticed it.
They had been too busy.

The fact was that their conversation reflected not so
much their own original ideas as a general wave of feeling
that was passing over the whole community.

There had come a moment, – quite suddenly it seemed, –
when it occurred to everybody at the same time that the
whole government of the city was rotten. The word is a
strong one. But it is the one that was used. Look at the
aldermen, they said, – rotten! Look at the city solicitor,
rotten! And as for the mayor himself, – phew!

The thing came like a wave. Everybody felt it at once.
People wondered how any sane, intelligent community
could tolerate the presence of a set of corrupt scoundrels
like the twenty aldermen of the city. Their names, it was
said, were simply a byword throughout the United States
for rank criminal corruption. This was said so widely that
everybody started hunting through the daily papers to try
to find out who in blazes *were* aldermen, anyhow. Twenty
names are hard to remember, and as a matter of fact, at the
moment when this wave of feeling struck the city, nobody
knew or cared who were aldermen, anyway.

To tell the truth, the aldermen had been much the same
persons for about fifteen or twenty years. Some were in the
produce business, others were butchers, two were grocers,
and all of them wore blue checkered waistcoats and red ties
and got up at seven in the morning to attend the vegetable

and other markets. Nobody had ever really thought about them, – that is to say, nobody on Plutoria Avenue. Sometimes one saw a picture in the paper and wondered for a moment who the person was; but on looking more closely and noticing what was written under it, one said, "Oh, I see, an alderman," and turned to something else.

"Whose funeral is that?" a man would sometimes ask on Plutoria Avenue. "Oh, just one of the city aldermen," a passer-by would answer hurriedly. "Oh I see, I beg your pardon, I thought it might be somebody important."

At which both laughed.

It was not just clear how and where this movement of indignation had started. People said that it was part of a new wave of public morality that was sweeping over the entire United States. Certainly it was being remarked in almost every section of the country. Chicago newspapers were attributing its origin to the new vigour and the fresh ideals of the middle west. In Boston it was said to be due to a revival of the grand old New England spirit. In Philadelphia they called it the spirit of William Penn. In the south it was said to be the reassertion of southern chivalry making itself felt against the greed and selfishness of the north, while in the north they recognised it at once as a protest against the sluggishness and ignorance of the south. In the west they spoke of it as a revolt against the spirit of the east and in the east they called it a reaction against the lawlessness of the west. But everywhere they hailed it as a new sign of the glorious unity of the country.

If therefore Mr. Newberry and Mr. Overend were found to be discussing the corrupt state of their city they only shared in the national sentiments of the moment. In fact in the same city hundreds of other citizens, as disinterested as themselves, were waking up to the realisation of what was going on. As soon as people began to look into the condition of things in the city they were horrified at what they found. It was discovered, for example, that Alderman

Schwefeldampf was an undertaker! Think of it! In a city with a hundred and fifty deaths a week, and sometimes even better, an undertaker sat on the council! A city that was about to expropriate land and to spend four hundred thousand dollars for a new cemetery, had an undertaker on the expropriation committee itself! And worse than that! Alderman Undercutt was a butcher! In a city that consumed a thousand tons of meat every week! And Alderman O'Hooligan – it leaked out – was an Irishman! Imagine it! An Irishman sitting on the police committee of the council in a city where thirty-eight and a half out of every hundred policemen were Irish, either by birth or parentage! The thing was monstrous.

So when Mr. Newberry said "It's worse than Russia!" he meant it, every word.

Now just as Mr. Newberry and Mr. Dick Overend were finishing their discussion, the huge bulky form of Mayor McGrath came ponderously past them as they sat. He looked at them sideways out of his eyes, – he had eyes like plums in a mottled face, – and, being a born politician, he knew by the very look of them that they were talking of something that they had no business to be talking about. But, – being a politician, – he merely said, "Good evening, gentlemen," without a sign of disturbance.

"Good evening, Mr. Mayor," said Mr. Newberry, rubbing his hands feebly together and speaking in an ingratiating tone. There is no more pitiable spectacle than an honest man caught in the act of speaking boldly and fearlessly of the evil-doer.

"Good evening, Mr. Mayor," echoed Mr. Dick Overend, also rubbing his hands; "warm evening, is it not?"

The mayor gave no other answer than that deep guttural grunt which is technically known in municipal interviews as refusing to commit oneself.

"Did he hear?" whispered Mr. Newberry as the mayor passed out of the club.

"I don't care if he did," whispered Mr. Dick Over-end.

Half an hour later Mayor McGrath entered the premises of the Thomas Jefferson Club, which were situated in the rear end of a saloon and pool room far down in the town.

"Boys," he said to Alderman O'Hooligan and Alderman Gorfinkel, who were playing freeze-out poker in the corner behind the pool tables, "you want to let the boys know to keep pretty dark and go easy. There's a lot of talk I don't like about the elections going round the town. Let the boys know that just for a while the darker they keep the better."

Whereupon the word was passed from the Thomas Jefferson Club to the George Washington Club and thence to the Eureka Club (coloured), and to the Kossuth Club (Hungarian), and to various other centres of civic patriotism in the lower parts of the city. And forthwith such a darkness began to spread over them that not even honest Diogenes with his lantern could have penetrated their doings.

"If them stiffs wants to make trouble," said the president of the George Washington Club to Mayor McGrath a day or two later, "they won't never know what they've bumped up against."

"Well," said the heavy mayor, speaking slowly and cautiously and eyeing his henchman with quiet scrutiny, "you want to go pretty easy now, I tell you."

The look which the mayor directed to his satellite was much the same glance that Morgan the buccaneer might have given to one of his lieutenants before throwing him overboard.

Meantime the wave of civic enthusiasm as reflected in the conversation of Plutoria Avenue grew stronger with every day.

"The thing is a scandal," said Mr. Lucullus Fyshe. "Why, these fellows down at the city hall are simply a pack of rogues. I had occasion to do some business there the other day (it was connected with the assessment of our soda factories) and do you know, I actually found that these fellows *take money!*"

"I say!" said Mr. Peter Spillikins, to whom he spoke, "I say! You don't say!"

"It's a fact," repeated Mr. Fyshe. "They take money. I took the assistant treasurer aside and said, 'I want such and such done,' and I slipped a fifty dollar bill into his hand. And the fellow took it, took it like a shot."

"He took it!" gasped Mr. Spillikins.

"He did," said Mr. Fyshe. "There ought to be a criminal law for that sort of thing."

"I say!" exclaimed Mr. Spillikins, "they ought to go to jail for a thing like that."

And the infernal insolence of them," Mr. Fyshe continued. "I went down the next day to see the deputy assistant (about a thing connected with the same matter), told him what I wanted and passed a fifty dollar bill across the counter and the fellow fairly threw it back at me, in a perfect rage. He refused it!"

"Refused it," gasped Mr. Spillikins, "I say!"

Conversations such as this filled up the leisure and divided the business time of all the best people in the city.

In the general gloomy outlook, however, one bright spot was observable. The "wave" had evidently come just at the opportune moment. For not only were civic elections pending but just at this juncture four or five questions of supreme importance would have to be settled by the incoming council. There was, for instance, the question of the expropriation of the Traction Company (a matter involving many millions); there was the decision as to the renewal of the franchise of the Citizens' Light Company, – a vital question; there was also the four hundred thousand dollar purchase of land for the new addition to the cemetery, a matter that must be settled. And it was felt, especially on

Plutoria Avenue, to be a splendid thing that the city was waking up, in the moral sense, at the very time when these things were under discussion. All the shareholders of the Traction Company and the Citizens' Light, – and they included the very best, the most high-minded, people in the city, – felt that what was needed now was a great moral effort, to enable them to lift the city up and carry it with them, or, if not all of it, at any rate as much of it as they could.

"It's a splendid movement!" said Mr. Fyshe (he was a leading shareholder and director of The Citizens' Light), "what a splendid thing to think that we shan't have to deal for our new franchise with a set of corrupt rapscallions like these present aldermen. Do you know, Furlong, that when we approached them first with a proposition for a renewal for a hundred and fifty years they held us up! Said it was too long! Imagine that! A hundred and fifty years (only a century and a half) too long for the franchise! They expect us to instal all our poles, string our wires, set up our transformers in their streets and then perhaps at the end of a hundred years find ourselves compelled to sell out at a beggarly valuation. Of course we knew what they wanted. They meant us to hand them over fifty dollars each to stuff into their rascally pockets."

"Outrageous!" said Mr. Furlong.

"And the same thing with the cemetery land deal," went on Mr. Lucullus Fyshe. "Do you realise that, if the movement hadn't come along and checked them, those scoundrels would have given that rogue Schwefeldampf four hundred thousand dollars for his fifty acres! Just think of it!"

"I don't know," said Mr. Furlong with a thoughtful look upon his face, "that four hundred thousand dollars is an excessive price, in and of itself, for that amount of land."

"Certainly not," said Mr. Fyshe, very quietly and decidedly, looking at Mr. Furlong in a searching way as he spoke. "It is *not* a high price. It seems to me, speaking purely as an outsider, a very fair, reasonable price for fifty acres of suburban land, if it were the *right* land. If, for example, it were a case of making an offer for that very fine stretch of land, about twenty acres, is it not, which I believe your Corporation owns on the *other* side of the cemetery, I should say four hundred thousand is a most modest price."

Mr. Furlong nodded his head reflectively.

"You had thought, had you not, of offering it to the city?" said Mr. Fyshe.

"We did," said Mr. Furlong, "at a more or less nominal sum, – four hundred thousand or whatever it might be. We felt that for such a purpose, almost sacred as it were, one would want as little bargaining as possible."

"Oh, none at all," assented Mr. Fyshe.

"Our feeling was," went on Mr. Furlong, "that if the city wanted our land for the cemetery extension, it might have it at its own figure, – four hundred thousand, half a million, in fact at absolutely any price, from four hundred thousand up, that they cared to put on it. We didn't regard it as a commercial transaction at all. Our reward lay merely in the fact of selling it to them."

"Exactly," said Mr. Fyshe, "and of course your land was more desirable from every point of view. Schwefeldampf's ground is encumbered with a growth of cypress and evergreens and weeping willows which make it quite unsuitable for an up-to-date cemetery; whereas yours, as I remember it, is bright and open, – a loose sandy soil with no trees and very little grass to overcome."

"Yes," said Mr. Furlong. "We thought too, that our ground, having the tanneries and the chemical factory along the further side of it, was an ideal place for, –" he paused, seeking a mode of expressing his thought.

"For the dead," said Mr. Fyshe, with becoming reverence.

And after this conversation Mr. Fyshe and Mr. Furlong senior understood one another absolutely in regard to the new movement.

It was astonishing in fact how rapidly the light spread.

"Is Rasselyer-Brown with us?" asked some one of Mr. Fyshe a few days later.

"Heart and soul," answered Mr. Fyshe. "He's very bitter over the way these rascals have been plundering the city on its coal supply. He says that the city has been buying coal wholesale at the pit mouth at three fifty, – utterly worthless stuff, he tells me. He has heard it said that everyone of these scoundrels has been paid from twenty-five to fifty dollars a winter to connive at it."

"Dear me," said the listener.

"Abominable, is it not?" said Mr. Fyshe. "But as I said to Rasselyer-Brown, what can one do if the citizens themselves take no interest in these things. 'Take your own case,' I said to him, 'how is it that you, a coal man, are not helping the city in this matter? Why don't *you* supply the city?' He shook his head, 'I wouldn't do it at three fifty,' he said. 'No,' I answered, 'but will you at five?' He looked at me for a moment and then he said, 'Fyshe, I'll do it; at five, or at anything over that they like to name. If we get a new council in they may name their own figure.' 'Good,' I said. 'I hope all the other business men will be animated with the same spirit.' "

Thus it was that the light broke and spread and illuminated in all directions. People began to realise the needs of the city as they never had before. Mr. Boulder, who owned, among other things, a stone quarry and an asphalt company, felt that the paving of the streets was a disgrace. Mr. Skinyer, of Skinyer and Beatem, shook his head and said that the whole legal department of the city needed reorganisation; it needed, he said, new blood. But he added always in a despairing tone, how could one expect to run a department with the head of it drawing only six thousand dollars; the thing was impossible. If, he argued, they could superannuate the present chief solicitor and get a man, a *good* man (Mr. Skinyer laid emphasis on this) at, say, fifteen thousand, there might be some hope.

"Of course," said Mr. Skinyer to Mr. Newberry in discussing the topic, "one would need to give him a proper staff of assistants so as to take off his hands all the *routine* work, – the mere appearance in court, the preparation of briefs, the office consultation, the tax revision and the purely legal work. In that case he would have his hands free to devote himself entirely to those things, which, – in fact to turn his attention in whatever direction he might feel it was advisable to turn it.

Within a week or two the public movement had found definite expression and embodied itself in the Clean Government Association. This was organised by a group of leading and disinterested citizens who held their first meeting in the largest upstairs room of the Mausoleum Club. Mr. Lucullus Fyshe, Mr. Boulder, and others keenly interested in obtaining simply justice for the stockholders of the Traction and the Citizens' Light were prominent from the start. Mr. Rasselyer-Brown, Mr. Furlong senior and others were there, not from special interest in the light or traction questions, but, as they said themselves, from pure civic spirit. Dr. Boomer was there to represent the university with three of his most presentable professors, cultivated men who were able to sit in a first class club and drink whiskey and soda and talk as well as any business man present. Mr. Skinyer, Mr. Beatem and others represented the bar. Dr. McTeague, blinking in the blue tobacco smoke, was there to stand for the church. There were all-round enthusiasts as well, such as Mr. Newberry and the Overend brothers and Mr. Peter Spillikins.

"Isn't it fine," whispered Mr. Spillikins to Mr. Newberry, "to see a set of men like these all going into a thing like this, not thinking of their own interests a bit?"

Mr. Fyshe, as chairman, addressed the meeting. He told them they were there to initiate a great free voluntary movement of the people. It had been thought wise, he said, to hold it with closed doors and keep it out of the newspapers. This would guarantee the league against the old underhand control by a clique that had hitherto disgraced every part of the administration of the city. He wanted, he said, to see everything done henceforth in broad day light: and for this purpose he had summoned them there at night to discuss ways and means of action. After they were once fully assured of exactly what they wanted to do and how they meant to do it, the league, he said, would invite the fullest and freest advice from all classes in the city. There were none, he said, amid great applause, that were so lowly that they would not be invited, – once the platform of the league was settled, – to advise and co-operate. All might help, even the poorest. Subscription lists would be prepared which would allow any sum at all, from one to five dollars, to be given to the treasurer. The league was to be democratic or nothing. The poorest might contribute as little as one dollar: even the richest would not be allowed to give more than five. Moreover he gave notice that he intended to propose that no actual official of the league should be allowed under its by-laws to give anything. He himself, – if they did him the honour to make him president as he had heard it hinted was their intention, – would be the first to bow to this rule. He would efface himself. He would obliterate himself, content in the interests of all, to give nothing. He was able to announce similar pledges from his friends, Mr. Boulder, Mr. Furlong, Dr. Boomer and a number of others.

Quite a storm of applause greeted these remarks by Mr. Fyshe, who flushed with pride as he heard it.

"Now, gentlemen," he went on, "this meeting is open for discussion. Remember it is quite informal, anyone may speak. I as chairman make no claim to control or monopolise the discussion. Let everyone understand –"

"Well then, Mr. Chairman," began Mr. Dick Overend.

"One minute, Mr. Overend," said Mr. Fyshe. "I want everyone to understand the he may speak as –"

"May I say then –" began Mr. Newberry.

"Pardon me, Mr. Newberry," said Mr. Fyshe, "I was

wishing first to explain that not only may *all* participate but that we *invite* –"

"In that case –" began Mr. Newberry.

"Before you speak," interrupted Mr. Fyshe, "let me add one word. We must make our discussion as brief and to the point as possible. I have a great number of things which I wish to say to the meeting and it might be well if all of you would speak as briefly and as little as possible. Has anybody anything to say?"

"Well," said Mr. Newberry, "what about organisation and officers?"

"We have thought of it," said Mr. Fyshe. "We were anxious above all things to avoid the objectionable and corrupt methods of a 'slate' and a prepared list of officers which have disgraced every part of our city politics until the present time. Mr. Boulder, Mr. Furlong and Mr. Skinyer and myself have therefore prepared a short list of offices and officers which we wish to submit to your fullest, freest consideration. It runs thus: Hon. President Mr. L. Fyshe, Hon. Vice-president, Mr. A. Boulder, Hon. Secretary Mr. Furlong, Hon. Treasurer Mr. O. Skinyer, et cetera, et cetera, – I needn't read it all. You'll see it posted in the hall later. Is that carried? Carried! Very good," said Mr. Fyshe.

There was a moment's pause while Mr. Furlong and Mr. Skinyer moved into seats beside Mr. Fyshe and while Mr. Furlong drew from his pocket and arranged the bundle of minutes of the meeting which he had brought with him. As he himself said he was too neat and methodical a writer to trust to jotting them down on the spot.

"Don't you think," said Mr. Newberry, "I speak as a practical man, that we ought to do something to get the newspapers with us?"

"Most important," assented several members.

"What do *you* think, Dr. Boomer?" asked Mr. Fyshe of the university president, "will the newspapers be with us?"

Dr. Boomer shook his head doubtfully. "It's an important matter," he said. "There is no doubt that we need, more than anything, the support of a clean, wholesome unbiassed press that can't be bribed and is not subject to money influence. I think on the whole our best plan would be to buy up one of the city newspapers."

"Might it not be better simply to buy up the editorial staff?" said Mr. Dick Overend.

"We might do that," admitted Dr. Boomer. "There is no doubt that the corruption of the press is one of the worst factors that we have to oppose. But whether we can best fight it by buying the paper itself or buying the staff is hard to say."

"Suppose we leave it to a committee with full power to act," said Mr. Fyshe. "Let us direct them to take whatever steps may in their opinion be best calculated to elevate the tone of the press, the treasurer being authorised to second them in every way. I for one am heartily sick of old underhand connection between city politics and the city papers. If we can do anything to alter and elevate it, it will be a fine work, gentlemen, well worth whatever it costs us."

Thus after an hour or two of such discussion the Clean Government League found itself organised and equipped with a treasury and a programme and a platform. The latter was very simple. As Mr. Fyshe and Mr. Boulder said there was no need to drag in specific questions or try to define the action to be taken towards this or that particular detail, such as the hundred and fifty year franchise, beforehand. The platform was simply expressed as Honesty, Purity, Integrity. This, as Mr. Fyshe said, made a straight, flat, clean issue between the league and all who opposed it.

This first meeting was of course confidential. But all that it did was presently done over again, with wonderful freshness and spontaneity at a large public meeting open to all citizens. There was a splendid impromptu air about everything. For instance when somebody away back in the hall said, "I move that Mr. Lucullus Fyshe be president of the league," Mr. Fyshe lifted his hand in unavailing protest as if this were the newest idea he had ever heard in his life.

After all of which the Clean Government League set itself to fight the cohorts of darkness. It was not just known where these were. But it was understood that they were there all right, somewhere. In the platform speeches of the epoch they figured as working underground, working in the dark, working behind the scenes, and so forth. But the strange thing was that nobody could state with any exactitude just who or what it was that the league was fighting. It stood for "honesty, purity, and integrity." This was all you could say about it.

Take for example the case of the press. At the inception of the league it had been supposed that such was the venality and corruption of the city newspapers that it would be necessary to buy one of them. But the word "clean government" had been no sooner uttered than it turned out that every one of the papers in the city was in favour of it: in fact had been working for it for years.

They vied with one another now in giving publicity to the idea. The *Plutorian Times* printed a dotted coupon on the corner of its front sheet with the words, "*Are you in favour of Clean Government? If so, send us ten cents with this coupon and your name and address.*" The *Plutorian Citizen* and *Home Advocate* went even further. It printed a coupon which said, "*Are you out for a clean city? If so send us twenty-five cents to this office. We pledge ourselves to use it.*"

The newspapers did more than this. They printed from day to day such pictures as the portrait of Mr. Fyshe with the legend below, "*Mr. Lucullus Fyshe, who says that government ought to be by the people, from the people, for the people and to the people*"; and the next day another labelled, "*Mr. P. Spillikins, who says that all men are born free and equal,*" and the next day a picture with the words, "*Tract of ground offered for cemetery by Mr. Furlong, showing rear of tanneries, with head of Mr. Furlong inserted.*"

It was of course plain enough that certain of the aldermen of the old council were to be reckoned as part of the cohort of darkness. That at least was clear. "We want no more men in control of the stamp of Alderman Gorfinkel and Alderman Schwefeldampf," so said practically every paper in the city. "The public sense revolts at these men. They are vultures who have feasted too long on the prostrate corpses of our citizens." And so on. The only trouble was to discover who or what had ever supported Alderman Gorfinkel and Alderman Schwefeldampf. The very organisations that might have seemed to be behind them were evidently more eager for clean government than the league itself.

"*The Thomas Jefferson Club Out for Clean Government,*" so ran the newspaper headings of one day; and of the next, "*Will help to clean up City Government. Eureka Club (Coloured) endorses the League; Is done with Darkness,*" and the day after that, "*Sons of Hungary Share in Good Work: Kossuth Club will vote with the League.*"

So strong, indeed, was the feeling against the iniquitous aldermen that the public demand arose to be done with a council of aldermen altogether and to substitute government by a Board. The newspapers contained editorials on the topic each day and it was understood that one of the first efforts of the league would be directed towards getting the necessary sanction of the legislature in this direction. To help to enlighten the public on what such government meant Professor Proaser of the university (he was one of the three already referred to) gave a public lecture on the growth of Council Government. He traced it from the Amphictionic Council of Greece as far down as the Oligarchical Council of Venice; it was thought that had the evening been longer he would have traced it clean down to modern times.

But most amazing of all was the announcement that was presently made, and endorsed by Mr. Lucullus Fyshe in an interview, that Mayor McGrath himself would favour clean government, and would become the official nominee of the league itself. This certainly was strange. But it would perhaps have been less mystifying to the public at large, had they been able to listen to certain of the intimate conversations of Mr. Fyshe and Mr. Boulder.

"You say then," said Mr. Boulder, "to let McGrath's name stand."

"We can't do without him," said Mr. Fyshe, "he has seven of the wards in the hollow of his hand. If we take his offer he absolutely pledges us every one of them."

"Can you rely on his word?" said Mr. Boulder.

"I think he means to play fair with us," answered Mr. Fyshe. "I put it to him as a matter of honour, between man and man, a week ago. Since then I have had him carefully dictaphoned and I'm convinced he's playing straight."

"How far will he go with us?" said Mr. Boulder.

"He is willing to throw overboard Gorfinkel, Schwefeldampf and Undercutt. He says he must find a place for O'Hooligan. The Irish, he says, don't care for clean government; they want Irish Government."

"I see," said Mr. Boulder very thoughtfully, "and in regard to the renewal of the franchise and the expropriation, tell me just exactly what his conditions are."

But Mr. Fyshe's answer to this was said so discreetly and in such a low voice, that not even the birds listening in the elm trees outside the Mausoleum Club could hear it.

No wonder then that if even the birds failed to know everything about the Clean Government League, there were many things which such good people as Mr. Newberry and Mr. Peter Spillikins never heard at all and never guessed.

Each week and every day brought fresh triumphs to the onward march of the movement.

"Yes, gentlemen," said Mr. Fyshe to the assembled committee of the Clean Government League a few days later, "I am glad to be able to report our first victory. Mr. Boulder and I have visited the state capital and we are able to tell you definitely that the legislature will consent to change our form of government so as to replace our council by a Board."

"Hear, hear!" cried all the committee men together.

"We saw the governor," said Mr. Fyshe. "Indeed he was good enough to lunch with us at the Pocahontas Club. He tells us that what we are doing is being done in every city and town of the state. He says that the days of the old-fashioned city council are numbered. They are setting up boards everywhere."

"Excellent!" said Mr. Newberry.

"The governor assures us that what we want will be done. The chairman of the Democratic State Committee (he was good enough to dine with us at the Buchanan Club) has given us the same assurance. So also does the chairman of the Republican State Committee, who was kind enough to be our guest in a box at the Lincoln Theatre. It is most gratifying," concluded Mr. Fyshe, "to feel that the legislature will give us such a hearty, such a thoroughly American support."

"You are sure of this, are you?" questioned Mr. Newberry. "You have actually seen the members of the legislature?"

"It was not necessary," said Mr. Fyshe. "The governor and the different chairmen have them so well fixed, – that is to say, they have such confidence in the governor and their political organisers that they will all be prepared to give us what I have described as a thoroughly American support."

"You are quite sure," persisted Mr. Newberry, "about the governor and the others you mentioned?"

Mr. Fyshe paused a moment and then he said very quietly, "We are quite sure," and he exchanged a look with Mr. Boulder that meant volumes to those who would read it.

"I hope you didn't mind my questioning you in that fashion," said Mr. Newberry, as he and Mr. Fyshe strolled home from the club. "The truth is I didn't feel sure in my own mind just what was meant by a 'Board,' and 'getting them to give us government by a Board.' I know I'm speaking like an ignoramus. I've really not paid as much attention in the past to civic politics as I ought to have. But what is the difference between a council and board?"

"The difference between a council and a board?" repeated Mr. Fyshe.

"Yes," said Mr. Newberry, "the difference between a council and a board."

"Or call it," said Mr. Fyshe reflectively, "the difference between a board and a council."

"Precisely," said Mr. Newberry.

"It's not altogether easy to explain," said Mr. Fyshe. "One chief difference is that in the case of a board, sometimes called a Commission, the *salary* is higher. You see the salary of an alderman or councillor in most cities is generally not more than fifteen hundred or two thousand dollars. The salary of a member of a board or commission is at least ten thousand. That gives you at once a very different class of men. As long as you only pay fifteen hundred you get your council filled up with men who will do any kind of crooked work for fifteen hundred dollars; as soon as you pay ten thousand you get men with larger ideas."

"I see," said Mr. Newberry.

"If you have a fifteen hundred dollar man," Mr. Fyshe went on, "you can bribe him at any time with a fifty dollar bill. On the other hand your ten thousand dollar man has a wider outlook. If you offer him fifty dollars for his vote on the board, he'd probably laugh at you."

"Ah, yes," said Mr. Newberry, "I see the idea. A fifteen hundred dollar salary is so low that it will tempt a lot of men into office merely for what they can get out of it."

"That's it exactly," answered Mr. Fyshe.

From all sides support came to the new league. The women of the city, – there were fifty thousand of them on the municipal voters list, – were not behind the men. Though not officials of the league they rallied to its cause.

"Mr. Fyshe," said Mrs. Buncomhearst, who called at the office of the president of the league with offers of support, "tell me what we can do. I represent fifty thousand women voters of this city, –"

(This was a favourite phrase of Mrs. Buncomhearst's, though it had never been made quite clear how or why she represented them.)

"We want to help, we women. You know we've any amount of initiative, if you'll only tell us what to do. You know, Mr. Fyshe, we've just as good executive ability as you men, if you'll just tell us what to do. Couldn't we hold a meeting of our own, all our own, to help the league along?"

"An excellent idea," said Mr. Fyshe.

"And could you not get three or four men to come and address it so as to stir us up?" asked Mrs. Buncomhearst anxiously.

"Oh, certainly," said Mr. Fyshe.

So it was known after this that the women were working side by side with the men. The tea rooms of the Grand Palaver and the other hotels were filled with them every day, busy for the cause. One of them even invented a perfectly charming election scarf to be worn as a sort of badge to show one's allegiance: and its great merit was that it was so fashioned that it would go with anything.

"Yes," said Mr. Fyshe to his committee, "one of the finest signs of our movement is that the women of the city are with us. Whatever we may think, gentlemen, of the question of woman's rights in general, – and I think we know what we *do* think, – there is no doubt that the influence of women makes for purity in civic politics. I am glad to inform the committee that Mrs. Buncomhearst and her friends have organised all the working women of the city who have votes. They tell me that they have been able to do this at a cost as low as five dollars per woman. Some of the women, – foreigners of the lower classes whose sense of political morality is as yet imperfectly developed, – have been organised at a cost as low as one dollar per vote. But of course with our native American women, with a higher standard of education and morality, we can hardly expect to do it as low as that."

Nor were the women the only element of support added to the league.

"Gentlemen," reported Dr. Boomer, the president of the university, at the next committee meeting, "I am glad to say that the spirit which animates us has spread to the students of the university. They have organised, entirely by themselves and on their own account, a Students' Fair Play League which has commenced its activities. I understand that they have already ducked Alderman Gorfinkel in a pond near the university. I believe they are looking for Alderman Schwefeldampf to-night. I understand they propose to throw him into the reservoir. The leaders of them, – a splendid set of young fellows, – have given me a pledge that they will do nothing to bring discredit on the university."

"I think I heard them on the street last night," said Mr. Newberry.

"I believe they had a procession," said the president.

"Yes, I heard them; they were shouting 'Rah! rah! rah! Clean Government! Clean Government! Rah! rah! It was really inspiring to hear them."

"Yes," said the president, "they are banded together to put down all the hoodlumism and disturbance on the street that has hitherto disgraced our municipal elections. Last night, as a demonstration they upset two street cars and a milk waggon."

"I heard that two of them were arrested," said Mr. Dick Overend.

"Only by an error," said the president. "There was a mistake. It was not known that they were students. The two who were arrested were smashing the windows of the car, after it was upset, with their hockey sticks. A squad of police mistook them for rioters. As soon as they were taken to the police station, the mistake was cleared up at once. The chief of police telephoned an apology to the university. I believe the league is out again to-night looking for Alderman Schwefeldampf. But the leaders assure me there will be no breach of the peace whatever. As I say, I think their idea is to throw him into the reservoir."

In the face of such efforts as these, opposition itself melted rapidly away. The *Plutorian Times* was soon able to announce that various undesirable candidates were abandoning the field. "Alderman Gorfinkel," it said, "who, it will be recalled, was thrown into a pond last week by the students of the college, was still confined to his bed when interviewed by our representative. Mr. Gorfinkel stated that he should not offer himself as a candidate in the approaching election. He was, he said, weary of civic honours. He had had enough. He felt it incumbent on him to step out and make way for others who deserved their turn as well as himself: in future he proposed to confine his whole attention to his Misfit Semi-Ready Establishment which he was happy to state was offering as nobby a line of early fall suiting as was ever seen at the price."

There is no need to recount here in detail the glorious triumph of the election day itself. It will always be remembered as the purest, cleanest election ever held in the precincts of the city. The citizens' organisation turned out in overwhelming force to guarantee that it should be so. Bands of Dr. Boomer's students, armed with baseball bats, surrounded the polls to guarantee fair play. Any man wishing to cast an unclean vote was driven from the booth: all those attempting to introduce any element of brute force or rowdysm into the election were cracked over the head. In the lower part of the town scores of willing workers, recruited often from the humblest classes, kept order with pickaxes. In every part of the city motor cars, supplied by all the leading business men, lawyers, and doctors of the city, acted as patrols to see that no unfair use should be made of other vehicles in carrying voters to the polls.

It was a foregone victory from the first, – overwhelming and complete. The cohorts of darkness were so completely routed that it was practically impossible to find them. As it fell dusk the streets were filled with roaring and surging crowds celebrating the great victory for clean government, while in front of every newspaper office huge lantern pictures of *Mayor McGrath, the Champion of Pure Government*, and *O. Skinyer, the People's Solicitor*, and the other nominees of the league, called forth cheer after cheer of frenzied enthusiasm.

They held that night in celebration a great reception at the Mausoleum Club on Plutoria Avenue, given at its own suggestion by the city. The city indeed insisted on it.

Nor was there ever witnessed even in that home of art and refinement a scene of greater charm. In the spacious corridor of the club a Hungarian band wafted Viennese music from Tyrolese flutes through the rubber trees. There was champagne bubbling at a score of sideboards where noiseless waiters poured it into goblets as broad and flat as floating water-lily leaves. And through it all moved the shepherds and shepherdesses of that beautiful Arcadia – the shepherds in their Tuxedo jackets, with vast white shirtfronts broad as the map of Africa, with spotless white waistcoats girdling their equators, wearing heavy gold watch-chains and little patent shoes blacker than sin itself, and the shepherdesses in foaming billows of silks of every colour of the kaleidoscope, their hair bound with glittering headbands or coiled with white feathers, the very symbol of municipal purity. One would search in vain the pages of pastoral literature to find the equal of it.

And as they talked the good news spread from group to group that it was already known that the new franchise of the Citizens' Light was to be made for two centuries so as to give the company a fair chance to see what it could do. At the word of it, the grave faces of manly bondholders flushed with pride, and the soft eyes of listening shareholders laughed back in joy. For they had no doubt or fear, now that clean government had come. They knew what the company could do.

Thus all night long, outside of the club, the soft note of the motor horns arriving and departing wakened the sleeping leaves of the elm trees with their message of good tidings. And all night long, within its lighted corridors, the bubbling champagne whispered to the listening rubber trees of the new salvation of the city. So the night waxed and waned till the slow day broke, dimming with its cheap prosaic glare the shaded beauty of the artificial light, and the people of the city – the best of them, – drove home to their well-earned sleep, and the others, – in the lower parts of the city, – rose to their daily toil.

FINIS

Afterword

BY GERALD LYNCH

Arcadian Adventures with the Idle Rich exposes to laughter and ridicule the crass materialism that the unrestricted practice of capitalism has thrown up in the form of an American metropolitan plutocracy. From Aristophanes to Mordecai Richler, the wise satirist, he whose work endures, has turned his light upon the undying sins: pride, greed, hypocrisy. In *Arcadian Adventures*, these enduring sins are satirized within the context of such early twentieth century phenomena as stock-market scams, the rage for mystical experience, the back-to-nature vogue, effete religiosity, doctrinal ditching efforts towards an expedient ecumenism, muck-raking politics, and the hypocritical movement for municipal reform. And it appears that these seemingly topical phenomena have themselves laid claim to a permanent place in human affairs – thus the enduring value of *Arcadian Adventures*.

To appreciate Leacock's achievement in *Arcadian Adventures* fully, readers need to know something of his earlier work, *Sunshine Sketches of a Little Town*. Both books are comprised of linked stories that humorously anatomize their subjects – the big anonymous American city and the small Canadian town of Mariposa at the turn of the century – portraying in roughly the same order such fundamental social and cultural institutions as business, religion, marriage, and politics. *Arcadian Adventures* begins in the Mausoleum Club; *Sunshine Sketches* ends in one. Considered as companion volumes, or as an extended work of fiction, the two books can thus be seen to turn about the closing sketch of *Sunshine Sketches*, "L'Envoi: The Train to Mariposa," in which two men, after a failed attempt to return imaginatively to Mariposa, find themselves sitting again in the posh chairs of a Mausoleum Club. The implied warning of "L'Envoi" is that if the "you" who is addressed throughout *Sunshine Sketches* does not find a way to recover the values that Leacock associated with the small Canadian community of Mariposa, "you" will remain entombed in a Mausoleum Club, with all the associations of cultural and spiritual death that the club's name carries. *Arcadian Adventures* shows us what sort of modern world ensues upon the loss of those anti-materialistic values – the values of community, charity, romance, and family. In *Essays and Literary Studies*, Leacock described these values as "all less tangible and provable forms of human merit, and less tangible aspirations of the human mind."

It may prove helpful to think of *Arcadian Adventures*' Plutoria Avenue (the main commercial thoroughfare of the unnamed American city) and *Sunshine Sketches*' Mariposa as supplying the two poles of Leacock's fictional landscape. Although portrayed ironically, Mariposa remains the ideal community of the Canadian humanist and tory, the community eulogized for its diversity in unity yet viewed with an acknowledgement of human fallibility. Plutoria is the twentieth century, a negative exemplar of modernity's tendencies towards obsessive individualism and materialism. What is worthwhile in Mariposa must be remembered, recovered, and brought into the present, if the extremes of mechanistic capitalism – Plutoria – are to be, if not defeated or avoided, at least opposed or countered.

The plutocrats of Plutoria Avenue, the wealthy inhabitants of an American city such as Chicago or New York, will do anything, and do everything, for money. Society, education, religion, romance, and of course business and politics are reduced to the all-consuming love of lucre, obsessive compulsive pecuniary acquisitiveness, the getting of green-backs, making a pile. *Arcadian Adventures* can be summed up that simply. *If* we leave out the humour. Which we can't. For who would want to exclude from any discussion of *Arcadian Adventures* the lucrative infants of Plutoria Avenue, such as the "little toddling princess in a rabbit suit who owns fifty distilleries in her own right"; or forget President Boomer's praise of such benefactors of Plutoria University as "the late Mr. Underbugg, who founded our lectures on the Four Gospels on the sole stipulation that henceforth any reference of ours to the four gospels should be coupled with his name"; or overlook the sham seer, Yahi-Bahi, who accepts six ten-dollar gold pieces arranged in the form of a mystic serpent and then prognosticates, "Many things are yet to happen before others begin"; or skip the corrupt Plutorian newspaper's unintentional pillorying of one of its scheming would-be politicians, when it captions a picture, "Tract of ground offered for cemetery by Mr. Furlong, showing rear of tanneries, with head of Mr. Furlong inserted."

Arcadian Adventures is arguably Leacock's funniest book. But Leacock described humour as "the kindly contemplation of the incongruities of life and the artistic expression thereof," and he seems in this book to violate his dictum of "kindliness." Readers should know, however, that for Leacock the word "kindliness" carried associations of *kin*ship, of shared humanity; the word was not synonymous with gentleness. Those characters who live in disregard of their humanity, those such as the plutocrats of *Arcadian Adventures*, become prime targets for Leacock's humorous satire.

As a traditional tory (as opposed to a neo-conservative) and humanist, Leacock believed in the nobility of his fellow man while remaining sensitive to his fallibility, to his need to be reminded of his social responsibilities. It would, therefore, be equally wrong to exclude from consideration the opening and closing references to the slum-dwellers and the working poor of the city, references which serve as a

kind of frame for *Arcadian Adventures*. The adventures of
these idle Plutorians take place within range of "slums"
that can be seen from the roof of the Mausoleum Club; and
the book concludes with reference to those "others – in the
lower parts of the city – [who] rose to their daily toil."
Behind the humorous satire of *Arcadian Adventures* is
Leacock the compassionate political economist who strove
to infuse humanitarianism into the capitalists and captains
of industry. "Few persons can attain to adult life without
being profoundly impressed by the appalling inequalities of
our human lot," he wrote in *The Unsolved Riddle of Social
Justice*. "Riches and poverty jostle one another upon our
streets. The tattered outcast dozes on his bench while the
chariot of the wealthy is drawn by. The palace is the
neighbour of the slum. We are, in modern life, so used to
this that we no longer see it." We are in modern life indeed.
Leacock was not, however, promoting a socialist state. He
was recommending his own brew of a traditional toryism
that already contained a sense of responsibility for the less
fortunate – a duty to find work for all willing members of a
society which should see as its first duty the care and
education of its children. The Soviet Union, which translated and published *Arcadian Adventures* for its incisive
critique of bourgeois capitalism (thus causing Leacock to
complain wryly till the end of his life that they owed him
bags of rubles), selectively ignored such remarks of Leacock's as, "This socialism, this communism, would work
only in Heaven where they don't need it, or in Hell where
they already have it." Leacock's social-political philosophy
is best described as a middle way between socialism and
liberalism.

Behind *Arcadian Adventures* also, though perhaps at a
greater distance than is often assumed, stands Thorstein
Veblen's incisive and at times humorous critique of modern
American society, *The Theory of the Leisure Class* (1899).
It was Veblen's presence at the University of Chicago that
attracted Leacock there to do his doctoral dissertation, a
critique entitled "The Doctrine of *Laissez Faire*" (1903),

and it is to Veblen we owe such phrases as "conspicuous consumption" and "conspicuous leisure." Even with only the argument of those fashionable phrases, we can feel Veblen's presence permeating the ostentatious Mausoleum Club and painting in lurid tones the expensive pursuits of Mrs. Rasselyer-Brown's society. Veblen is present in *Arcadian Adventures*, but it could as well be argued that Alexis de Tocqueville's mid-nineteenth-century look at America, *Democracy in America*, can be discerned behind Leacock's satire of the idle rich. For example, consider Lucullus Fyshe's little dinner or the meeting of the trustees of St. Asaph's and St. Osoph's churches in light of such remarks of de Tocqueville's as, "At first appearance this people seems to be a company of merchants gathered together for trade; and as one dips further into the national character of Americans, one sees that they have sought the value of all things in this world only in the answer to this one question: how much money will it bring in?"

More particularly, it might be said that *Arcadian Adventures* depicts the pursuit of money and power as, initially, the internally competitive and, ultimately, the concerted or monopolistic enterprise of a central clique of Plutorians. That is the unifying movement of this cycle of stories. The first adventure, "A Little Dinner with Mr. Lucullus Fyshe," concerns the competitive practices of those two financial animals, Fyshe and Mr. Asmodeus Boulder (whose surnames suggest the cold-blooded and the inanimate – definitely the sub-human); it ends in protracted acrimony and determined vengefulness. The next two adventures – "The Wizard of Finance" and "The Arrested Philanthropy of Mr. Tomlinson" – contrast the decadent, empowered metropolis of Plutoria and the rural ideal of the Tomlinson farm. (For a tory such as Leacock, agrarian enterprises should form the basis of society.) In effect, these two stories portray a kind of inverse alchemy at work: the Plutorians turn the green of Tomlinson's farm into a fool's gold; at the end the Tomlinsons turn the false gold back to green, so that "Nature reached out its hand and drew its

coverlet of green over the grave of the vanished Eldorado."
Throughout *Arcadian Adventures* the damaging effect of
the pursuit of gold in all its forms plays a destructive role.
"The Yahi-Bahi Oriental Society of Mrs. Rasselyer-Brown"
continues to chip away at the artificial Arcadia, with associations of pagan pastoral versus Judaeo-Christian that the
title of *Arcadian Adventures* itself contains. In the society
of Mrs. Rasselyer-Brown we see clearly the empty lives and
spurious culture – the conspicuous consumption and conspicuous leisure – that are supported by the plutorian
machine. In "The Love Story of Mr. Peter Spillikins,"
Plutoria asserts its dominion over romantic love itself.
Again Leacock presents a contrast between the gold and
the green, in the persons of Mrs. Everleigh with her dyed
blond hair and the "Little Girl in Green." The myopic
Spillikins mistakes the gold-digging Mrs. Everleigh for the
motherlode of love; the potential for true love and a natural
family that the "Green Girl" promises remains unfulfilled.
Thus Plutoria defeats a potentially redemptive love, a
defeat which can be seen to loom more ominously in light
of the redemptive role of romantic love in *Sunshine
Sketches*.

In the religious adventures – "The Rival Churches of St.
Asaph and St. Osoph" and "The Ministrations of the Rev.
Uttermost Dumfarthing" – Leacock's ostensible target is
financially expedient ecumenism. But the true object of the
satire in the religious adventures is monopoly capitalism.
The religious sketches subtly recall the opening story, "The
Little Dinner," in their portrayal of the concerted efforts of
those earlier competitive financial animals, Fyshe (St.
Asaph's) and Boulder (St. Osoph's), who are the prime
movers in the push for union. The church merger involves
the abandonment of doctrinal distinctions that have arisen
in response to genuine human needs; or as Skinyer of the
legal firm of Skinyer and Beatem would say, wasteful com-
petitiveness is ditched in favour of controlling the output of
the spiritual product. The reader of *Arcadian Adventures*
might well have wondered at this point in the book: If

business, society, culture, love, and religion have succumbed to the now-unified Plutorians, can rule by plutocracy be far behind? The final adventure, "The Great Fight
for Clean Government," answers this question with a
resounding, deadening negative.

Those in *Arcadian Adventures* who are close to the
values at the centre of Leacock's tory-humanist norm –
true manners (the Duke, the Little Girl in Green), agrarian
simplicity and virtuous action (the Tomlinsons), continuity
with the past (Concordia College), romantic love, the spirit
of religion (the Rev. McTeague), and the ideals of democracy – are subsumed by the ascendant plutocracy in a final
triumph of darkness. These "good people," as Leacock
calls them, offer but an ineffectual opposition to the
empowered plutocrats: they and what they represent are
rejected, defeated, or vulgarized beyond recognition. The
only real opposition to a plutocracy is suggested by the
closing words not of *Arcadian Adventures* but of *Sunshine
Sketches*: "the little Town in the Sunshine that once we
knew," referring, of course, to Mariposa. By recovering the
values of the small Canadian community, by knowing
again what once we knew, we will be able to avoid the dead
end that is so starkly depicted in *Arcadian Adventures*. In
Leacock's view, this is the only way for Canadian Mausoleum clubbers to re-route the Canadian train that may
careen southwards. Taken together, *Arcadian Adventures*
and *Sunshine Sketches* teach the need for a kind of memory-mining for the true gold of human community. As to
resisting the sort of plutocratic totalitarianism that dominates the close of *Arcadian Adventures*, all else is fool's
gold, as worthless finally as the beguiling stuff that is found
beside Tomlinson's creek and the deadly dye that glitters in
Mrs. Everleigh's hair.

BY STEPHEN LEACOCK

AUTOBIOGRAPHY
The Boy I Left Behind Me (1946)

BIOGRAPHY
Mark Twain (1932)
Charles Dickens: His Life and Work (1933)

DRAMA
"Q": A Farce in One Act [with Basil Macdonald] (1915)

ECONOMICS
Economic Prosperity in the British Empire (1930)
Back to Prosperity:
The Great Opportunity of the Empire Conference (1932)
The Gathering Financial Crisis in Canada:
A Survey of the Present Critical Situation (1936)

EDUCATION
The Pursuit of Knowledge: A Discussion of Freedom and
Compulsion in Education (1934)
Too Much College, or Education Eating Up Life (1939)

HISTORY
Baldwin, Lafontaine, Hincks:
Responsible Government (1907)

HUMOUR

*The Iron Man and the Tin Woman, with Other Such
Futurities* (1929)
*Wet Wit and Dry Humour: Distilled from the Pages of
Stephen Leacock* (1931)
The Dry Pickwick and Other Incongruities (1932)
Afternoons in Utopia: Tales of the New Time (1932)
*Hellements of Hickonomics in Hiccoughs of Verse Done in
Our Social Planning Mill* (1936)
Funny Pieces: A Book of Random Sketches (1936)
Here Are My Lectures (1937)
Model Memoirs, and Other Sketches from Simple to Serious
(1938)
My Remarkable Uncle, and Other Sketches (1942)
Happy Stories, Just to Laugh At (1943)
Last Leaves (1945)

LITERARY CRITICISM
Essays and Literary Studies (1916)
Humour: Its Theory and Technique (1935)
The Greatest Pages of American Humor (1936)
*Humour and Humanity: An Introduction to the Study of
Humour* (1937)
How to Write (1943)

POLITICAL SCIENCE
Elements of Political Science (1906)
The Unsolved Riddle of Social Justice (1920)
*My Discovery of the West:
A Discussion of East and West in Canada* (1937)
*While There Is Time:
The Case against Social Catastrophe* (1945)

TITLES BY STEPHEN LEACOCK
Available in the New Canadian Library

LITERARY LAPSES with an afterword by
Robertson Davies
7710-99835 $4.95 ☐

SUNSHINE SKETCHES OF A LITTLE TOWN
with an afterword by Jack Hodgins
7710-99843 $5.95 ☐

ARCADIAN ADVENTURES WITH THE IDLE RICH
with an afterword by Gerald Lynch
7710-99665 $5.95 ☐

MOONBEAMS FROM THE LARGER LUNACY
7710-91435 $4.95 ☐

WINNOWED WISDOM
7710-91745 $4.95 ☐

MY REMARKABLE UNCLE with an afterword by
Barbara Nimmo
7710-9965-7 $5.95 ☐

LAST LEAVES
7710-91699 $5.95 ☐

BUY THESE QUALITY BOOKS AT YOUR LOCAL BOOKSTORE OR
USE THIS CONVENIENT COUPON FOR ORDERING.

NEW CANADIAN LIBRARY McClelland & Stewart Inc.
25 Hollinger Road, Toronto, Ontario M4B 3G2

Please send me the book(s) I have checked above. I am enclosing a
cheque or money order for a total of $ _____
(no cash or C.O.D.s please). Or, please charge my
Visa account # _____ ,expiry date _____ .
Please add $1.50 to your first book to cover postage and handling, and
an additional 75 cents for each additional book you order.

Name _____

Address _____ Apt. _____

City _____

Province _____ Postal Code _____

Please make your cheque payable to McClelland & Stewart Inc. and allow 4 to
6 weeks for delivery. Prices and availability subject to change without notice.